Charnel House
and Other Stories

Charnel House
and Other Stories

Graham Masterton

Five Star • Waterville, Maine

Additional copyright information may be found on page 274.

Five Star First Edition Mystery Series.

Published in 2002 in conjunction with Tekno-Books and Ed Gorman.

Set in 11 pt. Plantin by Al Chase.

Printed in the United States on permanent paper.

Library of Congress Cataloging-in-Publication Data

Masterton, Graham.
Charnel House and other stories / Graham Masterton.
p. cm.—(Five Star first edition mystery series)
Contents: Underbed—The gray madonna—The ballyhooly boy—Charnel house.
ISBN 0-7862-4312-0 (hc : alk. paper)
1. Horror tales, English—Fiction. I. Title. II. Series.
PR6063.A834 C46 2002
823′.914—dc21 2002075470

For Wiescka, with all my love.

And for Ed Gorman, with affection and great respect.

Table of Contents

Introduction

In the spring of 1974 I quit my job as executive editor of *Penthouse* magazine so that I could write full time. Many of my friends thought I was mad. But I had already spent seven years in centerfold land and all I could see ahead of me was an endless procession of Pets of the Month until I reached retirement age. It was a great job, but it was Bob Guccione's vision, not mine.

My experience on *Penthouse* and *Penthouse Forum* had already given me the expertise and the contacts to publish several very successful "how-to" books on sex, notably *How a Woman Loves to Be Loved* by the very cute but pseudonymous "Angel Smith" and *How to Drive Your Man Wild in Bed*, under my own name, which is still in print after a quarter of a century.

But when I arrived in New York in 1975 with the manuscript for my next erotic manual, I was told by my publisher that the bottom had fallen out of the sex-book market, so to speak. I insisted, however, that they honor their contract (my wife Wiescka and I had a new baby on the way, and I badly needed the money). So I offered them a short horror novel which I had written for my own amusement, inspired by Wiescka's pregnancy and an article I had read as a boy in *The Buffalo Bill Annual 1951*.

This was *The Manitou*—the tale of a 300-year-old Native American wonder-worker who is reborn in modern-day New York to take his revenge on the white man. It was published in 1976 and almost immediately picked up by the late Bill Girdler (director of *Grizzly* and several blaxploitation movies). It was filmed with Tony Curtis, Burgess Meredith,

Michael Ansara, Stella Stevens, Susan Strasberg and Ann Sothern, and even though the special effects look hilarious today (a snowstorm was a blizzard of desiccated coconut) it established my credentials as a writer of supernatural fiction.

More than that, it established me as an interpreter of ancient evils visited on the modern world. After *The Manitou* came *The Djinn*, a tale of Arabian demons, and then *The Sphinx*, an eccentric frightener about a woman who was half-human and half-lioness.

But I was still fascinated by Native American legends, mainly because of the fact that they were exclusive to the American continent and hadn't been imported by European or Asian immigrants (like vampires or Golems or werewolves). With the active assistance and approval of several new Native American friends, including Sitting Bull's great-granddaughter, I researched the notorious Navaho demon Coyote.

There are countless stories about Coyote in Navaho lore, from his theft of Poop-man's anus to the violent raping of old women. He was the essence of evil and trickery, and his ceremonial name means First One to Use Words for Force. In other words, he was the embodiment of fury, without which there can be no war.

Coyote was a master trickster, and not even the most powerful of supernatural beings were safe from his deceit. He was also extremely lascivious, constantly and forcibly having sex with both humans and animals. He would lick animals between their legs to arouse them, and this is why two dogs will always do the same when they meet each other.

My working title for *Charnel House* was *In The Moon of the Demon*, to suggest the Native American calendar (such as the Drying Grass Moon in autumn). However my editor at Pinnacle Books, Andy Ettinger, considered this far too flowery, and came up with *Charnel House*, for which I am eternally grateful. The word "house" is very potent in horror fiction, as Stephen King and Peter Straub will tell you, and I used it again in *The House That Jack Built*.

I very much appreciate the interest and enthusiasm shown by my friend Ed Gorman in wanting to re-publish *Charnel House*. I hadn't read it myself since 1978, so it was a fascinating journey down memory lane. For you, however, I hope that it will take you to a journey on which anything is possible, no matter how terrifying—a journey from which there is no turning back.

Graham Masterton
Cork, Republic of Ireland, 2001
www.grahammasterton.co.uk

Underbed

As soon as his mother had closed the bedroom door, Martin burrowed down under the blankets. For him, this was one of the best times of the day. In that long, warm hour between waking and sleep, his imagination would take him almost anywhere.

Sometimes he would lie on his back with the blankets drawn up to his nose and his pillow on top of his forehead so—that only his eyes looked out. This was his spaceman game, and the pillow was his helmet. He travelled through sparkling light-years, passing Jupiter so close that he could see the storms raging on its surface, then swung on to Neptune, chilly and green, and Pluto, beyond. On some nights he would travel so far that he was unable to return to Earth, and he would drift further and further into the outer reaches of space until he became nothing but a tiny speck winking in the darkness and he fell asleep.

At other times, he was captain of a U-boat trapped thousands of feet below the surface. He would have to squeeze along cramped and darkened passageways to open up stopcocks, with water flooding in on all sides, and elbow his way along a torpedo tube in order to escape. He would come up to the surface into the chilly air of the bedroom, gasping for breath.

Then he would crawl right down to the very end of the bed, where the sheets and the blankets were tucked in really tight. He was a coalminer, making his way through the narrowest of fissures, with millions of tons of carboniferous rock on top of him.

He never took a flashlight to bed with him. This would

have revealed that the inside of his space-helmet didn't have any dials or knobs or breathing tubes; and that the submarine wasn't greasy and metallic and crowded with complicated valves; and that the grim black coal-face at which he so desperately hewed was nothing but a clean white sheet.

Earlier this evening he had been watching a programme on pot-holing on television and he was keen to try it. He was going to be the leader of an underground rescue team, trying to find a boy who had wedged himself in a crevice. It would mean crawling through one interconnected passage after another, then down through a water-filled sump, until he reached the tiny cavern where the boy was trapped.

His mother sat on the end of the bed and kept him talking. He was going back to school in two days' time and she kept on telling him how much she was going to miss him. He was going to miss her, too, and Tiggy, their golden retriever, and everything here at Home Hill. More than anything, he was going to miss his adventures under the blankets. You couldn't go burrowing under the bedclothes when you were at school. Everybody would rag you too much.

He had always thought his mother was beautiful and tonight was no exception, although he wished that she would go away and let him start his pot-holing. What made her beauty all the more impressive was the fact that she would be thirty-three next April, which Martin considered to be prehistoric. His best friend's mother was only thirty-three and she looked like an old lady by comparison. Martin's mother had bobbed brunette hair and a wide, generous face without a single wrinkle; and dark brown eyes that were always filled with love. It was always painful, going back to school. He didn't realize how much it hurt her, too: how many times she sat on his empty bed when he was away, her hand pressed against her mouth and her eyes filled with tears.

"Daddy will be back on Thursday," she said. "He wants to take us all out before you go back to school. Is there anywhere special you'd like to go?"

"Can we go to that Chinese place? The one where they give you those cracker things?"

"Pang's? Yes, I'm sure we can. Daddy was worried you were going to say McDonald's."

She stood up and kissed him. For a moment they were very close, face-to-face. He didn't realize how much he looked like her—that they were both staring into a kind of a mirror. He could see what he would have looked like, if he had been a woman; and she could see what she would have looked like, if she had been a boy. They were two different manifestations of the same person, and it gave them a secret intimacy that nobody else could understand.

"Good night," she said. "Sweet dreams." And for a moment she laid a hand on top of his head as if she could sense that something momentous was going to happen to him. Something that could take him out of her reach forever.

"Good night, Mummy," he said, and kissed her cheek, which was softer than anything else he had ever touched. She closed the door.

He lay on his back for a while, waiting, staring at the ceiling. His room wasn't completely dark: a thin slice of light came in from the top of the door, illuminating the white paper lantern that hung above his bed so that it looked like a huge, pale planet (which it often was). He stayed where he was until he heard his mother close the living room door, and then he wriggled down beneath the blankets.

He cupped his hand over his mouth like a microphone and said, "Underground Rescue Squad Three, reporting for duty."

"Hello, Underground Rescue Squad Three. Are we glad

you're here! There's a boy trapped in Legg's Elbow, 225 metres down, past Devil's Corner. He's seventeen years old, and he's badly injured."

"Okay, headquarters. We'll send somebody down there straight away."

"It'll have to be your very best man . . . it's really dangerous down there. It's started to rain and all the caves are flooding. You've probably got an hour at the most."

"Don't worry. We'll manage it. Roger and out."

Martin put on his equipment. His thermal underwear, his boots, his backpack and his goggles. Anybody who was watching would have seen nothing more than a boy-shaped lump under the blankets, wriggling and jerking and bouncing up and down. But by the time he was finished he was fully dressed for crawling his way down to Devil's Corner.

His last radio message was, "Headquarters? I'm going in."

"Be careful, Underground Rescue Squad Three. The rain's getting heavier."

Martin lifted his head and inhaled a lungful of chilly bedroom air. Then he plunged downwards into the first crevice that would take him down into the caves. The rock ceiling was dangerously low, and he had to crawl his way in like a commando, on his elbows. He tore the sleeve of his waterproof jacket on a protruding rock and he gashed his cheek, but he was so heroic that he simply wiped away the blood with the back of his hand and carried on crawling forward.

It wasn't long before he reached a tight, awkward corner, which was actually the end of the bed. He had to negotiate it by lying on his side, reaching into the nearest crevice for a handhold, and heaving himself forward inch by inch. He had only just squeezed himself around this corner when he came to another, and had to struggle his way around it in the same way.

The air in the caves was growing more and more stifling, and Martin was already uncomfortably hot. But he knew he had to go on. The boy in Legg's Elbow was counting on him, just like the rest of Underground Rescue Squad Three, and the whole world above ground, which was waiting anxiously for him to emerge.

He wriggled onwards, his fingers bleeding, until he reached the sump. This was a 10-metre section of tunnel which was completely flooded with black, chill water. Five pot-holers had drowned in it since the caves were first discovered, two of them experts. Not only was the sump flooded, it had a tight bend right in the middle of it, with rocky protrusions that could easily snag a pot-holer's belt or his backpack. Martin hesitated for a moment, but then he took a deep breath of stale air and plunged beneath the surface.

The water was stunningly cold, but Martin swam along the tunnel with powerful, even strokes until he reached the bend. Still holding his breath, he angled himself sideways and started to tug himself between the jagged, uncompromising rocks. He was almost through when one of the straps on his backpack was caught and he found himself entangled. He twisted around, trying to reach behind his back so that he could pull the strap free from the rock, but he succeeded only in winding it even more tightly. He tried twisting around the other way, but now the strap tightened itself into a knot.

He had been holding his breath for so long now that his lungs were hurting. Desperately, he reached into his pocket and took out his clasp knife. He managed to unfold the blade, bend his arm behind his back and slash at the tightened strap. He missed it with his first two strokes, but his third stroke managed to cut it halfway through. His eyes were bulging and he was bursting for air, but he didn't allow himself to give in. One more cut and the strap abruptly gave way.

Martin kicked both legs and swam forward as fast as he could. He reached the end of the sump and broke the surface, taking in huge grateful breaths of frigid subterranean air.

He had beaten the sump, but there were more hazards ahead of him. The rainwater from the surface was already beginning to penetrate the lower reaches of the cave system. He could hear water rushing through crevices and clattering through galleries. In less than half an hour, every pot-hole would be flooded, and there would be no way of getting back out again.

Martin pressed on, sliding on his belly through a fissure that was rarely more than 30 centimetres high. He was bruised and exhausted, but he had almost reached Devil's Corner. From there, it was only a few metres to Legg's Elbow.

Rainwater trickled from the low limestone ceiling and coursed down the side of the fissure, but Martin didn't care. He was already soaked and he was crawling at last into Devil's Corner. He slid across to the narrow vertical crevice called Legg's Elbow and peered down it, trying to see the trapped boy.

"Hallo!" he called. "Is anybody there? Hallo, can you hear me? I've come to get you out!"

Martin listened but there was no answer. There wasn't even an imaginary answer. He forced his head further down, so that he could see deeper into the crevice, but there was nobody there. Nobody crying; nobody calling out. No pale distressed face looking back up at him.

He had actually reached the bottom of the bed, and was looking over the edge of the mattress, into the tightly-tucked dead-end of blankets and sheets.

He had a choice, but there was very little time. Either he could climb down Legg's Elbow to see if he could find where the boy was trapped, or else he could give up his rescue mission and turn back. In less than twenty minutes, the caves would be completely flooded, and anybody down here would be drowned.

He decided to risk it. It would take him only seven or eight minutes to climb all the way down Legg's Elbow, and another five to crawl back as far as the sump. Once he was back through the sump, the caves rose quite steeply towards the surface, so that he would have a fair chance of escaping before they filled up with water.

He pushed his way over the edge of Legg's Elbow, and began to inch down the crevice. He could slip at any moment, and his arms and legs were shaking with effort. He could feel the limestone walls starting to move—a long slow seismic slide that made him feel as if the whole world were collapsing all around him. If Legg's Elbow fell in, he would be trapped, unable to climb back out, while more and more rainwater gushed into the underground caverns.

Panting with effort, he tried to cling on to the sides of the crevice. There was one moment when he thought he was going to be able to heave himself back. But then everything slid—sheets, blankets, limestone rocks, and he ended up right at the bottom of Legg's Elbow, buried alive.

For a moment, he panicked. He could hardly breathe. But then he started to pull at the fallen rockslide, tearing a way out of the crevice stone by stone. There had to be a way out. If there was a deeper, lower cavern, perhaps he could climb down to the foot of the hill and crawl out of a fox's earth or any other fissure he could locate. After all, if the rainwater could find an escape-route through the limestone, he was sure that *he* could.

He managed to heave all of the rocks aside. Now all he had to do was burrow through the sludge. He took great handfuls of it and dragged it behind him, until at last he felt the flow of fresh air into the crevice: fresh air, and wind. He crawled out of Legg's Elbow on his hands and knees, and found himself lying on a flat, sandy beach. The day was pearly-gray, but the sun was high in the sky and the ocean peacefully glittered in the distance. He turned around and saw that, behind him, there was nothing but miles and miles of gray tussocky grass. Somehow he had emerged from these tussocks like somebody emerging from underneath a heavy blanket.

He stood up and brushed himself down. He was still wearing his waterproof jacket and his pot-holing boots. He was glad of them, because the breeze was thin and chilly. Up above him, white gulls circled and circled, not mewing or crying, their eyes as expressionless as sharks' eyes. In the sand at his feet tiny iridescent shells were embedded.

For a moment, he was unable to decide what he ought to do next, and where he ought to go. Perhaps he should try to crawl back into the pot-hole, and retrace his route to the surface. But he was out in the open air here, and there didn't seem to be any point in it. Besides, the pot-hole was heavily covered in grass, and it was difficult to see exactly where it was. He thought he ought to walk inland a short way, to see if he could find a road or a house or any indication of where he might be.

But then, very far away, where the sea met the sky, he saw a small fishing boat drawing in to the shore, and a man climbing out of it. The fishing boat had a russet-coloured triangular sail, like a fishing boat in an old-fashioned watercolour. He started to walk towards it; and then, when he realized how far it was, he started to run. His waterproof jacket made a chuffing noise and his boots left deep impressions in the sand. The seagulls kept pace with him, circling and circling.

Running and walking, it took him almost twenty minutes to reach the fishing boat. A white-bearded man in olive-coloured oilskins was kneeling down beside it, stringing fat triangular fish on to a line. The fish were brilliant, and they shone with every colour of the rainbow. Some of them were still alive, thrashing their tails and blowing their gills.

Martin stopped a few yards away and watched and said nothing. Eventually the man stopped stringing fish and looked up at him. He was handsome, in an old-fashioned way—chiselled, like Charlton Heston. But his eyes were completely blank: the colour of sky on an overcast day. He reminded Martin of somebody familiar, but he couldn't think who he was.

Not far away, sitting cross-legged on a coil of rope, was a thin young boy in a hooded coat. He was playing a thin, plaintive tune on a flute. His wrists were so thin and the tune was so sad that Martin almost felt like crying.

"Well, you came at last," said the man with eyes the colour of sky. "We've been waiting for you."

"Waiting for me? Why?"

"You're a tunneller, aren't you? You do your best work underground."

"I was looking for a boy. He was supposed to be stuck in Legg's Elbow, but—I don't know. The whole cave system was flooded, and it seemed to collapse."

"And you thought that you escaped?"

"I did escape."

The man stood up, his waterproofs creaking. He smelled strongly of fresh-caught fish, all that slime on their scales. "That was only a way of bringing you here. We need you to help us, an experienced tunneller like you. What do you think of these fish?"

"I never saw fish like that before."

"They're not fish. Not in the strictest sense of the word. They're more like ideas."

He picked one up, so that it twisted and shimmered; and Martin could see that it was an idea, rather than a fish. It was an idea about being angry with people you loved, and how you could explain that you loved them, and calm them down. Then the man held up another fish; and this was a different fish altogether, a different idea. This was a glittering idea about numbers: how the metre was measured by the speed of light. If light could be compressed, then distance could, too—and the implications of that were quite startling.

Martin couldn't really understand how the fish managed to be ideas as well as fish; but they were; and some of the ideas were so beautiful and strange that he stood staring at them and feeling as if his whole life was turning under his feet.

The sun began to descend towards the horizon. The small boy put away his flute and helped the fisherman to gather the last of his lines and his nets. The fisherman gave Martin a large woven basket to carry, full of blue glass fishing floats and complicated reels. "We'll have to put our best foot forward, if we want to get home before dark."

They walked for a while in silence. The breeze blew the sand in sizzling snakes, and behind them the sea softly applauded, like a faraway audience. After four or five minutes, though, Martin said, "Why do you need a tunneller?"

The fisherman gave him a quick, sideways glance. "You may not believe it, but there's another world, apart from this one. A place that exists right next to us, like the world that you can see when you look in a mirror . . . essentially the same, but different."

"What does that have to do with tunnelling?"

"Everything, because there's only one way through to this world, and that's by crawling into your bed and through to the other side."

Martin stopped in his tracks. "What the hell are you talking about, *bed? I* tunnel into caves and pot-holes, not beds."

"There's no difference," said the fisherman. "Caves, beds, they're just the same . . . a way through to somewhere else."

Martin started walking again. "You'd better explain yourself." The sun had almost reached the horizon now, and their shadows were giants with stilt-like legs and distant, pin-size heads.

"There isn't much to explain. There's another world, beneath the blankets. Some people can find it, some can't. I suppose it depends on their imagination. My daughter Leonora always had the imagination. She used to hide under the blankets and pretend that she was a cave-dweller in prehistoric times; or a Red Indian woman, in a tent. But about a month ago she said that she had found this other world, right at the very bottom of the bed. She could see it, but she couldn't wriggle her way into it."

"Did she describe it?"

The fisherman nodded. "She said that it was dark, very dark, with tangled thorn-bushes and branchy trees. She said that she could see shadows moving around in it—shadows that could have been animals, like wolves; or hunched-up men wearing black fur cloaks."

"It doesn't sound like the kind of world that anybody would want to visit."

"We never had the chance to find out whether Leonora went because she wanted to. Two days ago my wife went into her bedroom to discover that her bed was empty. We thought at first that she might have run away. But we'd had no family arguments, and she really had no cause to. Then we stripped back her blankets and found that the lower parts of her sheets were torn, as if some kind of animal had been clawing at it." He paused, and then he said, with some difficulty, "We found blood, too. Not very much. Maybe she scratched herself on one of the thorns. Maybe one of the animals clawed her."

By now they had reached the grassy dunes and started to climb up them. Not far away there were three small cottages, two painted white and one painted pink, with lights in the windows, and fishing nets hung up all around them for repair.

"Didn't you try going after her yourself?" asked Martin.

"Yes. But it was no use. I don't have enough imagination. All I could see was sheets and blankets. I fish for rational ideas—for astronomy and physics and human logic. I couldn't imagine Underbed so I couldn't visit it."

"Underbed?"

The fisherman gave him a small, grim smile. "That's what Leonora called it."

They reached the cottage and laid down all of their baskets and tackle. The kitchen door opened and a woman came out, wiping her hands on a flowery apron. Her blond hair was braided on top of her head and she was quite beautiful in an odd, expressionless way, as if she were a competent oil painting rather than a real woman.

"You're back, then?" she said. "And this is the tunneller?"

The fisherman laid his hand on Martin's shoulder. "That's right. He came, just like he was supposed to. He can start to look for her tonight."

Martin was about to protest, but the woman came up and took hold of both of his hands. "I know you'll do everything you can," she told him. "And God bless you for coming here and trying."

They had supper that evening around the kitchen table—a rich fish pie with a crispy potato crust, and glasses of cold cider. The fisherman and his wife said very little, but scarcely took their eyes away from Martin once. It was almost as if they were frightened that he was going to vanish into thin air.

On the mantelpiece, a plain wooden clock loudly ticked out the time, and on the wall next to it hung a watercolour of a house that for some reason Martin recognized. There was a woman standing in the garden, with her back to him. He felt that if she were able to turn around he would know at once who she was.

There were other artifacts in the room that he recognized: a big green earthenware jug and a pastille-burner in the shape of a little cottage. There was a china cat, too, which stared at him with a knowing smile. He had never been here before, so he couldn't imagine why all these things looked so familiar. Perhaps he was tired, and suffering from *déjà vu*.

After supper they sat around the range for a while and the fisherman explained how he went out trawling every day for idea-fish. In the deeper waters, around the sound, there were much bigger fish, entire theoretical concepts, swimming in shoals.

"This is the land of ideas," he said, in a matter-of-fact way. "Even the swallows and thrushes in the sky are little whimsical thoughts. You can catch a swallow and think of something you once forgot; or have a small, sweet notion that you never would have had before.

"You—you come from the land of action, where things are *done,* not just discussed."

"And Underbed? What kind of a land is that?"

"I don't know. The land of fear, I suppose. The land of darkness, where everything always threatens to go wrong."

"And that's where you want me to go looking for your daughter?"

The fisherman's wife got up from her chair, lifted a photograph from the mantelpiece and passed it across to Martin without a word. It showed a young blond girl standing on the seashore in a thin summer dress. She was pale-eyed and captivatingly pretty. Her bare toes were buried in the sand. In the distance, a flock of birds were scattering, and Martin thought of "small, sweet notions that you never would have had before."

Martin studied the photograph for a moment and then gave it back. "Very well, then," he said. "I'll have a try." After all, it was his duty to rescue people. He hadn't been able to find the boy trapped in Legg's Elbow: perhaps he could redeem himself by finding Leonora.

Just after eleven o'clock they showed him across to her room. It was small and plain, except for a pine dressing table crowded with dolls and soft toys. The plain pine bed stood right in the middle of the longer wall, with an engraving of a park hanging over it. Martin frowned at the engraving more closely. He was sure that the park was familiar. Perhaps he had visited it when he was a child. But here, in the land of ideas?

The fisherman's wife closed the red gingham curtains and folded down the blankets on the bed.

"Do you still have the sheets from the time she disappeared?" Martin asked her.

She nodded, and opened a small pine linen chest at the foot of the bed. She lifted out a folded white sheet and spread it out on top of the bed. One end was ripped and snagged, as if it had been caught in machinery, or clawed by something at least as big as a tiger.

"She wouldn't have done this herself," said the fisherman. "She *couldn't* have done."

"Still," said Martin. "If she didn't do it, what did?"

By midnight Martin was in bed, wearing a long white borrowed nightshirt, and the cottage was immersed in darkness. The breeze persistently rattled the window-sash like somebody trying to get in; and beyond the dunes Martin could hear the sea. He always thought that there was nothing more lonely than the sea at night.

He didn't know whether he believed in Underbed or not. He didn't even know whether he believed in the land of ideas or not. He felt as if he were caught in a dream—yet how could he be? The bed felt real and the pillows felt real and he could just make out his pot-holing clothes hanging over the back of the chair.

He lay on his back for almost fifteen minutes without moving. Then he decided that he'd better take a look down at the end of the bed. After all, if Underbed didn't exist, the worst that could happen to him was that he would end up half-stifled and hot. He lifted the blankets, twisted himself around, and plunged down beneath them.

Immediately, he found himself crawling in a low, peaty crevice that was thickly tangled with tree roots. His nostrils were filled with the rank odour of wet leaves and mould. He must have wriggled into a gap beneath the floor of a wood forest. It was impenetrably dark, and the roots snared and scratched his face. He was sure that he could feel beetles crawling across his hands and down the back of his collar. He wasn't wearing nightclothes any longer. Instead, he was ruggedly dressed in a thick checkered shirt and heavy duty jeans.

After 40 or 50 metres, he had to crawl right beneath the bole of a huge tree. Part of it was badly rotted, and as he inched his way through the clinging taproots, he was unnervingly aware that the tree probably weighed several tons and if he disturbed it, it could collapse into this subterranean and crush him completely. He had to dig through peat and soil, and at one point his fingers clawed something both crackly and slimy. It was the decomposed body of a badger that must have become trapped underground. He stopped for a moment, suffocated and sickened, but then he heard the huge tree creaking and showers of damp peat fell into his hair, and he knew that if he didn't get out of there quickly he was going to be buried alive.

He squirmed out from under the tree, pulling aside a thick curtain of hairy roots, and discovered that he was out in the open air. It was still nighttime, and very cold, and his breath smoked in the way that he and his friends had pretended to smoke on winter mornings when they waited for the bus for school—which was, when? Yesterday? Or months ago? Or even years ago?

He stood in the forest and there was no moon, yet the forest was faintly lit by an eerie phosphorescence. He imagined that aliens might have landed behind the trees. A vast spaceship filled with narrow, complicated chambers where a space mechanic might get lost for months, squeezing his pelvis through angular bulkheads and impossibly-constricted service-tunnels.

The forest was silent. No insects chirruped. No wind disturbed the trees. The only sound was that of Martin's footsteps, as he made his way cautiously through the brambles, not sure in which direction he should be heading. Yet he felt he was going the right way. He felt drawn: *magnetized,* almost, like a quivering compass needle. He was plunging deeper and deeper into the land of Underbed: a land of airlessness and claustrophobia, a land in which most people couldn't even breathe. But to him, it was a land of closeness and complete security.

Up above him, the branches of the trees were so thickly entwined together that it was impossible to see the sky. It could have been daytime up above, but here in the forest it was always night.

He stumbled onwards for over half an hour. Every now and then he stopped and listened, but the forest remained silent. As he walked on he became aware of something pale, flickering behind the trees, right in the very corner of his eye. He stopped again, and turned around, but it disappeared, whatever it was.

"Is anybody there?" he called out, his voice muffled by the encroaching trees. There was no answer, but now Martin was certain that he could hear dry leaves being shuffled, and twigs being softly snapped. He was certain that he could hear somebody *breathing.*

He walked further, and he was conscious of the pale shape following him like a paper lantern on a stick, bobbing from tree to tree, just out of sight. But although it remained invisible, it became noisier and noisier, its breath coming in short, harsh gasps, its feet rustling faster and faster across the forest floor.

Suddenly, something clutched at his shirtsleeve—a hand, or a claw—and ripped the fabric. He twisted around and almost lost his balance. Standing close to him in the phosphorescent gloom was a girl of sixteen or seventeen, very slender and white-faced. Her hair was wild and straw-like, and backcombed into a huge birds nest, decorated with thorns and holly and moss and shiny maroon berries. Her irises were charcoal-gray—night-eyes, with wide black pupils. Eyes that could see in the dark. Her face was starved-looking but mesmerically pretty. It was her white, white skin that had made Martin believe that he was being followed by a paper lantern.

Her costume was extraordinary and erotic. She wore a short blouse made of hundreds of bunched-up ruffles of grubby, tattered lace. Every ruffle seemed to be decorated with a bead or a medal or a rabbit's-foot, or a bird fashioned out of cooking-foil. But her blouse reached only as far as her navel, and it was all she wore. Her feet were filthy and her thighs were streaked with mud.

"What are you searching for?" she asked him, in a thin, lisping voice.

Martin was so confused and embarrassed by her half-nakedness that he turned away. "I'm looking for someone, that's all."

"Nobody looks for *anybody* here. This is Underbed."

"Well, *I'm* looking for someone. A girl called Leonora."

"A girl who came out from under the woods?"

"I suppose so, yes."

"We saw her passing by. She was searching for whatever it is that makes her frightened. But she won't find it here."

"I thought this was the land of fear."

"Oh, it is. But there's a difference between fear, isn't there, and what actually makes you frightened?"

"I don't understand."

"It's easy. Fear of the dark is only a fear. It isn't anything real. But what about things that really do hide in the dark? What about the coat on the back of your chair that isn't a coat at all? What about your dead friend standing in the corner, next to your wardrobe, waiting for you to wake?"

"So what is Leonora looking for?"

"It depends what's been frightening her, doesn't it? But the way she went, she was heading for Under-Underbed; and that's where the darkest things live."

"Can you show me the way?"

The girl emphatically shook her head so that her beads rattled and her ribbons shook. "You don't know what the darkest things are, do you?" She covered her face with her hands, her fingers slightly parted so that only her eyes looked out. *"The darkest things are the very darkest things; and once you go to visit them in Under-Underbed, they'll know which way you came, they'll be able to smell you, and they'll follow you back there."*

Martin said, "I still have to find Leonora. I promised."

The girl stared at him for a long, long time, saying nothing, as if she were sure that she would never see him again and wanted to remember what he looked like. Then she turned away and beckoned him to follow.

They walked through the forest for at least another twenty minutes. The branches grew sharper and denser, and Martin's cheeks and ears were badly scratched. All the same, with his arms raised to protect his eyes, he followed the girl's thin, pale back as she guided him deeper and deeper into the trees. As she walked, she sang a high-pitched song.

The day's in disguise

It's wearing a face I don't recognize

It has rings on its fingers and silken roads in its eyes

Eventually they reached a small clearing. On one side the ground had humped up, and was thickly covered with sodden green moss. Without hesitation the girl crouched down and lifted up one side of the moss, like a blanket, revealing a dark, root-wriggling interior.

"Down there?" asked Martin, in alarm.

The girl nodded. "But remember what I said. Once you find them, they'll follow you back. That's what happens when you go looking for the darkest things."

"All the same, I promised."

"Yes. But just think *who* you promised, and why. And just think who Leonora might be; and who I am; and what it is you're doing here."

"I don't know," he admitted; and he didn't. But while the girl held the moss blanket as high as she could manage, he climbed on to his side and worked his way underneath it, feet first, as if he were climbing into bed. The roots embraced him, they took him into their arms like thin-fingered women, and soon he was buried in the mossy hump up to his neck. The girl knelt beside him and her face was calm and regretful.

For some reason her nakedness didn't embarrass him any more. It was almost as if he knew her too well. But without saying anything more, she lowered the blanket of moss over his face and his world went completely dark.

He took a deep, damp-tasting breath, and then he began to insinuate his way under the ground. At first, he was crawling quite level, but he soon reached a place where the soil dropped sharply away into absolute blackness. He thought he could feel a faint draft blowing, and the dull sound of hammering and knocking. This must be it: the end of Underbed, where Under-Underbed began. This was where the darkest things lived. Not just the fear, but the reality.

For the first time since he had set out on his rescue mission he was tempted to turn back. If he crawled back out of the moss blanket now, and went back through the forest, then the darkest things would never know that he had been here. But he knew that he had to continue. Once you plunged into bed, and Underbed, and Under-Underbed, you had committed yourself.

He swung his legs over the edge of the precipice, clinging with both hands on to the roots that sprouted out of the soil like hairs on a giant's head. Little by little, he lowered himself down the face of the precipice, his shoes sliding in the peat and bringing down noisy cascades of earth and pebbles. The most frightening part about his descent was that he couldn't see anything at all. He couldn't even see how far down he had to climb. For all he knew, the precipice went down and down forever.

Every time he clutched at a root, he couldn't help himself from dragging off its fibrous outer covering, and his hands soon became impossibly slippery with sap.

Below him, however, the hammering had grown much louder, and he could hear echoes too, and double echoes.

He grasped at a large taproot, and immediately his hand slipped. He tried to snatch a handful of smaller roots, but they all tore away, with a sound like rotten curtains tearing. He clawed at the soil itself, but there was nothing that he could do to stop himself from falling. He thought, for an instant: *I'm going to die.*

He fell heavily through a damp, lath-and-plaster ceiling. With an ungainly wallop he landed on a sodden mattress, and tumbled off it on to a wet carpeted floor. He lay on his side for a moment, winded, but then he managed to twist himself around and climb up on to his knees. He was in a bedroom—a bedroom which he recognized, although the wallpaper was mildewed and peeling, and the closet door was tilting off its hinges to reveal a row of empty wire hangers.

He stood up, and went across to the window. At first he thought it was nighttime, but then he realized that the window was completely filled in with peat. The bedroom was buried deep below the ground.

He began to feel the first tight little flutters of panic. What if he couldn't climb his way out of here? What if he had to spend the rest of his life buried deep beneath the surface, under layers and layers of soil and moss and suffocating blankets? He tried to think what he ought to do next, but the hammering was now so loud that it made the floor tremble and the hangers in the closet jingle together.

He had to take control of himself. He was an expert, after all: a fully-trained pot-holer, with thirty years' experience.

His first priority was to find Leonora, and see how difficult it was going to be to get her back up the precipice. Perhaps there was another way out of Under-Underbed which didn't involve 20 or 30 metres of dangerous climbing?

He opened the bedroom door and found himself confronted by a long corridor with a shiny linoleum floor. The walls were lined with doors and painted, with a tan dado, like a school or a hospital. A single naked light hung at the very far end of the corridor, and under this light stood a girl in a long white nightgown. Her blond hair was flying in an unfelt wind, and her face was so white that it could have been sculpted out of chalk.

The hem of her nightgown was ripped into tatters and spattered with blood. Her calves and her feet were savagely clawed, with the skin hanging down in ribbons, and blood running all over the floor.

"Leonora?" said Martin, too softly for the girl to be able to hear. Then, "Leonora!"

She took one shuffling step towards him, and another, but then she stopped and leaned against the side of the corridor. It was the same Leonora whose photograph he had seen in the fisherman's cottage, but three or four years older, maybe more.

Martin started to walk towards her. As he passed each door along the corridor, it seemed to fly open by itself. The hammering was deafening now, but the rooms on either side were empty, even though he could see armchairs and sofas and coffee tables and paintings on the walls. They were like tableaux from somebody's life, year by year, decade by decade.

"Leonora?" he said, and took her into his arms. She was very cold, and shivering. "Come on, Leonora, I've come to take you home."

"There's no way out," she whispered, in a voice like blanched almonds. "The darkest things are coming and there's no way out."

"There's always a way out. Come on, I'll carry you."

"There's no way out!" she screamed at him, right in his face. *"We're buried too deep and there's no way out!"*

"Don't panic!" he shouted back at her. "If we go back to the bedroom we can find a way to climb back up to Underbed! Now, come on, let me carry you!"

He bent down a little, and then heaved her up on to his shoulder. She weighed hardly anything at all. Her feet were badly lacerated. Two of her left toes were dangling by nothing but skin, and blood dripped steadily on to Martin's jeans.

As they made their way back down the corridor, the doors slammed shut in the same way that they had flown open. But they were still 10 or 11 metres away from the bedroom door when Leonora clutched him so tightly round the throat that she almost strangled him, and screamed. *"They're here! The darkest things! They're following us!"*

Martin turned around, just as the lightbulb at the end of the corridor was shattered. In a single instant of light, however, he had seen something terrible. It looked like a tall, thin man in a gray monkish hood. Its face was as beatifically perfect as the effigy of a saint. Perfect, that is, except for its mouth, which was drawn back in a lustful grin, revealing a jungle of irregular, pointed teeth. And below that mouth, in another lustful grin, a second mouth, with a thin tongue-tip that lashed from side to side as if it couldn't wait to start feeding.

Both its arms were raised, so that its sleeves had dropped back, exposing not hands but hooked black claws.

This was one of the darkest things. The darkest thing that

Leonora had feared, and had to face.

In the sudden blackness, Martin was disoriented and thrown off balance. He half-dropped Leonora, but he managed to heft her up again and stumble in the direction of the bedroom. He found the door, groped it open and then slammed it shut behind them and turned the key.

"Hurry!" he said. "You'll have to climb on to the bedhead, and up through the ceiling!"

They heard a thick, shuffling noise in the corridor outside, and an appalling screeching of claws against painted plaster walls. The bedroom door shook with a sudden collision and plaster showered down from the lintel. There was another blow, and then the claws scratched slowly down the doorpanels. Martin turned around. In spite of her injured feet, Leonora had managed to balance herself on the brass bedrail, and now she was painfully trying to pull herself through the hole in the damaged ceiling. He struggled up on to the mattress to help her, and as the door was shaken yet again, she managed to climb through. Martin followed, his hands torn by splintered laths. As he drew his legs up, the bedroom door racketed open and he glimpsed the hooded gray creature with its upraised claws. It raised its head and looked up at him and both its mouths opened in mockery and greed.

The climb up the precipice seemed to take months. Together, Martin and Leonora inched their way up through soft, collapsing peat, using even the frailest of roots for a handhold. Several times they slipped back. Again and again they were showered with soil and pebbles and leaf-mould. Martin had to spit it out of his mouth and rub it out of his eyes. And all the time they knew that the darkest thing was following them, hungry and triumphant, and that it would always follow them, wherever they went.

Unexpectedly, they reached the crest of the precipice. Leonora was weeping with pain and exhaustion, but Martin took hold of her arm and dragged her through the roots and the soft, giving soil until at last they came to the blanket of moss. He lifted it up with his arm, trembling with exhaustion, and Leonora climbed out from under it and into the clearing. Martin, gasping with effort, followed her.

There was no sign of the forest-girl anywhere, so Martin had to guess the way back. Both he and Leonora were too tired to speak, but they kept on pushing their way through the branches side by side, and there was no doubt of their companionship. They had escaped from Under-Underbed, and now they were making their way back through Underbed and up to the worlds of light and fresh air.

It took Martin far longer than he thought to find the underground cavity which would take them back to Leonora's world. But a strong sense of direction kept him going: a sense that they were making their way upwards. Just when he thought that they were lost for good, he felt his fingers grasping sheets instead of soil, and he and Leonora climbed out of her rumpled bed into her bedroom. Her father was sitting beside the bed, and when they emerged he embraced them both and skipped an odd little fisherman's dance.

"You're a brave boy, you're a brave boy, bringing my Leonora back to me."

Martin smeared his face with his hands. "She's going to need treatment on her feet. Is there a doctor close by?"

"No, but there's lady's smock and marigolds; and myrtle, for dismissing bad dreams."

"Her toes are almost severed. She needs stitches. She needs a doctor."

"An idea will do just as well as a doctor."

"There's something else," said Martin. "The thing that

hurt her . . . I think it's probably following us."

The fisherman laid his hand on Martin's shoulder and nodded. "We'll take care of that, my young fellow."

So they stood by the shore in the mauvish light of an early summer's evening and they set fire to Leonora's bed, blankets and sheets and all, and they pushed it out to sea like an Arthurian funeral barge. The flames lapped into the sky like dragons' tongues, and fragments of burned blanket whirled into the air.

Leonora with her bandaged feet stood close to Martin and held his arm; and when it was time for him to go she kissed him and her eyes were filled with tears. The fisherman gratefully clasped his hand. "Always remember," he said. "What might have been is just as important as what actually was."

Martin nodded; and then he started walking back along the shoreline, to the tussocky grass that would lead him back to Legg's Elbow and the caves. He turned around only once, but by then it was too dark to see anything but the fire burning from Leonora's bed, 300 metres out to sea.

His mother frantically stripped back his sheets and blankets in the morning and found him at the bottom of the bed in his red-and-white striped pajamas, his skin cold and his limbs stiff with rigor mortis. There was no saving him: the doctor said that he had probably suffocated some time after midnight, and by the time his mother found him he had been dead for seven-and-a-half hours.

When he was cremated, his mother wept and said that it was just as if Martin's was a life that had never happened.

But who could say such a thing? Not the fisherman and his family, who went back to their imaginary cottage and said a prayer for the tunneller who rescued their daughter. Not a wild, half-naked girl who walked through a forest that never was, thinking of a man who dared to face the darkest things. And not the darkest thing which heaved itself out from under the moss and emerged at last in the world of ideas from a smoking, half-sunken bed; a hooded gray shape in the darkness.

And, in the end, not Martin's mother, when she went back into his bedroom after the funeral to strip the bed.

She pulled back the blankets one by one; then she tugged off the sheets. But it was just when she was dragging out the sheets from the very end of the bed that she saw six curved black shapes over the end of the mattress. She frowned, and walked around the bed to see what they were.

It was only when she looked really close that she realized they were claws.

Cautiously, she dragged down the sheet a little further. The claws were attached to hands and the hands seemed to disappear into the crack between sheet and mattress.

This was a joke, she thought. Some really sick joke. Martin had been dead for less than a week and someone was playing some childish, hurtful prank. She wrenched back the sheet even further and seized hold of one of the claws, so that she could pull it free.

To her horror, it lashed out at her, and tore the flesh on the back of her hand. It lashed again and again, ripping the mattress and shredding the sheets. She screamed, and tried to scramble away, her blood spotting the sheets. But something rose out of the end of the bed in a tumult of torn foam and ripped-apart padding—something tall and gray with a face like a saint and two parallel mouths crammed with shark's teeth. It rose up and up, until it was towering above her and it was cold as the Arctic. It was so cold that even *her* breath fumed.

"There are some places you should never go," it whispered at her, with both mouths speaking in unison. "There are some things you should never think about. There are some people whose curiosity will always bring calamity, especially to themselves, and to the people they love. You don't need to go looking for your fears. Your fears will always follow you, and find you out."

With that, and without hesitation, the darkest thing brought down its right-hand claw like a cat swatting a thrush and ripped her face apart.

Before she could fall to the carpet, it ripped her again, and then again, until the whole bedroom was decorated with blood.

It bent down then, almost as if it were kneeling in reverence to its own cruelty and its own greed, and it firmly seized her flesh with both of its mouths. Gradually, it disappeared back into the crevice at the end of the bed, dragging her with it, inch by inch, one lolling leg, one flopping arm.

The last to go was her left hand, with her wedding ring on it.

Then there was nothing but a torn, bloodstained bed in an empty room, and a faint sound that could have been water, trickling down through underground caves, or the sea, whispering in the distance, or the rustling of branches in a deep, dark forest.

The Gray Madonna

Bruges, Belgium

Although it is such a crowded and popular tourist town, Bruges hasn't lost its feeling of medieval mysticism, especially on chill, autumnal days when the fog hangs over the canals, and the footsteps of unseen people clatter through its winding, cobbled streets. The capital of West Flanders, Bruges has kept its old city walls and its fortified gates, and the old city has some of the grandest Gothic buildings in Europe, especially the 14th-century cathedral of St. Saveur and the church of Notre Dame. It was while I was walking through the statue collection in the church of Notre Dame that I was first inspired to write about the gray madonna. I had already seen the stone virgins that adorn the street corners of Bruges, but here was Michelangelo's Virgin & Child*—a statue that seems to have a life of its own. When you reach out to touch the Virgin's hand, you can hardly believe that it isn't going to be warm.*

Go to Bruges for its lace and its embroidery and its freshly made chocolates. Enjoy its cafés and its restaurants, and eat as many steamed mussels and as much waterzooi *chicken stew as you want. Take a boat trip around the canals, visit its art galleries and walk in its parks. But be careful of going down its side streets alone, and always look around you to see who might be following.*

He had always known that he would have to return to Bruges. This time, however, he chose winter, when the air was foggy and the canals had turned to the colour of breathed-on pewter, and the narrow medieval streets were far less crowded with shuffling tourists.

He had tried to avoid thinking about Bruges for three

years now. Forgetting Bruges—really forgetting—was out of the question. But he had devised all kinds of ways of diverting his attention away from it, of mentally changing the subject, such as calling his friends or turning on the TV really loud or going out for a drive and listening to Nirvana with the volume set on Deaf.

Anything rather than stand on that wooden jetty again, opposite the overhanging eaves and boathouses of the 14th-century plague hospital, waiting for the Belgian police frogmen to find Karen's body. He had stood there so many times in so many dreams, a bewildered sun-reddened American tourist with his shoulder bag and his camcorder, while diseased-looking starlings perched on the steep, undulating tiles up above him, and the canal slopped and gurgled beneath his feet.

Anything rather than watch the medical examiner with her crisp, white uniform and her braided blond hair as she unzipped the black vinyl body bag and Karen's face appeared, not just white but almost green. "She would not have suffered much," in that guttural back-of-the-throat Flemish accent. "Her neck was broken almost at once."

"By what?"

"By a thin ligature, approximately eight millimetres in diameter. We have forensic samples, taken from her skin. It was either hemp or braided hair."

Then Inspector Ben De Buy from the Politie resting a nicotine-stained hand on his arm and saying, "One of the drivers of the horse-drawn tourist carriages says that he saw your wife talking to a nun. This was approximately ten minutes before the boatman noticed her body floating in the canal."

"Where was this?"

"Hoogstraat, by the bridge. The nun turned the corner around Minderbroederstraat and that was the last the driver saw of her. He did not see your wife."

"Why should he have noticed my wife at all?"

"Because she was attractive, Mr. Wallace. All of these drivers have such an eye for good-looking women."

"Is that all? She talked to a nun? Why should she talk to a nun? She's not a Catholic." He had paused, and then corrected himself. "She wasn't a Catholic."

Inspector De Buy had lit up a pungent Ernte 23 cigarette, and breathed smoke out of his nostrils like a dragon. "Perhaps she was asking for directions. We don't know yet. It shouldn't be too difficult to find the nun. She was wearing a light gray habit, which is quite unusual."

Dean had stayed in Belgium for another week. The police came up with no more forensic evidence; no more witnesses. They published photographs of Karen in the newspapers, and contacted every religious order throughout Belgium, southern Holland and northern France. But nobody came forward. Nobody had seen how Karen had died. And there were no nunneries where the sisters wore gray, especially the whitish-gray that the carriage driver claimed to have seen.

Inspector De Buy had said, "Why not take your wife back to America, Mr. Wallace? There's nothing more you can do here in Bruges. If there's a break in the case, I can fax you, yes?"

Now Karen was lying in the Episcopal cemetery in New Milford, Connecticut, under a blanket of crimson maple leaves, and Dean was back here, in Bruges, on a chilly Flanders morning, tired and jet-lagged, and lonelier than he had ever felt before.

He crossed the wide, empty square called 't Zand, where fountains played and clusters of sculptured cyclists stood in the fog. The real cyclists were far busier jangling their bells and pedalling furiously over the cobbles. He passed cafés with steamy, glassed-in verandahs, where doughy-faced Belgians sat drinking coffee and smoking and eating huge cream-filled pastries. A pretty girl with long black hair watched him pass, her face as white as an actress in a European art movie. In an odd way, she reminded him of the way that Karen had looked, the day that he had first met her.

With his coat collar turned up against the cold and his breath fuming, he walked past the shops selling lace and chocolates and postcards and perfume. In the old Flemish tradition, a flag hung over the entrance of every shop, bearing the coat of arms of whoever had lived there in centuries gone by. Three grotesque fishes, swimming through a silvery sea. A man who looked like Adam, picking an apple from a tree. A white-faced woman with a strange suggestive smile. Dean reached the wide cobbled marketplace. On the far side, like a flock of seagulls, twenty or thirty nuns hurried silently through the fog. Up above him, the tall spire of Bruges' Belfry loomed through the fog, six hundred tightly spiralling steps to the top. Dean knew that because he and Karen had climbed up it, panting and laughing all the way. Outside the Belfry the horse-drawn tourist carriages collected, as well as ice cream vans and hot dog stalls. In the summer, there were long lines of visitors waiting to be given guided tours around the town, but not today. Three carriages were drawn up side by side, while their drivers smoked and their blanketed horses dipped their heads in their nose-bags.

Dean approached the drivers and lifted one hand in greeting.

"Tour, sir?" asked a dark-eyed unshaven young man in a tilted straw hat.

"Not today, thanks. I'm looking for somebody . . . one of your fellow drivers." He took out the folded newspaper clipping. "His name is Jan De Keyser."

"Who wants him? He's not in trouble, is he?"

"No, no. Nothing like that. Can you tell me where he lives?"

The carriage drivers looked at each other. "Does anybody know where Jan De Keyser lives?"

Dean took out his wallet and handed them 100 francs each. The drivers looked at each other again, and so Dean gave them another 100.

"Oostmeers, about halfway down, left-hand side," said the unshaven young man. "I don't know the number but there's a small delicatessen and it's next to that, with a brown door and brown glass vases in the window."

He coughed, and then he said, "You want a tour, too?"

Dean shook his head. "No, thanks. I think I've seen everything in Bruges I ever want to see, and more."

He walked back along Oude Burg and under the naked lime trees of Simon Stevin Plein. The inventor of decimal currency stood mournfully on his plinth, staring at a chocolate shop across the street. The morning was so raw now that Dean wished he had brought a pair of gloves. He crossed and recrossed the canal several times. It was smelly and sullen and it reminded him of death.

They had first come to Bruges for two reasons. The first was to get over Charley. Charley hadn't even talked, or walked, or seen the light of day. But a sound-scan had shown that Charley would be chronically disabled, if he were ever born; a nodding, drooling boy in a wheelchair, for all of his life. Dean and Karen had sat up all evening and wept and drank wine, and finally decided that Charley would be happier if he remained a hope; and a memory; a brief spark that illuminated the darkness, and died. Charley had been terminated and now Dean had nobody to remember Karen by. Her china collection? Her clothes? One evening he had opened her underwear drawer and taken out a pair of her panties and desperately breathed them in, hoping to smell her, hoping to smell her. But the panties were clean and Karen was gone; as if she had never existed.

They had come to Bruges for the art, too: for the Groeninge Museum with its 14th-century religious paintings and its modern Belgian masters, for Rubens and Van Eycks and Magrittes. Dean was a veterinarian, but he had always been a keen amateur painter; and Karen had designed wallpaper. They had first met nearly seven years ago, when Karen had brought her golden retriever into Dean's surgery to have its ears checked out. She had liked Dean's looks right from the very beginning. She had always liked tall, gentle, dark-haired men ("I would have married Clark Kent if Lois Lane hadn't gotten in first.").

But what had really persuaded her was the patience and affection with which he had handled her dog Buffy. After they were married, she used to sing *Love Me, Love My Dog* to him, and accompany herself on an old banjo.

Buffy was dead now, too. Buffy had pined so pitifully for Karen that Dean had eventually put him down.

Oostmeers was a narrow street of small, neat, row houses, each with its shining front window and its freshly painted front door and its immaculate lace curtains. Dean found the delicatessen easily because—apart from an antique dealers—it was the only shop. The house next door was much shabbier than most of its neighbours, and the brown glass vases in the window were covered in a film of dust. He rang the doorbell, and clapped his hands together to warm them up.

After a long pause, he heard somebody coming downstairs, and then coughing, and then the front door was opened about two inches. A thin, soapy-looking face peered out at him.

"I'm looking for Jan De Keyser."

"That's me. What do you want?"

Dean took out the newspaper cutting and held it up. "You were the last person to see my wife alive."

The young man frowned at the cutting for nearly half a minute, as if he needed glasses. Then he said, "That was a long time ago, mister. I've been sick since then."

"All the same, can I talk to you?"

"What for? It's all in the paper, everything I said."

"I'm just trying to understand what happened."

Jan De Keyser gave a high, rattling cough. "I saw your wife talking to this nun, that's all, and she was gone. I turned around in my seat, and saw the nun walk into Minderbroederstraat, into the sunshine, and then she was gone, too, and that was all."

"You ever see a nun dressed in gray like that before?" Jan De Keyser shook his head.

"You don't know where she might have come from? What order? You know, Dominican or Franciscan or whatever?"

"I don't know about nuns. But maybe she wasn't a nun."

"What do you mean? You told the police that she was a nun."

"What do you think I was going to say? That she was a statue? I have two narcotics offences already. They would have locked me up, or sent me to that bloody stupid hospital in Kortrijk."

Dean said, "What are you talking about, statue?"

Jan De Keyser coughed again, and started to close the door. "This is Brugge, what do you expect?"

"I still don't understand."

The door hovered on the point of closing. Dean took out his wallet again, and ostentatiously took out a £100 note, and held it up. "I've come a long way for this, Jan. I need to know everything."

"Wait," said Jan De Keyser; and closed the door. Dean waited. He looked down the foggy length of Oostmeers, and he could see a young girl standing on the corner of Zonnekemeers, her hands in her pockets. He couldn't tell if she were watching him or not.

After two or three minutes, Jan De Keyser opened the door again and stepped out into the street, wearing a brown leather jacket and a chequered scarf. He smelled of cigarettes and linament. "I've been very sick, ever since that time. My chest. Maybe it was nothing to do with the nun; maybe it was. But you know what they say: once a plague, always a plague."

He led Dean back the way he had come, past the canals, past the Gruuthuuse Museum, along Dijver to the Vismarkt. He walked very quickly, with his narrow shoulders hunched. Horses and carriages rattled through the streets like tumbrils; and bells chimed from the Belfry. They had that high, strange musical ring about them that you only hear from European bells. They reminded Dean of Christmases and wars; and maybe that was what Europe was really all about.

They reached the corner of Hoogstraat and Minderbroederstraat; by the bridge. Jan De Keyser jabbed his finger one way, and then the other. "I am carrying Germans; five or six-member German family. I am going slow because my horse is tired, yes? I see this woman in tight white shorts, and a blue T-shirt, and I look at her because she is pretty. That was your wife, yes? She has a good figure. Anyway, I turn and watch because she is not only pretty, she is talking to a nun. A nun in gray, quite sure of that. And they are talking as if they are arguing strongly. You know what I mean? Like, arguing, very fierce. Your wife is lifting her arms, like this, again and again, as if to say, 'What have I done? What have I done?' And the nun is shaking her head."

Dean looked around, frustrated and confused. "You said something about statues, and the plague."

"Look up," said Jan De Keyser. "You see on the corner of almost every building, a stone madonna. Here is one of the largest, life-size."

Dean raised his eyes, and for the first time he saw the arched niche that had been let into the corner of the building above him. In this niche stood a Virgin Mary, with the baby Jesus in her arms, looking sadly down at the street below.

"You see?" said Jan De Keyser. "There is so much to see in Brugge, if you lift your head. There is another world on the second storey. Statues and gargoyles and flags. Look at that building there. It has the faces of thirteen devils on it. They were put there to keep Satan away; and to protect the people who lived in this building from the Black Death."

Dean leaned over the railings, and stared down into the water. It was so foggy and gelid that he couldn't even see his own face; only a blur, as if somebody had taken a black-and-white photograph of him, and jogged the camera.

Jan De Keyser said, "In the 14th Century, when the plague came, it was thought that the people of Brugge were full of sin, yes? And that they were being given a punishment from God. So they made statues of the Holy Mary at every corner, to keep away the evil; and they promised the Holy Mary that they would always obey her, and worship her, if she protected them from plague. You understand this, yes? They made binding agreement."

"And what would happen if they didn't stick to this binding agreement?"

"The Holy Virgin would forgive; because the Holy Virgin always forgives. But the statue of the Holy Virgin would give punishment."

"The statue? How could the statue punish anybody?"

Jan De Keyser shrugged. "They made it, in the false belief. They made it with false hopes. Statues that are made with false hopes will always be dangerous; because they will turn on the people who made them; and they will expect the payment for their making."

Dean couldn't grasp this at all. He was beginning to suspect that Jan De Keyser was not only physically sick but mentally unbalanced, too; and he was beginning to wish that he hadn't brought him here.

But Jan De Keyser pointed up to the statue of the Virgin Mary; and then at the bridge; and then at the river, and said, "They are not just stone; not just carving. They have all of people's hopes inside them, whether these hopes are good hopes; or whether these hopes are wicked. They are not just stone."

"What are you trying to tell me? That what you saw—?"

"The gray madonna," said Jan De Keyser. "If you offend her, you must surely pay the price."

Dean took out another £100 bill, folded it, and stuffed it into Jan De Keyser's jacket pocket. "Thanks, pal," he told him. "I love you, too. I flew all the way from New Milford, Connecticut, to hear that my wife was killed by a statue. Thank you. Drink hearty."

But Jan De Keyser clutched hold of his sleeve. "You don't understand, do you? Everybody else has told you lies. I am trying to tell you the truth."

"What does the truth matter to you?"

"You don't have to insult me, sir. The truth has always mattered to me; just like it matters to all Belgians. What would I gain from lying to you? A few euros, so what?"

Dean looked up at the gray madonna in her niche in the wall. Then he looked back at Jan De Keyser. "I don't know," he said, flatly.

"Well, just give me the money, and maybe we can talk about morals and philosophy later."

Dean couldn't help smiling. He handed Jan De Keyser his money; and then stood and watched him as he hurried away, his hands in his pockets, his shoulders swinging from side to side. *Jesus,* he thought, *I'm getting old. Either that, or Jan De Keyser has deliberately been playing me along.*

All the same, he stood across the street, cater-corner from the gray madonna, and watched her for a long, long time, until the chill began to get to his sinuses, and his nose started to drip. The gray madonna stared back at him with her blind stone eyes, calm and beautiful, with all the sadness of a mother who knows that her child must grow up, and that her child will be betrayed, and that for centuries to come men and women will take His name in vain.

Dean walked back along Hoogstraat to the marketplace, and he went into one of the cafés beside the entrance to the Belfry. He sat in the corner, underneath a carved wooden statue of a *louche*-looking medieval musician. He ordered a small espresso and an Asbach brandy to warm him up. A dark-looking girl on the other side of the café smiled at him briefly, and then looked away. The jukebox was playing *Guantanamera.*

He was almost ready to leave when he thought he saw a gray nun-like figure passing the steamed-up window.

He hesitated, then he got up from his table and went to the door, and opened it. He was sure that he had seen a nun. Even if it wasn't the same nun that Karen had been talking to, on the day when she was strangled and thrown into the canal, this nun had worn a light gray habit, too. Maybe she came from the same order, and could help him locate the original nun, and find out what Karen had said to her.

A party of schoolchildren were crossing the gray fan-patterned cobbles of the market, followed by six or seven teachers. Behind the teachers, Dean was sure that he could glimpse a gray robed figure, making its way swiftly toward the arched entrance to the Belfry. He started to walk quickly across the marketplace, just as the carillon of bells began to ring, and starlings rose from the rooftops all around the square. He saw the figure disappear into the foggy, shadowy archway, and he broke into a jog.

He had almost reached the archway when a hand snatched at his sleeve, and almost pulled him off balance. He swung around. It was the waiter from the café, palefaced and panting.

"You have to pay, sir," he said.

Dean said, "Sure, sorry, I forgot," and hurriedly took out his wallet. "There—keep the change. I'm in a hurry, okay?"

He left the bewildered waiter standing in the middle of the square and ran into the archway. Inside, there was a large, deserted courtyard. On the right-hand side, a flight of stone steps led to the interior of the Belfry tower itself. There was nowhere else that the nun could have gone.

He vaulted up the steps, pushed open the huge oak door, and went inside. A young woman with upswept glasses and a tight braid on top of her head was sitting behind a ticket window, painting her nails.

"Did you see a nun come through here?"

"A nun? I don't know."

"Give me a ticket anyway."

He waited impatiently while she handed him a ticket and leaflet describing the history of the Belfry. Then he pulled open the narrow door which led to the spiral stairs, and began to climb up them in leaps and bounds.

The steps were extravagantly steep, and it wasn't long before he had to slow down. He trudged around and around until he reached a small gallery, about a third of the way up the tower, where he stopped and listened. If there *were* a nun climbing the steps up ahead of him, he would easily be able to hear her.

And—yes—he could distinctly make out the *chip-chip-chip* sound of somebody's feet on worn stone steps. The sound echoed down the staircase like fragments of granite dropping down a well. Dean seized the thick, slippery rope that acted as a handrail, and renewed his climbing with even more determination, even though he was soaked in chilly sweat, and he was badly out of breath.

As it rose higher and higher within the Belfry tower, the spiral staircase grew progressively tighter and narrower, and the stone steps were replaced with wood. All that Dean could see up ahead of him was the triangular treads of the steps above; and all he could see when he looked down was the triangular treads of the steps below. For more than a dozen turns of the spiral, there were no windows, only dressed stone walls, and even though he was so high above the street, he began to feel trapped and claustrophobic. There were still hundreds of steps to climb to reach the top of the Belfry, and hundreds of steps to negotiate if he wanted to go back down again.

He paused for a rest. He was tempted to give it up. But then he made the effort to climb up six more steps and found that he had reached the high-ceilinged gallery which housed the clock's carillon and chiming mechanism—a gigantic medieval musical box. A huge drum was turned by clockwork, and a complicated pattern of metal spigots activated the bells.

The gallery was silent, except for the soft, weary ticking of a mechanism that had been counting out the hours without interruption for nearly five hundred years. Columbus's father could have climbed these same steps, and looked at this same machinery.

Dean was going to rest a moment or two longer, but he heard a quick, furtive rustling sound on the other side of the gallery, and caught sight of a light gray triangle of skirt just before it disappeared up the next flight of stairs.

"Wait!" he shouted. He hurried across the gallery and started to climb. This time he could not only hear the sound of footsteps, he could hear the swishing of well-starched cotton, and once or twice he actually saw it.

"Wait!" he called. "I don't mean to frighten you—I just want to talk to you!"

But the footsteps continued upward at the same brisk pace, and with each turn in the spiral the figure in the light gray habit stayed tantalizingly out of sight.

At last the air began to grow colder and fresher, and Dean realized that they were almost at the top. There was nowhere the nun could go, and she would *have* to talk to him now.

He came out onto the Belfry's viewing gallery, and looked around. Barely visible through the fog he could distinguish the orange rooftops of Bruges, and the dull gleam of its canals. On a clear day the view stretched for miles across the flat Flanders countryside, toward Ghent and Kortrijk and Ypres. But today Bruges was secretive and closed in; and looked more like a painting by Brueghel than a real town. The air smelled of fog and sewers.

To begin with, he couldn't see the nun. She must be here, though: unless she had jumped off the parapet. Then he stepped around a pillar, and there she was, standing with her back to him, staring out toward the Basilica of the Holy Blood.

Dean approached her. She didn't turn around, or give any indication that she knew that he was here. He stood a few paces behind her and waited, watching the faint breeze stirring the light gray cloth of her habit.

"Listen, I'm sorry if I alarmed you," he said. "I didn't mean to give you the impression that I was chasing you or anything like that. But three years ago my wife died here in Bruges, and just before she died she was seen talking to a nun. A nun in a light gray habit, like yours."

He stopped and waited. The nun remained where she was, not moving, not speaking.

"Do you speak English?" Dean asked her, cautiously. "If you don't speak English, I can find somebody to translate for us."

Still the nun remained where she was. Dean began to feel unnerved. He didn't like to touch her, or to make any physical attempt to turn her around. All the same, he wished she would speak, or look at him, so that he could see her face. Maybe she belonged to a silent order. Maybe she was deaf. Maybe she just didn't want to talk to him, and that was that.

He thought of the gray madonna, and of what Jan De Keyser had told him: *"They are not just stone; not just carving. They have all of people's hopes inside them; whether these hopes are good hopes, or whether these hopes are wicked."*

For some reason that he couldn't quite understand, he shivered, and it wasn't only the cold that made him shiver. It was the feeling that he was standing in the presence of something really terrible.

"I, er—I wish you'd say something," he said, loudly, although his voice sounded off balance.

There was a very long silence. Then suddenly the carillon of bells started to ring, so loudly that Dean was deafened, and could literally feel his eyeballs vibrating in their sockets. The nun swivelled around—didn't turn, but smoothly swivelled, as if she were standing on a turntable. She stared at him, and

Dean stared back, and the fear rose up inside him like ice-cold sick.

Her face was a face of stone. Her eyes were carved out of granite, and she couldn't speak because her lips were stone, too. She stared at him blind and sad and accusing, and he couldn't even find the breath to scream.

He took one step backward, then another. The gray madonna came gliding after him, blocking his way to the staircase. She reached beneath her habit and lifted out a thin braided ligature, made of human hair, the kind of ligature that depressed and hysterical nuns used to plait out of their own hair, and then use to hang themselves. Better to meet your Christ in Heaven than to live in fear and self-loathing.

Dean said, "Keep away from me. I don't know *what* you are, or *how* you are, but keep away from me."

He was sure that she smiled, very faintly. He was sure that she whispered something.

"What?" he asked. *"What?"*

She came closer and closer. She was stone, and yet she breathed, and she smiled, and she whispered, *"Charley, this is for Charley."*

Again, he screamed at her, *"What?"*

But she caught hold of his left arm in a devastatingly strong grip, and she stepped up onto the platform that ran around the parapet, and with one irresistible turn of her back she rolled herself over the parapet and slid down the orange-tiled roof.

Dean shouted, "No" and tried to tug himself free from her; but she wasn't an ordinary woman. She gripped him so tight and she weighed so much that he was dragged over the parapet after her. He found himself sliding and bumping over the fog-moist tiles, and at the end of the tiles was a lead gutter and then a sheer drop down to the cobbles of the market, one hundred and seventy feet below.

With his right hand, he scrabbled to get a grip on the tiles. But the gray madonna was far too heavy for him. She was solid granite. Her hand was solid granite; no longer pliable, but still holding him fast.

She tumbled over the edge of the roof. Dean caught hold of the guttering, and for one moment of supreme effort he swung from it, with the gray madonna revolving around him, her face as calm as only the face of the Virgin Mary could be. But the guttering was medieval lead, soft and rotten, and slowly it bent forward under the weight, and then gave way.

Dean looked down and saw the market square. He saw horse-drawn carriages and cars and people walking in every direction. He heard the air whistling in his ears.

He clung to the gray madonna because that was the only solid thing he had to cling to. He embraced her as he fell. Hardly anybody saw him falling, but those who did lifted up their hands in horror in the same way that serious burns victims lift up their hands.

He dropped and dropped the whole height of Bruges' Belfry, two dark figures falling through the fog, holding each other tight, like lovers. Dean thought for one illogical instant that everything was going to be all right, that he was going to fall forever and never hit the ground. But then suddenly he saw the rooftops much closer and the cobbles expanded faster and faster. He hit the courtyard with the gray madonna on top of him. She weighed over half a ton, and she exploded on impact, and so did he. Together, they were like a bomb bursting. Their heads flew apart. Stone arms and flesh arms jumped up into the air.

Then there was nothing but the muffled sound of traffic, and the echoing flap of starlings' wings as they resettled on the rooftops, and the jangling of bicycle bells.

* * * * *

Inspector Ben De Buy stood amongst the wreckage of man and madonna and looked up at the Belfry, cigarette smoke and fog vapour fuming from his nose.

"He fell from the very top," he told his assistant, Sergeant Van Peper.

"Yes, sir. The girl who collects the tickets can identify him."

"And was he carrying the statue with him, when he bought his ticket?"

"No, sir, of course not. He couldn't even have lifted it. It was far too heavy."

"But it was up there with him, wasn't it? How did he manage to take a life-size granite statue of the Virgin Mary all the way up those stairs? It's impossible. And even if it was possible, why would he do it? You might need to weight yourself down to drown yourself, but to jump from the top of a belfry?"

"I don't know, sir."

"No, well, neither do I, and I don't think I really want to know."

He was still standing amongst the blood and the broken stone when one of his youngest detectives appeared, carrying something grayish-white in his arms. As he came closer, Inspector De Buy realized that it was a baby, made of stone.

"What's this?" he demanded.

"The infant Jesus," said the officer, blushing. "We found it on the corner of Hoogstraat, up in the niche where the stone madonna used to stand."

Inspector De Buy stared at the granite baby for a while, then held out his arms. "Here," he said, and the officer handed it over to him. He lifted it over his head, and then he smashed it onto the cobbles as hard as he could. It shattered into half a dozen lumps.

"Sir?" asked his sergeant, in puzzlement.

Inspector De Buy patted him on the shoulder. "Thou shalt worship no graven image, Sergeant Van Peper. And now you know why."

He walked out of the Belfry courtyard. Out in the market square, an ambulance was waiting, its sapphire lights flashing in the fog. He walked back to Simon Stevin Plein, where he had left his car. The bronze statue of Simon Stevin loomed over him, black and menacing in his doublet and hat. Inspector De Buy took out his car keys and hesitated for a moment. He was sure that he had seen Simon Stevin move slightly.

He stood quite still, right next to his Citroën, his key lifted, not breathing, listening, waiting. Anybody who saw him then would have believed that he was a statue.

The Ballyhooly Boy

Rain came dredging down the street in misty gray curtains as we drew up outside the narrow terraced house in the middle of Ballyhooly. All of the houses in the row were painted different colors: sunflower yellows, crimsons, pinks and greens. In sullen contrast, Number 15 was painted as brown as peat.

Mr. Fearon switched off the engine of his eight-year-old Rover and peered at the house through his circular James Joyce glasses. "I'll admit it doesn't look like much. But prices have been very buoyant lately. You could get eighty-five thousand for it easy, if you put it on the market today."

I took in the peeling front door, the darkened and dusty front windows, the sagging net curtains in one of the upstairs rooms. I guessed that I could sell it straight away; but then it might be worth smartening it up a little. A coat of paint and a new bathroom suite from Hickey's could make all the difference between £100,000 and £150,000.

I climbed out of the car, tugging up my collar against the rain. A small brindled dog barked at me for invading its territory without asking. I shaded my eyes and looked in through the front window. It was too grimy to see much, but I could just make out a black fireplace and a tipped-over chair. The living room was very small, but that didn't matter. I might redecorate Number 15, but I certainly wouldn't be living in it. Not here in Ballyhooly, which was little more than a crossroads ten miles north of Cork, with two pubs and a shop and a continuous supply of rain.

Mr. Fearon made a fuss of finding the right key and unlocked the front door. He had to kick the weatherboard to open it; and it gave a convulsive shudder, like a donkey, when it's kicked. The doormat was heaped with letters and free newspapers and circulars. Inside the hallway, there was a strong smell of damp, and the brown wallpaper was peppered with black specks of mold.

"It'll need some airing out, of course, but the roof's quite sound, and that's your main thing."

I stepped over the letters and looked around. Next to the front door stood a Victorian coat and umbrella stand, with a blotchy, yellowed mirror, in which Mr. Fearon and I looked as if we had both contracted leprosy. On the opposite wall hung a damp, faded print of a dark back street in some unidentifiable European city, with a cathedral in the background, and hooded figures concealed in its Gothic doorways. The green-and-brown diamond-patterned linoleum on the floor must have dated from the 1930s.

The sitting room was empty of furniture except for that single overturned wheelback chair. A broken glass lampshade hung in the center of the room.

"No water penetration," Mr. Fearon remarked, pointing to the ceiling. But in one corner, there were six or seven deep scratchmarks close to the coving.

"What do you think caused those?" I asked him.

He stared at them for a long time and then shrugged.

We went through to the kitchen, which was cold as a mortuary. Which *felt* like a mortuary. Under the window there was a thick, old-fashioned sink, with rusty streaks in it. A gas cooker stood against the opposite wall. All of the glass in the cream-painted kitchen cabinets had been broken, and some of the frames had dark brown strips running down them, as if somebody had smashed the glass on purpose, in a rage, and cut their hands open.

Outside, I could see a small yard crowded with old sacks of

cement and bricks and half a bicycle, and thistles that grew almost chest-high. And the rain, gushing from the clogged-up guttering, so that the wall below it was stained with green.

"I still can't imagine why your woman wanted to give me this place," I said, as we climbed the precipitous staircase. Halfway up, there was a stained-glass window, in amber, with a small picture in the center of a winding river, and a dark castle, with rooks flying around its turrets.

"You'll be watching for the stair-carpet," Mr. Fearon warned me. "It's ripped at the top."

Upstairs, there were two bedrooms, one of them overlooking the street and a smaller bedroom at the back.

In the smaller bedroom, against the wall, stood a single bed with a plain oak bedhead. It was covered with a yellowing sheet. Above it hung a damp, rippled picture of the Cork hurling team, 1976. I went to the window and looked down into the yard. For some reason I didn't like this room. There was a sour, unpleasant smell in it, boiled vegetables and Dettol. It reminded me of nursing homes and old, pale people seen through rainy windows. It was the smell of hopelessness.

"Mrs. Devlin wasn't a woman to explain herself," said Mr. Fearon. "Her estate didn't amount to much, and she left most of it to her husband. But she insisted that this house should come to you. She said she was frightened of what would happen to her if it didn't."

I turned away from the window. "But she wouldn't explain why?"

Mr. Fearon shook his head. "If I had any inkling, I'd tell you."

I still found it difficult to believe. Up until yesterday morning, when Mr. Fearon had first called me, I had never heard of Mrs. Margaret Devlin. Now I found myself to be one of the beneficiaries of her will, and the owner of a shabby terraced property in the rear end nowhere in particular.

Not that I was looking a gift horse in the mouth. My Italian-style café in Academy Street in Cork hadn't been doing too well lately. Only three weeks ago I had lost my best chef Carlo, and I had always been badly under-financed. I had tried to recoup some of my losses by buying a £1,250 share in a promising-looking yearling called Satan's Pleasure, but it had fallen last weekend at Galway and broken its leg. No wonder Satan was pleased. He was probably laughing all the way back to hell.

We left the house. Mr. Fearon slammed the front door shut behind us—twice—and handed me the keys. "Well, I wish you joy of it," he said.

As I opened the car door, a white-haired priest came hurrying across the road in the rain. "Good morning to you!" he called out. He came up and offered me his hand. "Father Murphy, from St. Bernadette's." He was a stocky man, with a large head, and glasses that enormously magnified his eyes.

"You must be Jerry Flynn," he said. "You're very welcome to Ballyhooly, Jerry."

I shook his hand. "Difficult place to keep a secret, Ballyhooly?"

"Oh, you'd be surprised. We have plenty of secrets here, believe me. But everybody knew who Margaret Devlin was going to give her house to."

"Everybody except me, apparently."

Father Murphy gave me an evasive smile. "Do you know what she said? She said it was destiny. I have to bequeath my house to Jerry Flynn. The wheel turning the full circle, so to speak."

"And what do you think she meant by that?"

"I believe that she was making her peace before God. The world is a strange place, Jerry. Doors may open, but they don't always lead us where we think they're going to."

"And this door?" I asked, nodding toward Number 15.

"Well, who knows? But when you're back, don't forget to drop in to see me. My housekeeper makes the best tea brack in Munster. And we can talk. We really ought to talk."

I hadn't planned on going back to Ballyhooly for at least ten days. I was interviewing new chefs and I was also trying to borrow some more money from the bank so that I could keep my café afloat. I had already re-mortgaged my flat in Wellington Road, and even when I told my bank manager about my unexpected bequest he shook his head from side to side like a swimmer trying to dislodge water out of his ears.

But only two nights later the phone rang at half-past two in the morning. I sat up. The bedroom was completely dark, except for a diagonal line of sodium street-crossing the ceiling. I scrabbled around my nightstand and knocked my glass of water onto the floor, the whole lot. The phone kept on ringing until I managed to pick it up. I don't like calls in the middle of the night: they're always bad news. Your father's dead. Your son's been killed in a car crash.

"Who is it?" I asked.

There was nothing on the other end of the line except for a thin, persistent crackling.

"Who is it? Is anybody there?"

The crackling went on for almost half a minute and then the caller hung up. Click. Silence.

I tried to get back to sleep, but I was wide awake now. I switched on the bedside light and climbed out of bed. My cat Charlie stared at me through slitted eyes as if I were mad. I went to the bathroom and refilled my glass of water. In the mirror over the washbasin I thought I looked strangely pale, as if a vampire had visited me when I was asleep. Even my lips were white.

The phone rang again. I went back into the bedroom and picked it up. I didn't say anything, just listened. At first I heard nothing but that crackling noise again, but then a woman's voice said, "Is that Mr. Jerry Flynn?"

"Who wants him?"

"Is that Mr. Jerry Flynn who has the house in Ballyhooly?"

"Who wants him? Do you know what time it is?"

"You have to go to your house, Jerry. You have to do what needs to be done."

"What are you talking about? What needs to be done?"

"It can't go on, Jerry. It has to be done."

"Look, who is this? It's two-thirty in the morning and I don't understand what the hell you're talking about."

"Go to your house, Jerry. Number Fifteen. It's the only way."

The woman hung up again. I stared at the receiver for a while, as if I expected it to say something else, and then I hung up, too.

For a change, it wasn't raining the next morning when I drove back to Ballyhooly, but the hills were covered with low gray clouds. The road took me over the Nagle mountains and across the long stone bridge that spans the Blackwater river. I drove for almost twenty minutes and saw nobody, except for a farmhand driving a tractor heaped with sugar-beet. For some reason, they reminded me of rotting human heads.

When I reached Ballyhooly, I parked outside Number 15 and climbed out of my car. I hesitated for a few moments before I opened the front door, pretending to be searching for my keys. Then I turned around quickly to see if I could catch anybody curtain-twitching. But the street was empty, except for two young boys with runny noses and a dog that was trotting off on some self-appointed errand.

I pushed open the shuddering front door. The house was damp and silent. No new mail, only a circular advertising Dunne's Stores Irish bacon promotion. I walked through to the kitchen. It was so cold in there that my breath smoked. I opened one or two drawers. All I found was a rusty can opener, a ball of twine and a half-empty packet of birthday-cake candles.

I went through to the living room. Out on the street, an old man in a brown raincoat was standing on the opposite corner, watching the house and smoking. I picked up the fallen chair and set it straight.

The silence was uncanny. A truck drove past, then a motorcycle, but I couldn't hear them at all. I felt as if I had gone completely deaf.

I returned to the hallway and inspected myself in the blotchy Victorian mirror. I certainly didn't look well, although I couldn't think why. I felt tired, but that was only natural after an interrupted night. More than that, though, I felt unsettled, as if something were going to happen that I wasn't going to be able to control. Something unpleasant.

It was then that I glanced up the stairs. I said "Jesus!" out loud, and my whole body tingled with fright.

Standing on the landing was a white-faced boy, staring at me intensely. He looked about eight or nine, with short brown hair that looked as if it had been cut with the kitchen scissors, and protuberant ears. He wore a gray sweater with darned elbows and long gray-flannel shorts.

And he stared at me, in utter silence, without even blinking.

"What are you doing here?" I asked him. "You almost gave me a heart attack."

He didn't say anything, but continued to stare at me, almost as if he were trying to stare me into non-existence.

"Come on," I said. "You can't stay here. This house belongs to me now. What have you been doing, playing? I used to do that, when I was your age. Play in this old derelict house. Ghost-hunters."

Still the boy didn't speak. His fists were tightly clenched, and he breathed through his mouth, quite laboriously, as if he were suffering from asthma.

"Listen," I told him, "I'm supposed to be back in Cork by eleven. I don't know how you got in here, but you really have to leave."

The boy continued to stare at me in silence. I started to climb up the steep, narrow staircase toward him. As soon as I did so, he turned around and walked quite quickly across the landing, and disappeared into the smaller bedroom at the back of the house.

"Come on, son," I called him. I was beginning to lose my patience. I climbed up the rest of the stairs and followed him through the bedroom door. "Breaking into other people's houses, that's trespass."

The bedroom was empty. There was nobody there. Only the bed with the yellowed sheet and the dull view down to the yard, with its weeds and its cement sacks.

I knelt down and looked under the bed. The boy wasn't there. I felt around the walls to see if there was a secret door, but all I felt was damp wallpaper. The sash window was jammed up with years of green paint, and the floor was covered in thin brown underlay, so the boy couldn't have lifted up any of the floorboards. I even looked up the chimney, but that was ridiculous, and I felt ridiculous even when I was doing it. The flue was so narrow that even a hamster couldn't have climbed up it.

My irritation began to rearrange itself into a deeply disturbing sense of creepiness. If the boy hadn't hidden under the bed, and he hadn't climbed up the chimney, and he certainly hadn't escaped through the window, then where had he gone?

He couldn't have been a ghost. I refused to believe in ghosts. Besides, he had looked far too solid to be a ghost. Too normal, too real. What ghost has falling-down socks and darns in his sweater?

But he wasn't here. I had seen him standing at the top of the stairs. I had heard him breathing. But he wasn't here.

I went from room to room, searching them all. I didn't go up in the attic because I didn't have a ladder, but then the boy hadn't had a ladder, either, and there was a cobweb in the corner of the attic door which he would have had to have broken, even if he had found some miraculous way of getting up there. The house was empty. No boy, anywhere. I even opened up the gas oven.

I left the house much later than I had meant to, almost half an hour later. As I came out, and slammed the door shut, a woman approached me. She probably wasn't much older than 35, but she looked 40 at least. Her brown hair was tightly permed and she had the pinched face of a heavy smoker. She wore a cheap purple coat and a long black skirt with a fraying hem.

"Well, Jerry," she said, without any introduction, "you've seen what you have to do."

"Was it you who phoned me last night?"

"It doesn't matter who phoned you. You've seen what you have to do."

"I haven't the slightest idea what I have to do."

"You should be here at night then. When the screaming starts."

"Screaming? What screaming? What are you talking about?"

The woman took out a pack of Carroll's and lit one, and sucked it so hard that her cheeks were all drawn in. "We've been living next door to that for twenty-five years and what are we supposed to do? That house is all we've got. But my daughter's a nervous wreck and my husband tried to take his own life. And who can we tell? We'd never sell the property if everybody knew about it. Number seventeen they're the same. Nobody can stand it any more."

It started to rain again, but neither of us made any attempt to find shelter. "What's your name?" I asked her.

"Maureen," she said, blowing smoke.

"Well, tell me about this screaming, Maureen."

"It doesn't happen all the time. Sometimes we can go for weeks and we don't hear anything. But it's November now, and that's the anniversary, and then we hear it more and more, and sometimes it's unbearable, the screaming. You never heard such screaming in your whole life."

"The anniversary?" I asked her. "The anniversary of what?"

"The day the boy killed his whole family and then himself. In that house. Nobody found them till two days later. The gardai thought the house was painted red, until they realized it was blood. I saw them carry the mother and the daughters out myself. I saw it myself. And you never saw such a frightful thing. He used his father's razor, and he almost took their heads off."

I looked away, down Ballyhooly's main road. I could see Father Murphy, not far away, white-haired, leaning against the rain, talking to a woman in a blue coat.

"Can't the priest help you?"

"Him? He's tried. But this is nothing to do with God, believe me."

"I don't see what I can do. I was bequeathed this house, by

somebody I never even knew, and that's it. I run a café. I'm not an exorcist."

"You've seen the boy, though?"

I didn't say anything, but the woman tilted her head sideways and looked at me closely. "You've seen the boy, I can tell."

"I've seen—I don't know what I've seen."

"You've seen him. You've seen the boy. You can't deny it." She sucked at her cigarette again, more triumphantly this time.

"All right, yes. Is he a local boy?"

"He's the very same boy. The boy who killed his family, and then himself."

I didn't know what to say. I was beginning to suspect that Maureen had been drinking. But she kept on smoking and nodding as if she had proved her point beyond a shadow of a doubt, and that I was just being perverse to question the feasibility of a dead schoolboy walking around my newly-acquired house.

"I have to get back to Cork now," I told her. "I'm sorry."

"You've seen him and you're just going to leave? You don't think that you were given this house by accident? That your name was picked out with a pin?"

"Quite frankly I don't know why it was given to me."

"You were chosen, that's why. That's what Margaret always used to say to me—Mrs. Devlin. She was chosen and there was nothing she could do about it, except to pass it on."

I unlocked my car. Maureen started to become agitated, tossing her cigarette away and wiping her hands on the front of her coat, over and over, as if she couldn't get them clean.

"You mustn't go. Please."

"I'm sorry. I have a business to run."

But it was then that I saw one of the grubby upstairs curtains being drawn aside. Standing in the bedroom window, staring at me, was the white-faced boy. Somehow he must have hidden from me when I was searching the house, and here he was, mocking me.

I kicked open the front door and ran upstairs. I hurtled into the front bedroom but the boy was gone. He wasn't in the back bedroom, either. There was a tiny linen cupboard between the two rooms, but it was empty except for two folded sheets and a 60-watt lightbulb. I slapped the walls in both bedrooms, to see if they were hollow. I lifted up the mattress in the smaller bedroom, in case it was hollowed-out, and the boy had been concealing himself in there. It was stained, and damp, but it hadn't been tampered with.

Underneath it, however, lying on the bedsprings, I discovered a book. It was thin, like an exercise book, with a faded maroon cover, and it was disturbingly familiar. I picked it up and angled it toward the window, so that I could see what was printed on the front.

Bishop O'Rourke Memorial School, Winter 1976. The same junior school that I had attended, in Cork. I opened it up and leafed through it. I could even remember this particular yearbook. The sports reports. The opening of the new classroom extension. The visit from the Taoiseach. And right at the back, the list of names of everybody in the school. Familiar names, all of them, but I couldn't remember many of their faces. And there was my name, too. Class III, Gerald Flynn, between Margaret Flaherty and Kevin Foley.

But what was it doing here, this book, hidden under the mattress in this run-down little house in Ballyhooly?

I looked around one more time. I still couldn't figure out how the boy had managed to elude me, but I would make sure that he never got in here again. Tomorrow morning I would change the locks, front and back, and check that none of the windows could be opened from the outside.

As I left the house, Father Murphy came over.

"Everything in order?" he asked me, with that same evasive smile. A real priest's smile, always waiting for you to commit yourself.

"You said we ought to talk."

"We should," he said. "Come across and have a glass with me."

We crossed the street and went into a small pub called The Roundy House. Inside, there was a small bar, and a sitting room with armchairs and a television, just like somebody's private home. Two young men sat at the bar, smoking, and they acknowledged Father Murphy with a nod of their heads.

We sat in the corner by the window. The afternoon light strained through net curtains the color of cold tea. Father Murphy clinked my half of Guinness, and then he said, "Maureen hasn't been upsetting you?"

"She told me that she could hear screaming."

"Well, yes. She's right. I've heard it myself."

"I've seen a boy, too. I saw him in the house, twice. I don't know how he got in there."

"He got in there because he's always there."

"What are you trying to tell me, that he's a ghost?"

Father Murphy shook his head. "I don't believe in ghosts and I don't suppose that you do, either. But he's not alive in the way that you and I are alive. You can see him because he will occupy that house until he gets justice for what happened to him. That's my theory, anyway."

"You really think it's the same boy who killed his family? That's not possible, is it? I mean, how can that be possible? He killed himself, too, and even if he hadn't, he'd be my age by now."

Father Murphy wiped foam from his upper lip. "What's been happening in that house isn't recognized by the teachings of the Church, Jerry. I've tried twice to exorcise it. The second time I brought down Father Griffin from Dublin. He said afterwards that no amount of prayer or holy water could cleanse that property, because it isn't possessed of any devil.

"It's possessed instead by the rage of a nine-year-old boy who was driven to utter despair. A child of God, not of Satan. His father was a drunk who regularly beat him. His mother neglected him and fed him on nothing but chips, if she fed him at all. His older sister had Down's Syndrome and he was expected to do everything for her, change her sheets when she wet the bed, everything. He lived in hell, that boy, and he had nobody to help him.

"My predecessor here did whatever he could, but it isn't easy when the parents are so aggressive. And he wasn't alone, this boy. He was only one of thousands of children all over the country whose parents abuse them, and who don't have anywhere to turn.

"Whatever it is in your house, Jerry—whatever kind of force it is—it's the force of revenge. A sense of rage and injustice so strong that it has taken on a physical shape."

"Even if that's true, father—what can I do about it?"

"You were chosen. I don't know why. Margaret Devlin said that *she* was chosen, too, when she inherited Number Fifteen. And before her, Martin Donnolly. I never knew what became of him."

"So what happened to Margaret Devlin? How did she die?"

"Well, it was a tragedy. She took her own life. I believe she was separated from her husband or something of the kind. She took an overdose of paracetamol. Lay dead in the house for over a week."

* * * * *

On the drive back to Cork, under a late-afternoon sky as black as a crow's wing, I kept thinking about what Father Murphy had told me. *A sense of rage and injustice so strong that it has taken on a physical shape.* It didn't really make any scientific sense, or any theological sense, either, but in a way I could understand what he meant. We all get angry and frustrated from time to time, and when we do, we can all feel the uncontrollable beast that rises up inside us.

Katharine was waiting for me when I got back to my flat. She was a neat, pretty girl with a pale pre-Raphaelite face and long black hair. She helped me in the café from time to time, but her real job was making silver jewelry. We had nearly had an affair once, after a friend's party and too many bottles of Chilean sauvignon, but she was such a good friend that I was always glad that we had managed to resist each other. Mainly by falling asleep.

She wanted to know if I wanted to come to an Irish folk evening in McCurtain Street. She was dressed for it: with a blue silk scarf around her head and a long flowing dress with patterns of peacock feathers on it, and dozens of jangly silver bracelets. But I didn't feel in the mood for *Whiskey in the Jar* and *Goodbye Mrs. Durkin.* I poured us a glass of wine and sat down on my big leather sofa, tossing Bishop O'Rourke's Memorial Junior School yearbook onto the coffee table.

"What's wrong?" asked Katharine. "The bank didn't turn you down, did they?"

"As a matter of fact they did, but that's not it."

She sat close to me, and she had some perfume like a pomander, cinnamon and cloves and orange-peel. "You've got something on your mind. I can tell."

I told her about Number 15 and the boy that I had seen on the landing. I told her about Maureen, too, and the screaming, and what Father Murphy had said about revenge.

"You don't believe any of it, do you? It sounds like a prime case of mass hysteria."

"I wasn't hysterical, but I saw the boy as clear as I can see you now. And I couldn't find how the hell he managed to get in and out of the house. There just wasn't any way."

She picked up the yearbook. "This is spooky though, isn't it—finding your old junior school yearbook under the mattress?"

She read through the list of names in Class III. "Linda Ahern, remember her?"

"Fat. Freckles. The reddest hair you've ever seen. But when she turned fourteen, she was a cracker."

"Donal Coakley?"

"Thin. Weedy. We all used to chase him round the playground and pinch his biscuits."

"What a mean lot you were."

"Oh, you know what schoolkids are like."

"Ellen Collins?"

"Don't remember her."

"Martin Donnolly?"

I frowned at her. "Who did you say?"

"Martin Donnolly."

"I don't remember him, but that was the name of the man who owned Number 15 before Margaret Devlin."

"It's a common enough name, for goodness' sake."

"Yes, but who comes next? Margaret Flaherty. I wonder if she could have changed her name to Devlin when she married."

"Isn't there somebody you could ask?"

I called my old friend Tony O'Connell—the only former classmate from Bishop O'Rourke's who I still saw from time to time. He ran an auto repair business on the Patrick

Mills Estate out at Douglas.

"Tony, you remember Margaret Flaherty?"

"How could I ever forget her? I was in love with her. I picked her a bunch of dandelions once and she threw them away and called me an idiot."

"Do you know if she married?"

"Oh, yes. She married some fellow much older than herself. A real waste of space. Estate agent, I think he was. Frank Devlin."

"And Martin Donnolly? Do you know what happened to him?"

"Martin? He moved to Fermoy or somewhere near there. They found him drowned in the Blackwater."

I put down the phone. "I may be making a wild assumption here," I told Katharine, "but it looks as if Number 15 is being passed from one pupil of Bishop O'Rourke's to the next, alphabetically, down the class list. And everybody who owns it ends up dead."

"You'd better check some more," Katharine suggested. "See if you can find out what happened to Linda Ahern and Donal Coakley."

It took another hour. Outside, it started to grow dark, that strange foggy disappearance of light that happens over Cork some evenings, because the River Lee brings in cold seawater from the Atlantic, the same reaches where the *Lusitania* was sunk, and the city turns chilly and quiet, as if it remembers the dead.

I found Ita Twomey, who was Linda Ahern's best friend when they were at school, by calling her mother. Ita was Mrs. Desmond now, and lived in Bishopstown. "Linda was a single mother. But she inherited a house, I believe. But she was killed in a car accident on the N20 . . . both herself and her kiddie. They burned to death. The gardai said that she drove her car deliberately into a bridge."

And Donal Coakley? I managed at last to find Vincent O'Brien, our class teacher at Bishop O'Rourke's. "You'll have to forgive me for sounding so hoarse. I was diagnosed with cancer of the larynx only two months ago. I'll be having a laryngectomy by Christmas, God willing."

"I'm trying to find out what happened to a classmate of mine called Donal Coakley."

"Donal? I remember Donal. Poor miserable kid. I don't know what happened to him. He was always very unhappy at school. All of the other kids used to bully him, every day. I don't suppose you did, Jerry, but you know how cruel children can be to each other, without even realizing what they're doing. He was always playing truant, young Donal, because he didn't want to stay at home and he didn't want to stay at school. Poor miserable kid. They were always stealing his lunch money and taking his sweeties and hitting him around. You never know why, do you? Just because his parents were poor and he always smelled a bit and had holes in his socks."

"But do you know what happened to him, after he left school?"

"I couldn't tell you. He never finished Bishop O'Rourke's. He left at mid-term. He couldn't take the bullying any longer. I think his parents moved. There was some trouble with the social services. I never heard where they went."

My mouth was as dry as if I had woken up from drinking red wine all night. "Donal was bullied that badly?"

"It happens in every school, doesn't it? It's kids, they have a sort of pack instinct. Anybody who doesn't fit in, they go for, and they never let up. Donal had second-hand shoes and jumpers with holes in them and of course that made him a prime target. I'm not talking about you, Jerry. I know you were very protective of the weaker kids. But it was a fact."

Protective? I thought of the time that I had snatched the Brennan's bread wrapper in which Donal's mother had packed his jam sandwiches for him, and stamped on it. I thought of the time that five of us had cornered him by the boys' toilets and punched him and beaten him with sticks and rulers until he knelt down on the tarmac with his grubby hands held over his head to protect himself, not even crying, not even begging for mercy, though we kept on shouting and screaming at him.

Donal Coakley. My God. The shame of it made my cheeks burn, even after all these years. The day it was raining and we found out that he had lined his shoes with newspaper because they had holes in the soles. Wet pages from the *Evening Echo* folded beneath his socks.

"Is that all you wanted to know?" asked Vincent O'Brien.

I could hardly speak to him. "I'd forgotten Donal. I'd forgotten him. I don't think I wanted to remember."

I put down the phone and Katharine was staring at me in the strangest way. Or perhaps she wasn't. Perhaps I had suddenly realized what I had done, and everything was different.

"I—ah, I have to go back to Ballyhooly," I told her.

"You're not *crying,* are you?"

"Crying? What are you talking about? I have to go back to Ballyhooly, that's all."

"Tonight?"

"Yes, tonight. Now."

"Let me come with you. Something's happened, hasn't it? You'd be better off with somebody with you."

"Katharine—this is something I have to deal with on my own."

She took hold of my hands between hers. She stroked my fingers, trying to calm me down. "But you must tell me," she said. "It's something to do with Donal Coakley, isn't it?"

I nodded. I couldn't speak. She was right, damn it. She was right. I was crying. The boy on the landing was Donal Coakley. I had bullied him and tortured him and stolen his money and trodden on his lunch, and what had he ever had to go home to, except a drunken father who punched him and a mother who expected him to lay the fire and take care of his handicapped sister; and that damp bedroom in Ballyhooly.

I could have befriended him. I could have taken care of him. But I was worse than any of the others. No wonder his father's razor had seemed like the only way out.

You don't know how dark it is in the Cork countryside at night, unless you've been there. Only a speckle of distant flickering lights as we drove over the Nagle mountains. It was cold but at least it was dry. We arrived in the middle of Ballyhooly at 11:37 and the Roundy House was emptying out, three or four locals laughing and swearing and a small brown-and-white dog barking at them disapprovingly.

"I don't know what you expect to find here," said Katharine.

"I don't know, either."

I helped her out of the car, but all the time I couldn't take my eyes off Number 15. Its windows looked blacker than ever; and in the orange light of Ballyhooly's main street, its paintwork looked even more scabrous and diseased.

"Is this it?" Katharine asked. "It looks derelict."

"It is." I unlocked the front door and kicked the weatherboard to open it. I switched on the light and, miraculously, it worked, even though it was only a single bare bulb. I had called the ESB only yesterday afternoon to have Number 15 reconnected. The damp smell seemed even stronger than ever, and I was sure that I could hear a dripping noise.

"This is a seriously creepy house," said Katharine, looking around. "How many people died here?"

"That night? All four of them. Donal's father and mother, Donal's sister, and Donal himself. And Margaret Flaherty died here, too."

"It smells like death."

"It smells more like dry rot to me," I said. But then I took two or three cautious steps into the hallway and sniffed again. "Dry rot, and something dead. Probably a bird, stuck down the chimney."

"What are you going to do?" asked Katharine.

"I don't know. But I have to do *something.*"

We took a look in the living room. The broken ceiling light cast a diagonal shadow, which made the whole room appear to be sloping sideways, and distorted its perspective. The wind blew a soft lament down the chimney.

"What are those scratches?" asked Katharine, pointing up at the covering. "It looks like a lion's been loose."

"I asked the estate agent."

"And?"

"Either he didn't know or he didn't want to tell me."

I took Katharine into the kitchen. It was deadly cold, as always. I didn't really know what I was looking for. Just some sign of what was really happening here. Just some indication of what I could do to break the cycle of Donal Coakley's revenge.

If it *was* Donal Coakley, and not some madman playing games with us.

"Nothing here," said Katharine, opening the larder door and peering inside. Only an old bottle of Chef sauce, with a rusty, encrusted cap.

We went upstairs together. I hadn't realized how much the stairs creaked until now. Every one of them complained as if their nails were slowly being drawn out of them, like teeth. The landing was empty. The front bedroom was empty. The back bedroom was empty, too. The chill was intense: that damp, penetrating chill that characterizes bedrooms in old Irish houses.

"I think you should sell," said Katharine. "Get rid of the place as soon as you can. And make sure that you don't sell it to the next person on your class register."

"You may be right. And there was me, thinking this was going to solve all of my problems."

Katharine took a last look around the bedroom. "Come on," she said. "There's no point in staying here. There's nothing you can do."

But at that moment, we heard an appalling scream from downstairs. It was a woman's scream, but it was so shrill that it was almost like an animal's. Then it was joined by another scream—a man's. He sounded as if he were being fatally hurt, and he knew it.

"Oh my God," Katharine gasped. "Oh my God what is it?"

"Stay here," I told her.

"I'm coming with you. I just want to get out of here."

"*Stay here!* We don't know what the hell could be down there."

"Oh, God," she repeated; but her voice was drowned out by another agonized scream, and then another, and then another.

I started downstairs, ducking my head so that I could see through the banisters into the hallway. I was so frightened that I was making a thin pathetic whining noise, like a child.

The screams were coming from the living room. The door was half-open, and the light was still on, but I couldn't see anything at all. No shadows, nothing. I reached the bottom of the stairs and edged my way along the hall until I was right beside the living room door. The screams were hideous, and in between the screams I could hear a woman begging for her life.

I tried to peer in through the crack in the door, but I still couldn't see anything. I thought: there's only one thing for it. I've just got to crash into the room and surprise him, whoever it is, and hope that he isn't stronger and quicker and that he doesn't have a straight-razor.

I took a deep breath. Then I took a step back, lowered my shoulder and collided against the door. It slammed wide open, and juddered a little way back again. The screams abruptly stopped.

I was standing in a silent room—alone, with only a chair for company. Either we had imagined the screaming, or else it was some kind of trick.

I was still standing there, baffled, when I heard the bedroom door slamming upstairs, and more screaming. Only this time, I recognized who it was. Katharine, and she was shouting out, *"Jerry! Jerry! Jerry for God's sake help me Jerry for God's sake!"*

I vaulted back up the stairs, my vision jostling like a hand-held camera. The door to the smaller bedroom was shut—brown-painted wood, with a cheap plastic handle. I tried to open it but it was locked or bolted. And all the time Katharine was screaming and screaming.

"Katharine!" I yelled back. "Katharine, what's happening! I can't open the door!"

But all she could do was scream and weep and babble something incomprehensible, like *"no-no-no-you-can't-you-can't-be-you-can't—"*

I hurled myself against the door, shoulder-first, but all I did was bruise my arm. Katharine's screams reached a crescendo and I was mad with panic, panting and shaking. I propped my hands against the landing walls to balance myself, and I kicked at the door-lock—once, twice—and then the door-jamb splintered and the door shuddered open.

Katharine was lying on the bed. She was struggling and staring at me, her eyes wide open. She looked as if she were fastened onto the mattress with thick brown sticks—trapped, unable to move. But beside the bed stood a huge and complicated creature that I could hardly even begin to understand. It almost filled the room with arms and legs like an immense spider; and glossy brown sacs hung from its limbs like some kind of disgusting fruit. In the middle of it, and part of it, all mixed up in it, his head swollen out of proportion and his eyes as black as cellars stood Donal Coakley, in his gray flannel shorts and his patched-up jumper, his lips drawn back as if they had been nailed to his gums. He floated, almost, borne up above the threadbare carpet by the thicket of tentacles that sprouted out of his back.

The thick brown sticks that fastened Katharine to the bed were spider's legs—or the legs of the thing that Donal Coakley had created out of his need for revenge. This was revenge incarnate. This was what revenge looked like, when it reached such an intensity that it took a life of its own.

In his right hand, Donal held a straight-razor, with a bloodied blade. It was only an inch above Katharine's neck. He had already cut her once, a very light cut, right across her throat, and blood was running into the collar of her green sweater.

I approached him as near as I dared. The whole room was a thicket of spider-like legs, and there was nothing on Donal's face to indicate that he could see me; or that he had any human emotions at all.

"What do you want me to do?" I asked him. "What do you

want me to say? You want me to apologize, for bullying you? I bullied you, yes, and I'm sorry for it. I wish I'd never done it. But we were all young and ignorant in those days. We never guessed that you were so unhappy, and even if we'd known, I don't think that we would have cared.

"It's life, Donal. It's life. And you don't ease your own pain by inflicting it on others."

Donal raised his head a little. I didn't know whether he could see me or not. The criss-cross-spider's-legs that surrounded him twitched and trembled, as if they were eager to scuttle toward me.

"You don't know the meaning of pain," he said; and his voice sounded exactly as it had, all those years ago, in the playground of Bishop O'Rourke's. "You never suffered pain, any of you."

"Oh God," said Katharine, "please help me."

But without any hesitation at all, Donal swept the straight-razor from one side of her neck to the other. If you hadn't been paying any particular attention, you wouldn't have realized immediately what he had done. But he had sliced her neck through, almost to the vertebrae, and from that instant there was no chance at all of her survival. Blood suddenly sprayed everywhere, all over the bed, all up the walls, all over the carpet. No wonder the gardai had broken into this house and thought that it was all decorated red.

Katharine twitched and shuddered. One hand tried to reach out for me. But I knew that Donal had killed her—and so, probably, did she. The blood was unbelievable: pints of it, pumped out everywhere.

Donal's hands were smothered in it, and it was even splattered across his face.

I shall never know to this day exactly what happened next. But if you can accept that men and women become physically transformed, whenever they're truly vengeful, then you can understand it, even if you don't completely believe it. When Donal cut Katharine's throat, something happened to me. I'm not saying that it was similar to what happened to Donal. But my mind suddenly boiled over with the blackest of rages. I felt hatred, and aggression, but I also felt enormous power. I felt myself lifted up, surged forward, as if I had legs and arms that I had never had before, as if I had unimaginable power. I hurled myself at Donal, and the thicket of limbs that surrounded him, and grasped him around the waist.

He slashed at my face with his straight-razor. I knew he was cutting me. I could feel the blood flying. He struggled and screamed like a girl. But I forced him backward. I gripped his hair and clawed at his face. His spidery arms and legs were flailing at me, but I had spidery arms and legs that were more than the equal of his, and we fought for one desperate moment like two giant insects. My urge for revenge, though, was so much fiercer than his. I hurled him back against the bedroom window.

The glass cracked. The glazing-bars cracked. Then both of us smashed through the window and into the yard, falling fifteen feet onto bricks and bags of cement and window frames. I lifted my head. I could feel the blood dripping from my lips. I felt bruised all over, as if I had been trampled by a horse. I could hear shouting in the street, and a woman screaming.

Donal Coakley was staring at me, only inches away, and his face was as white as the face of the moon.

"I've got you now, Jerry," he said; and he managed the faintest of smiles.

And that's my testimony; and that's all that I can tell you. You can talk to Father Murphy, for what it's worth. You can talk to Maureen. If she doesn't admit to the screaming, then it's only because she's worried about the value of her house. But it's all true; and I didn't touch Katharine, I swear.

If you can't find any trace of Donal, then I don't mind that, because it means that he's finally gone to his rest. But I'd be careful of who I bullied, if I were you; and I'd steer clear of white-faced boys in second-hand shoes. And I wouldn't have a vengeful thought in my head, not one. Not unless you want to find out what vengeance really is.

Charnel House

ONE

The old man came into my office and closed the door. He was wearing a creased linen jacket and green bowtie, and in his liver-spotted hands he held a Panama hat that had turned brown as a London broil from years of California sun. One side of his face was still prickly with white stubble, so I guessed he couldn't shave too well.

He said, almost apologetically, "It's my house. It's breathing."

I smiled and said, "Sit down."

He sat on the edge of the chrome-and-plastic chair, and licked his lips. He had one of those concerned old faces that make you wish you had a grandfather as nice as that. He was the kind of old guy it would've been satisfying to play chess with, idling away some fall afternoon on a balcony overlooking the beach.

"You don't have to believe me if you don't want to, young feller. But I called before, and I said the same thing," he insisted.

I turned over the appointment list on my desk.

"Sure. You telephoned last week, right?"

"And the week before."

"And you told the girl your house was—"

I paused and looked at him, and he looked back at me. He didn't finish my sentence for me; and I guess that was because he wanted to hear me say it, too. I gave him a tight, bureaucratic smile.

He said, in his gentle, crumbly voice, "I moved into the house from my sister's old apartment up on the hill. I sold some stock, and bought it for cash. It was going pretty cheap, and I've always wanted to live around Mission Street. But now, well . . ."

He dropped his eyes, and fiddled with the brim of his hat.

I picked up my pen. "Could you tell me your name please?"

"Seymour Wallis. I'm a retired engineer. Bridges, mainly."

"And your address?"

"Fifteen-fifty-one Pilarcitos."

"Okay. And your problem is noise?"

He looked up again. His eyes were the color of faded cornflowers pressed between the leaves of a book.

"Not noise," he said softly. "Breathing."

I sat back in my black simulated-leather revolving armchair, and tapped my ballpen against my teeth. I was pretty used to complaints in the sanitation department. We had a woman who came in regular, saying that dozens of alligators that kids had flushed toilets in the 1960s had made their way to the sewers beneath her apartment on Howard and Fourth and were trying to make their way back up the S-bend to eat her. Then there was the young pothead who believed that his water heater was giving off dangerous rays.

But, cranks or not, I was paid to be nice to them and to listen patiently to whatever they had to say, and try to reassure them that San Francisco was not harboring alligator swarms or hidden lumps of green Kryptonite.

"Isn't it possible you made a mistake?" I said. "Maybe it's your own breathing you can hear."

The old man shrugged a little, as if to say that was possible, yes, but not really likely.

"Maybe you have a downdraft in your chimney," I suggested. "Sometimes the air comes down an old stack and finds its way through cracks in the bricks where the fireplaces are blocked up."

He shook his head.

"Well," I asked him, "if it's not your own breathing, and it's not a draft in your chimney, could you tell me what you think it may be?"

He coughed and took out a clean but frayed handkerchief to dab his mouth.

"I think it's breathing," he said. "I think there's some kind of animal trapped in the walls."

"Do you hear scratching? Feet pattering? That kind of thing?"

He shook his head again.

"Just breathing?"

He nodded.

I waited to hear if he had anything else to say, but he obviously didn't. I stood up and walked across to my window, which overlooked the apartment block next door. On warm days, you'd occasionally see off-duty air hostesses sunning themselves on the roof-garden, in bikinis that made me consider that flying United had to be the best way. But all that was on show today was an aged Mexican gardener, repotting geraniums.

"If you did have an animal trapped between your walls, it could only survive for so long without food and water. And if it wasn't trapped, you'd hear it running around," I said.

Seymour Wallis, engineer, stared at his hat. I was beginning to realize that he wasn't a crank, in fact, he was rather a plain, practical man, and that coming down here to the sanitation department with stories of disembodied breathing must have taken quite a lot of careful consideration. He didn't want to look a fool. But then, who does?

He said, quietly but firmly, "It sounds like an animal breathing. I know it's hard to credit, but I've heard it for three months now, almost the whole time I've lived there, and it's quite unmistakable."

I turned back from the window. "Are there any odors? Any unpleasant deposits? I mean, you're not finding animal excrement in your cupboard or anything like that?"

"It *breathes,* that's all. Like a German shepherd on a hot day. Pant, pant, pant, all night long, and sometimes in the daytime as well."

I returned to my desk and sat myself back in my chair. Seymour Wallis looked at me expectantly, as if I could pull some kind of magical solution out of my bottom left drawer; but the truth was that I was authorized to exterminate rats, cockroaches, termites, wasps, lice, fleas, bedbugs, but so far my authority didn't extend to breathing.

"Mr. Wallis," I said, as kindly as I could, "are you sure you've come to the right department?"

He coughed. "Do you have any *other* suggestions?"

As a matter of fact, I was beginning to wonder if a psychiatrist might be a good idea, but it's kind of hard to tell a nice old gentleman straight out that he might be going cuckoo. In any case, supposing there was breathing?

I looked across at the contemporary red-and-green print on the opposite side of the room. There was a time, before our offices were redecorated, when all I had on the wall was a tatty poster warning against handling food with unwashed hands, but these days the sanitation department was far more tasteful. There had even been talk about calling us "environmental maintenance executives."

"If there's no dirt, and there are no visible signs of what's causing the breathing, then I don't quite see why you're worried. It's probably just some unusual phenomenon caused by the way your house is built," I told him.

Seymour Wallis listened to this with a look on his face that meant, *you're a bureaucrat, you have to say all these reassuring things, but I don't believe a word of it.* When I'd finished, he sat back in the plastic chair and nodded for a while in reflective silence.

"If there's anything else you need," I said. "If you want your roaches wiped out or your rats rounded up . . . well, you're very welcome."

He gave me a hard, unimpressed glance.

"I'll tell you the truth," he said hoarsely. "The truth is that I'm frightened. There's something about that breathing that scares the pants off me. I've only come here because I didn't know where else to turn. My doctor says my hearing is fine. My plumber says my drainpipes are A-Okay. My builder says my house is sound and my psychiatrist says there are no imminent signs of senility. All that reassurance, and I can still hear it and I'm still frightened."

"Mr. Wallis," I told him, "there's nothing I can do. Breathing just isn't my bag."

"You could come listen."

"To breathing?"

"Well, you don't have to."

I spread my hands sympathetically. "It's not that I don't *want* to. It's just that I have more pressing matters of city sanitation to deal with. We have a backed-up sewer on Folsom, and the folks around there are naturally more interested in their own breathing than anyone else's. I'm sorry, Mr. Wallis, there's nothing I can do to help you."

He rubbed his forehead wearily, and then he stood up.

"All right," he said, in a defeated voice. "I can understand your priorities."

I walked around my desk and opened the door for him. He put on his old Panama hat, and stood there for a moment, as if he was trying to find the words to say something else.

"If you hear anything else, like pattering feet, or if you find excrement—" I told him.

He nodded. "I know, I'll call you. The trouble with the way things are these days, everybody specializes. You can clean out sewers but you can't listen to something as strange as a house that breathes."

"I'm sorry."

He reached out and gripped my wrist. His bony old hand was surprisingly strong, and it felt as if I'd been suddenly seized by a bald eagle.

"Why not stop being sorry and do something positive?" he said. He came so close I could see the red tracery of veins in his cloudy eyes. "Why not come around when you're finished up here, and just listen for five minutes? I have some Scotch whisky my nephew brought back from Europe. We could have a drink, and then you could hear it."

"Mr. Wallis—"

He let go of my wrist, and sighed, and adjusted his hat. "You'll have to forgive me," he said flatly. "I guess it's been kind of a strain on the nerves."

"That's okay," I said. "Listen, if I find a few minutes after work, I'll come by. I can't promise, and if I don't make it, don't worry. I have a late meeting this evening, so it won't be early. But I'll try."

"Very well," he said, without looking at me. He didn't like losing control of his feelings and right now he was doing his best to gather them up, like a tumbled skein of loose wool.

Then he said, "It could be the park, you know. It could be

something to do with the park."

"The park?" I asked blankly.

He frowned, as if I'd said something totally irrelevant. "Thanks for your time, young man," and walked off down the long polished corridor. I stood at my open door watching him go. All of a sudden in the air-conditioned chill, I began to shiver.

As usual, the evening's meeting was dominated by Ben Pultik, the executive in charge of garbage disposal. Pultik was a short, wide-shouldered man who looked like a small wardrobe in a plaid jacket. He had been in garbage ever since the general strike of 1934, and he considered its collection and eventual disposal to be one of the highest callings of mankind, which in some ways it was, but not in the sense of "highest" that he meant it.

We sat around the conference table and smoked too much and drank stale coffee out of Styrofoam cups while outside the windows the sky was curtained with purple and faded gold, and the towers and pyramids of San Francisco settled into the glittering grainy Pacific night. Pultik was complaining that the owners of ethnic restaurants were failing to wrap kitchen refuse in black plastic garbage bags, and that his clean-up crews were having their coveralls soiled by exotic foods.

"Some of my men are Jewish," he said, relighting his burned-down stogie. "The last thing they want is to be soiled all over with food that ain't kosher-prepared."

Morton Meredith, the head of the department, sat in his chair at the top of the table with a wan, twitchy smile on his face, and stifled a yawn behind his hand. The only reason we convened meetings was because city hall insisted on interstaff stimulation, but the idea of being stimulated by Ben

Pultik was like the idea of ordering *moules farcies* at McDonald's. It just wasn't on the menu.

Eventually, at nine o'clock, after a tedious report from the extermination people, we left the building and walked out into the warm night air. Dan Machin, a young beanpole of a guy from the health research laboratory, came pushing across the plaza toward me and clapped me on the back.

"You fancy a drink?" he asked me. "Those meetings are enough to turn your throat into a desert preservation zone."

"Sure," I told him. "All I have to kill is time."

"Time *and* fleas," Dan reminded me.

I don't particularly know why I liked Dan Machin. He was three or four years younger than me, and yet he had his hair crew cut like a Kansas wheat field, and he wore big unfashionable eyeglasses which always looked as if they were about to drop off the end of his snubbed-up nose. He wore loose-fitting jackets with patched leather elbows, and his shoes were always scuffed, yet he had a funny oblique sense of humor which tickled me, and even though his face was pallid from spending too many hours indoors, he played a good game of tennis and he knew as many old facts and figures as the editors of Ripley.

Maybe Dan Machin reminded me of my safe suburban upbringing in Westchester, where all the houses had coach lamps, and all the housewives had blond lacquered hair and drove their children around in Buick station wagons, and every fall the smell of burning leaves would signal the season of roller-skating and, trick-or-treat. A lot of hard things had happened to me since then, not the least of which was a messy divorce and a fierce but absurd affair, and it was nice to know that such an America still existed.

We crossed the street and walked up the narrow sidewalk of Gold Street to Dan's favorite bar, the Assay Office. It was a high-ceilinged room with an old-style balcony, and the wood-and-brass furniture of a long-gone San Francisco. We found a table next to the wall, and Dan ordered us a couple of Coors.

"I meant to go up to Pilarcitos this evening," I told him, lighting a cigarette.

"Fun or business?"

I shrugged. "I'm not sure. Not much of either."

"Sounds mysterious."

"It is. An old guy came into the office today and said he had a house that breathed."

"Breathed?"

"That's right. In fact, it panted like Lassie. He wanted to know if I could do something about it."

The beers arrived and Dan took a long swallow, leaving himself with a white foamy moustache that quite suited him.

"It isn't a downdraft in the chimney," I told him. "Nor is it any kind of creature trapped inside the wall cavities. In fact, it's a genuine case of inexplicable respiration."

That was meant to be a wisecrack, but Dan seemed to take it seriously. "Did he say anything more? Did he tell you when it happened? What time of day?"

I set down my glass. "He said it was all the time. He'd only lived in the place for a few months, and it's been happening ever since he moved in. He's real frightened. I guess the old coot thinks it's some kind of a ghost."

"Well, it could be," said Dan.

"Oh, sure. And Ben Pultik's grown tired of garbage."

"No, I mean it," insisted Dan. "I've heard of cases like that before, when people have heard voices and stuff like that. Under certain conditions, the sounds that were uttered in an old room can be heard again. Sometimes, people have claimed to hear conversations that could only have been spoken a century before."

"Where did you find all this out?"

Dan tugged at his tiny nose as if he was trying to make it grow longer, and I could swear that he faintly blushed. "As a matter of fact," he said, embarrassed, "I've always been pretty interested in spirit manifestations. It kind of runs in the family."

"A hard-boiled scientist like you?"

"Now, come on," said Dan, "it's not as nutty as it seems, all this spirit-world stuff. There have been some pretty astounding cases. And anyway, my aunt used to say that the ghost of Buffalo Bill Cody came and sat by her bedside every night to tell her stories of the Old West."

"Buffalo Bill?"

Dan pulled a self-deprecating face. "That's what she said. Maybe I shouldn't have believed her."

I sat back my chair. There was a friendly hubbub of chatter in the bar, and they were bringing out pieces of fried chicken and spareribs, which reminded me that I hadn't eaten since breakfast.

"You think I should go up there?" I asked Dan, eyeing a girl in a tight white T-shirt with "Oldsmobile Rocket" printed across her breasts.

"Well, let's put it this way, I'd go. In fact, maybe we should go up there together. I'd love to hear a house that breathes."

"You would, huh? Okay, if you want to split the taxi fare, we'll go. But don't think I can guarantee this guy. He's very old, and he may be just hallucinating."

"An hallucination is a trick of the eyes."

"I'm beginning to think that girl in the T-shirt is a trick of the eyes."

Dan turned around, and the girl caught his eye, and he blushed a deep shade of red. "You always do that," he complained irritably. "They must think I'm some kind of sex maniac in here."

We finished up our beers and caught a taxi up to Pilarcitos Street. It was one of those short sloping streets where you park your car when you're visiting a Japanese restaurant on the main drag, and which, queasy on too much tempura and sake, you can never find again afterward. The houses were old and silent, with turrets and gables and shadowy porches, and considering that Mission Street was only a few yards away, they seemed to be strangely brooding and out of touch with time. Dan and I stood outside 1551 in the evening breeze, looking up at the Gothic tower and the carved balcony, and the grayish paint that flaked off it like the scales from a dead fish.

"You don't believe a house like this could breathe?" he asked me, sniffing.

"I don't believe any house can breathe. But it smells like he needs his drains checked."

"For Christ's sake," Dan complained. "No shop talk after hours. You think I go round cocktail parties looking through my guests' hair for lice?"

"I wouldn't put it past you."

There was a rusted wrought-iron gate, and then five angled steps that led up to the porch. I pushed the gate open, and it groaned like a dying dog. Then we went up the steps and searched around in the gloom of the porch for the front doorbell. All the downstairs windows overlooking the street were shuttered and locked, and so there didn't seem much point in whistling or calling out. Down the hill, a police car sped past with its siren warbling, and a girl was laughing as she pranced along the street with two young boys. All this was happening within sight and earshot, and yet up here in the entrance of 1551, there was nothing but shadowy silence, and a feeling that lost years were eddying past us, leaking out of the letter box and from under the elaborate front door like sand seeping out of a bucket.

"There's a knocker here," Dan said. "Maybe I should give it a couple of raps."

I peered into the darkness. "As long as you don't quote 'Nevermore' at the same time."

"Jesus," said Dan. "Even the knocker's creepy."

I stepped forward and took a look at it. It was a huge old knocker, black with age and weathering. It was fashioned like the head of a strange snarling creature, something between a wolf and a demon, and I didn't find it at all encouraging. Somebody who could happily hang something like that on his front door couldn't be altogether normal, unless he actually enjoyed having nightmares. Under the knocker there was engraved the single word: *"Return."*

While Dan was hesitating, I took hold of the knocker and banged it two or three times. The sound echoed flatly inside the house, and we waited patiently on the porch for Seymour Wallis to answer.

"What do you think that is? That thing on the knocker?" Dan asked.

"Don't ask me. Some kind of a gargoyle, I guess."

"It looks more like a goddamned werewolf to me."

I reached in my pocket for a cigarette. "You've been watching too many old horror pictures."

I was just about to bang the knocker again, when I heard footsteps shuffling toward us from inside the house. Bolts were pulled back at the top of the door, and at the bottom, and then it shuddered open an inch or two, until it was stopped by a security chain. I saw the pale face of Seymour

Wallis peering around it cautiously, as if he was expecting muggers, or Mormons.

"Mr. Wallis?" I said. "We came to hear the breathing."

"Oh, it's you," he said, with obvious relief. "Just hold on a moment there and I'll open the door."

He slipped the chain and the door shuddered wider still. Seymour Wallis was wearing a bathrobe and slippers and his thin, bare, hairy legs were showing. "I hope we haven't caught you at a bad moment," Dan said.

"No, no. Come in. I was only getting ready to take a bath."

"I sure like your knocker," I said. "It's kind of scary, though, isn't it?"

Seymour Wallis gave me a flicker of a smile. "I suppose so. It came with the house. I don't know what it's meant to be. My sister thinks it might be the devil, but I'm not so sure. And why it should say *'Return'* I shall never know."

We found ourselves in a high, musty hallway, carpeted in threadbare brown, and with dozens of yellowing prints and engravings and framed letters all over the walls. Some of the frames were empty and others were cracked, but most of them contained sepia views of Mount Taylor and Cabezon Peak, or foxed and illegible maps, lists of statistics written in crabbed and faded handwriting.

Beside us, the newel post of the stairs was carved out of dark mahogany, and on top of it was a bronze bear, standing upright, with a woman's face instead of a snout. The stairs themselves, tall and narrow, rose toward the darkness of the second floor like an escalator into the gloomiest recesses of the night.

"You'd better come this way," Seymour Wallis said, leading us down the hall toward a door at the end. There was a shabby stag's head hanging over it with dusty antlers and only one eye. Dan said, "After *you,*" and I wasn't sure if he was joking about the house or not. It couldn't have been much creepier.

We entered a small, airless study. There were shelves all around that must have been lined with books at one time, but were now empty. The brownish-figured wallpaper behind them was marked with the shadows of where they had once been. In the corner, under a doleful painting of early San Francisco, was a stained leather-topped desk and a wooden stockbroker's chair with two slats missing. Seymour Wallis had kept the shutters closed, and the room was suffocating and stale. It smelled of cats, lavender bags, and roach powder.

"I hear the noises in here more than in any other room," Wallis explained. "It comes at night mostly, when I'm sitting here writing letters, or finishing my accounts. At first there's nothing, but then I start straining my ears and I'm sure I can hear it. Soft breathing, just as if somebody's walked into the room, and is standing a little ways away watching me. I try, well, I've *tried* not to turn around. But I'm afraid that I always do. And of course there's nobody there."

Dan walked across the worn-out rug. The floorboards creaked under his feet. He picked up an astral calendar from Seymour Wallis's desk, and examined it for a moment or two. "Do you believe in the supernatural, Mr. Wallis?"

"It depends what you mean by the supernatural."

"Well, ghosts."

Wallis glanced at me and then back to Dan. I think he was afraid that we were putting him on. In his maroon bathrobe, he looked like one of those elderly men who insist on taking a dip in the ocean on Christmas Day.

"I was telling my colleague here that some houses act as receivers for sounds and conversation from the past. If anything particularly stressful has happened inside them, they kind of store up the sound in the texture of their walls and play it back like a tape recorder, over and again. There was a case in Massachusetts, only last year, where a young couple claimed to have heard a man and a woman arguing in their living room at night, but whenever they went downstairs there was nobody there. They heard actual names being shouted, though, and when they went to their local church register and looked them up, they found that the people they could hear had lived in their house in 1860."

Seymour Wallis rubbed his bristly chin. "You're trying to say that when I hear breathing, it's a ghost?"

"Not exactly a ghost," said Dan. "It's just an echo from the past. It might be frightening, but it is no more dangerous than the sound you can hear from your television. It's just *sound,* that's all."

Wallis sat slowly down on the old stockbroker's chair and looked at us gravely. "Can I get it to leave me alone?" he asked. "I mean, can you exorcise it?"

"I don't think so," said Dan. "Not without knocking the house down. What you're hearing is within the fabric of the house itself."

I coughed and said politely, "I'm afraid there's a city ordinance against knocking down these old houses for meretricious reasons. Sub-section eight."

Seymour Wallis looked very tired. "You know something," he said, "I've wanted one of these houses for years. I used to walk by here and admire their age and their character and their style. At last I've managed to get one. It means a great deal to me, this house. It represents everything I've done in my life to maintain the old true standards against the easy, false, beguiling modern world. Look at this place. There isn't a foot of Formica, an ounce of plastic, or a scrap of fiberglass. Those moldings around the ceiling are real plaster, and these floorboards came from an old sailing ship. Look how wide they are. Now look at those doors. They're solid and they hang true. The hinges are brass."

He raised his head, and when he spoke there was a great deal of emotion in his voice.

"This house is mine," he said. "And if there's a ghost in it, or a noise in it, I want it out. I'm the master of this place, and, by God, I'll fight any supernatural oddity for the right to say that."

"I don't like to sound as if I don't believe you," I said, "because I'm sure you heard what you say you did. But don't you think you've been over-working? Maybe you're just tired."

Seymour Wallis nodded. "I'm tired. But I'm not so tired that I won't fight to keep what's mine."

Dan looked around the room. "Maybe you could come to some arrangement with this breathing. You know, strike some kind of compromise."

"I don't understand."

"Well, I'm not sure that I do, either. But lots of spiritualists seem to believe that you can do deals with the spirit world to have yourself left alone. I mean, the whole reason a place gets itself haunted is because the spirit isn't free to get itself off to wherever spirits hang out. So maybe this breathing spirit is trying to get you to help it accomplish something. I don't know. It's just a thought. Maybe you ought to try and talk to it."

I raised an eyebrow.

"What do you suggest I say?" asked Wallis cautiously.

"Be blunt. Ask it what it wants."

"Oh, come on, Dan," I butted in. "This is ridiculous."

"No, it isn't. If Mr. Wallis here can hear the breathing, then maybe whatever's doing the breathing can hear him."

"We don't yet know that there is any breathing."

"But supposing there is."

Wallis stood up. "I guess the only way I'm going to convince you is if you hear it for yourself. Why not have a glass of Scotch? Then maybe we can sit down here for a half hour, if you can spare it, and we'll listen."

"Sure, I'd love to," said Dan.

Wallis shuffled out of the room and came back a few moments later with two bentwood chairs. We sat down, upright and uncomfortable, while he shuffled off again to fetch his decanter.

I sniffed the musty air. It was hot and stuffy in that tiny library, and I was beginning to wish I was back in the Assay Office drinking a cold Coors. Dan rubbed his hands together in a businesslike kind of way. "This is going to be wild."

"You mean you think we're going to hear it?"

"Sure I think we're going to hear it. I told you. I believe in this stuff. I nearly saw a ghost once."

"You *nearly* saw it? What does that mean?"

"I was staying at an old hotel in Denver, and I was going back to my room one night when I saw the maid coming out of it. I put my key in the door, and she said, 'Are you sure you have the right room, sir? There's a gentlemen taking a bath in there!' Well, I checked my key number, and it was the right room, so I went inside. The maid followed in to check, and when I looked in the bathroom there was nobody taking a bath, no water in the tub, no nothing. Hotels are great places for ghosts."

"Sure, and the sanitation department is a great place for liars."

Right then, old man Wallis came back with a tarnished silver tray, bearing a decanter of whisky and three tumblers. He sat them down on the table and poured us each a generous glassful. Then he sat in his chair and sipped the Scotch as if he was testing it for hemlock.

Outside in the hallway, a clock that I hadn't seen when I walked in struck ten. *Bong-chirr-bong-chirr-bong-chirr . . .*

"Do you have any ice, Mr. Wallis?" Dan asked.

Wallis looked at him in confusion, then shook his head. "I'm sorry. The icebox is broken. I've been meaning to have it fixed. I eat out mostly, so I haven't felt the need."

Dan lifted his glass. "Well, here's to the breathing, whoever it is."

I swallowed warm, neat Scotch and grimaced.

We waited there in silence for almost ten minutes. It's surprising how much noise you can make drinking whisky in total quiet. After a while, I could hear that invisible clock ticking out there in the hallway, and even the distant murmur of traffic on Mission. And there was that rushing sound of my own blood circulating in my ears. Wallis suppressed a cough, "More whisky?"

Dan held his glass out, but I said, "If I have any more, I'll be hearing bells, not breathing."

We settled back on our chairs again, with an awkward creaking of wood. Dan asked, "Do you know anything about the history of this house, Mr. Wallis? Anything that might help you identify *who* this mystery breather might be?"

Seymour Wallis nervously rearranged the things on his desk—pen, letter opener, calendar—then looked at Dan with that same defeated look he'd had on his face when he first came into my office.

"I looked at the deeds and they go back to 1885 when the house was built. It was owned by a seed merchant and then by a naval captain. But there wasn't anything unusual. Nothing to make you think there might have been stress here. No murders or anything like that."

Dan swallowed some more whisky. "Maybe the breather

sticks around because he was happy here. That sometimes happens. A ghost haunts a house trying to recapture its old joy."

"The happy breather?" I asked in disbelief.

"Sure," retorted Dan defensively. "It's been known."

We lapsed into silence again. Both Dan and I sat there reasonably still, but Seymour Wallis seemed to twitch and scratch, as if he was really unsettled. The clock struck the half hour, and still we waited, and still we heard nothing. All around us, the dark bulk of the old house remained hushed, with not even the sound of a roof timber creaking or a window rattling. Over a hundred years, this building had done all the settling it was going to, and now it was dead, immobile, and quiet.

I laid down my whisky glass on the edge of Seymour Wallis's desk. He glanced up at me briefly, and I smiled, but he simply turned away, biting his lip. Perhaps he was worried that there wouldn't be any breathing tonight, in which case he was either lying or going out of his mind.

Just then, Dan said, "Ssshh."

I froze and listened, "I don't hear anything."

Wallis lifted his hand. "At first it's very soft," he said, "but it grows louder. Listen."

I strained my ears. There was still the ticking of the clock outside, still the distant murmur of traffic. But there was something else, too, something so faint that all of us were frowning in concentration as we tried to hear it.

It was like a sibilant whispering at first like the wind tossing a piece of soft tissue across a room. But gradually it grew more distinct, and all I could do was turn to look at Dan to see if he was hearing what I was hearing, to make sure that it wasn't auto-suggestion or a trick of the wind.

It was breathing. Slow, deep breathing, like the breathing

of someone asleep. It went in and out, in and out, with measured respiration, as if lungs were being endlessly filled and emptied with hopeless regularity, the breathing of someone who slept and slept and would never reach morning.

Now I knew why Seymour Wallis was frightened. This sound, this breathing, could make your skin prickle with cold. It was the breathing of someone who could never wake up. It had more to do with death than with life, and it went on and on and on, louder and louder, until we no longer had to strain our ears, but simply sat there, staring at each other in horror and fright.

It was impossible to say where the breathing came from. It was all around. I even looked at the walls to make sure that they weren't sagging in and out with every breath. Wallis was right. The house was breathing. The house itself was not dead, as it had first appeared, but asleep.

I whispered, "Dan, *Dan!*"

"What is it?"

"Challenge it, Dan, like you said. Ask it what it wants!"

Dan licked his lips. All around us, the breathing went on, slow and heavy. Sometimes I thought it was going to stop, but then another deep breath would come, and another, and if it had been breathing like this for more than a hundred years, it was probably going to go on forever.

Dan coughed. "I can't," he said hoarsely. "I don't know what to say."

Wallis himself just sat there, tense and still for the first time this evening, his whisky untouched in his hand.

Slowly, cautiously, I stood up. The breathing didn't falter. It was as loud now as if I was sleeping next to someone in the same bed and they had turned to face me in the darkness.

"Who's there?" I asked.

There was no response. The breathing went on.

"Who's there?" I said, louder. "What do you want? Tell us what you want and we'll help you!"

The breathing continued, although for some reason I thought it sounded harsher. It was quicker, too.

"Don't, for God's sake!" Dan pleaded.

I ignored him. I walked into the center of the room and called out. "Whoever's breathing, listen! We want to help you! Tell us what to do and we'll help you. Give us a sign! Show us that you know we're here!"

Seymour Wallis said, "Please, I think this is dangerous. Let's just listen and leave it alone."

I shook my head. "How can we? Dan here believes in ghosts, and you say it scares you. Well, I can hear it, too, and if I can hear it that means there's something there, because I don't believe in ghosts and I'm not particularly scared."

The breathing grew quicker and quicker. It was still the breathing of a sleeper, but of a sleeper who dreams, or a sleeper who is going through nightmares. Wallis stood up, his face drawn and pale. "My God, it's never been as loud as this before. Please, don't say any more. Just leave it alone, and it'll go away."

"Whoever's breathing!" I called crisply. "Whoever's there! Listen! We can help you! We can help you leave this house!"

The breathing was almost frantic now, panting, whining. Seymour Wallis, terrified, put his hands over his ears, and Dan was sitting rigid in his chair, his face white. As for me, I may not have been scared before, but this was insane. It was like a hideous fantasy. The breathing was mounting and mounting as if it was working up toward a climax, the peak of some grotesque effort.

Soon it was the screaming breath of a runner who runs too far and too fast, the breath of a terrified animal. And then suddenly, there was a roar of sound and energy that made me cover my eyes, and sent Dan Machin hurtling off his chair and halfway across the room. Seymour Wallis shrieked like a woman and dropped to his knees. I heard a blizzard of splintering glass from someplace in the house and things clattering and falling. Then there was silence.

I opened my eyes. Wallis was crouched on the floor, shaken but unhurt. It was Dan I was worried about. He was lying on his back, unmoving, and his face was a ghastly white. I picked up his fallen chair, then knelt beside him and patted his cheek.

"Dan? Are you okay? Dan!"

"Maybe I'd better call an ambulance," Wallis offered.

I raised one of Dan's eyelids with my thumb. His twitching eyeball showed that he was still alive, but he must have been in a deep state of concussion or shock. They'd taught me that much in the Army, apart from how to blow up paddy fields and defoliate twenty-five acres in just as many minutes.

While Wallis called the emergency service, I covered Dan with my jacket and switched on the beat-up old electric heater to keep him warm. Dan didn't tremble or shake. He just lay there flat on his back, white and still, and when I listened close to his lips I could only just hear his breathing. I slapped him, a couple of times, but it was just like slapping a lump of baker's dough.

"They'll be right here," reported Wallis, setting down the phone.

I lifted my head. For a moment, I thought I heard that breathing again, that soft, rustling breath. But it was only Dan, struggling to keep himself alive. The house itself seemed to have gone back to its ancient secret sleep.

Wallis knelt slowly and arthritically down beside me. "Do you have any idea what that was?" he asked me. "That noise?

All that power? I couldn't believe it. It's never happened before."

"I don't know. Maybe some kind of pressure release. Maybe you've got some kind of air pressure that sometimes needs to get free. I don't know what the hell it is."

"Do you still think it's a ghost?"

I glanced at him. "Do you?"

Wallis thought for a moment, and then shook his head. "If it's a ghost then it's a damned powerful ghost. I never heard of a ghost that could lay people flat."

He looked down at Dan's pallid face and bit his lip. "Do you think he's going to be all right?" he asked me.

I didn't know what to say. All I could do was shrug, and kneel in that dingy library, and wait for the ambulance.

He was sitting propped up in bed when I went to visit him the following morning. He had a bright green-painted private room overlooking the Bay, and the nurses had filled the room with flowers. He was still pale, and the doctors were keeping him under observation, but he was cheerful enough. I gave him a copy of *Playboy* and that morning's *Examiner*, and I pulled up a tubular steel-and-canvas chair.

He opened the *Playboy* centerspread and took a quick and critical look at a brunette with gigantic breasts.

"Just what I need," he said dryly. "A short burst of over-adrenalization."

"I thought it might work better than Benzedrine," I told him. "How do you feel?"

He laid the magazine down. "I'm not sure. I feel okay, in myself. No worse than if someone had knocked me on the head with a baseball bat."

He paused, and looked at me. The pupils of his eyes, even behind his Clark Kent glasses seemed unusually tiny. Maybe it was just the drugs they'd given him. Maybe he was still in a mild state of concussion. But somehow he didn't look quite like the same Dan Machin that I had met for a drink the previous evening. There was something *starey* about him, as if his mouth was saying one thing but his mind was thinking another.

"You don't look yourself," I told him. "Is that what you mean?"

"I don't *feel* myself. I don't know what it is, but I feel definitely odd."

"Did you feel anything strange when that explosion happened?" I asked him.

He shrugged. "I don't even remember. I remember the breathing, and the way it built up, but after that, well, I just don't recall. I get the feeling I was attacked."

"*Attacked?* By what?"

"I don't know," said Dan. "It's real hard to explain. If I knew how to tell you, I would. But I can't."

"Do you still think it was a ghost, or a spirit?"

He ran his hand through his crew cut. "I'm not too sure. It could have been some kind of poltergeist, you know, the kind of spirit that hurls things around. Or it may even have been an earth tremor. Perhaps there's a fault directly under the house."

"Suddenly you're looking for rational explanations again," I told him. "I thought of that, and there's no tremor reported in the paper today. I asked around at the office, too, and nobody else felt one."

Dan reached over and helped himself to a glass of water.

"In that case I haven't a clue. Maybe it was a ghost. But I always believed that ghosts were pretty harmless, on the whole. You know, they walk around with their heads under their arms, clanking their chains, but that's about it."

I walked over to the window and looked down at the midmorning traffic crossing the Golden Gate. The fog had lifted but a last haze still clung around the uprights of the bridge, smudging them like a watercolor painting.

"I've arranged to go back to the house this evening," I said. "I really want to take a good look all around, and see what's going on there. I'm taking Bryan Corder from the engineering department, too. I had a talk with him this morning, and he guessed it might be some kind of katabatic draft."

Dan, when I turned around again, didn't appear to have heard. He was sitting up in bed, staring absentmindedly across the room, and his lower jaw had dropped open slack.

"Dan?" I said. "Did you hear that?"

He blinked at me.

"Dan?"

I walked quickly across to the bed and took his arm.

"Dan, are you okay? You look real ill."

He licked his lips as if they were very dry.

"Sure," he said uncertainly. "I'm okay. I guess I need some rest, that's all. Once I came out of the concussion, I didn't sleep too good. I kept having dreams."

"Well, why don't you ask the nurse for a sleeping pill?"

"I don't know. I just kept having these dreams, that was all."

I sat down again, and looked at him intently.

"What kind of dreams? Nightmares?"

Dan took off his eyeglasses and rubbed his eyes. "No, no, they weren't nightmares. I guess they were kind of scary, but they didn't seem to frighten me. I dreamed about that doorknocker, you know, that one at old man Wallis's house. But it wasn't a doorknocker at all. I dreamed it was hanging on the door, but it was talking to me. Instead of metal, it was made of real hair and real flesh, and it was talking to me, trying to explain something to me, in this kind of quiet, whispery voice."

"What was it saying? Don't light fires in the forest?"

Dan didn't seem to see the joke. He shook his head seriously. "It was trying to tell me to go somewhere, to find something; but I couldn't make out what it was. It kept explaining and explaining, and I could never understand. It was something to do with that bear on Mr. Wallis's stairs, you know, that little statue of the bear with a face like a woman. But I couldn't get the connection at all."

I frowned at Dan's white, grave face for a while, but then I grinned and gripped his wrist in a friendly squeeze.

"You know what you're suffering from, Dan old buddy? Post-ghost delusion. It's an occult type of post-natal depression. Have a few days' rest and you won't even remember what you were worried about."

Dan grimaced. He didn't seem to believe me at all.

"Listen," I told him, "we're going to go over that house tonight with a fine-tooth comb, and whatever it was that laid you out, we'll find it. We won't only find it, we'll bring it back alive, and you can keep it in a jar in your laboratory."

Dan attempted a smile, but it wasn't much of one. "Okay," he said quietly. "Do what you like."

I sat there for a few more minutes, but Dan didn't seem to be in a conversational mood. So I gave him one more friendly squeeze of the hand. "I'll drop in tomorrow. 'Round about the same time."

Dan nodded, without looking up.

I left him, and went out into the hospital corridor. A doctor was on his way to Dan's room, and he brushed past me as I came out. As he opened the door, I said, "Doctor?"

The doctor looked at me impatiently. He was a short, sandy-haired man with a pointed nose and purple bags under his eyes like the drapes of an old-fashioned theater curtain. A badge on his lapel said *Doctor James T. Jarvis.*

I nodded toward Dan's room. "I don't like to intrude. I'm only a friend of Mr. Machin's, not a relative or anything. But I just wanted to know if he was okay. I mean, he seemed pretty strange today."

"What do you mean by strange?"

"Well, you know. Not quite himself."

Doctor Jarvis shook his head. "That's not unusual after severe concussion. Give him a few days to get over it."

"Was that really all it was? Concussion?"

The doctor lifted his clipboard and checked it out. "That's all. Apart from the asthma."

"Asthma? What asthma? He doesn't have asthma."

The doctor stared at me baldly. "You're trying to tell me my job?"

"Of course not. But I play tennis with Dan. He doesn't suffer from asthma. He never has, as far as I know."

The doctor kept his hand on the handle of Dan's door. "Well, that's your view, Mr.—"

"What's your view?" I asked him.

The doctor smirked. "I'm afraid that's confidential between me and my patient. But if he doesn't have asthma, he certainly does have a severe respiratory complaint. It was exacerbated by the concussion, and he spent three or four hours last night with a breathing mask on. I don't think I've ever come across a case quite as severe."

A pretty brunette nurse in a tight white uniform came along the corridor with a tray of hypodermic syringes and bottles of medicine. "I'm sorry I'm behind, Dr. Jarvis," she said. "Mrs. Walters needed changing again."

"That's all right," said Dr. Jarvis. "I've just been having a top-level medical conference with Mr. Machin's learned friend here. I'm learning so much, I'm almost reluctant to drag myself away."

He opened Dan's door wider. But I said, "Please, just one thing," and held his arm. He paused, and looked down at my hand as if something nasty had just dropped on his sleeve from a passing buffalo.

"Listen," he said sourly, "I don't know what kind of native expertise you have in the field of diagnostic medicine, but I have to continue with your friend's treatment program right away. So please excuse me."

"It's just the breathing," I said. "It could be important."

"Of course it's important," retorted Dr. Jarvis sarcastically. "If our patients don't breathe, we get seriously concerned."

"Will you hear me out?" I snapped. "Last night, Dan and I got ourselves involved with something to do with breathing. I need to know what made you think he had an asthma attack."

"What the hell are you talking about? Something to do with breathing? You mean you were sniffing glue, something like that?"

"I can't explain. It wasn't drugs. But it could be real important."

Dr. Jarvis closed the door again, and sighed with exaggerated exasperation. "All right, if you really need to know, Mr. Machin was panting and gasping. Every ninety minutes or so, he began to breathe heavily, finally working up to a real climax of panting. That was all. It was severe, and it was unusual, but there was nothing to suggest that it wasn't a regular attack of asthma."

"I've just told you. He doesn't have asthma."

Dr. Jarvis lowered his head. "Will you get out of here?" he said quietly. "Visiting time is over, and the last thing I need is homespun advice. Okay?"

I was about to say something else, but then I checked myself. I guess I would have been just as irked if somebody had strayed into my office and tried to tell me how to exterminate bugs. I raised my hands in a conciliatory gesture. "Okay. I get you. I'm sorry."

The nurse opened the door and went in, while I turned to leave. "I really didn't mean to be rude," Dr. Jarvis apologized. "But I do know what I'm doing. You can come back again at five if you want to. We should know some more by then."

At that second, there was a shrill and horrified shriek from inside Dan's room. Dr. Jarvis looked at me, and I looked at him, and we both banged the door wide open and pushed our way inside. What I saw right then I couldn't believe. It was there, in front of my eyes, but I couldn't believe it.

The nurse was standing, rigid with shock, by the side of Dan Machin's bed. Dan himself was sitting upright in bed, in his blue-striped hospital pajamas, as normal and ordinary as you could think of. But his eyes were terrifying. His glasses had fallen to the floor, and his eyes were total blazing red, the eyes of a vicious dog caught in a searchlight at night, or the eyes of a demon. What's more, he was breathing, in and out, in and out, with the deep groaning breaths that we had all heard in Seymour Wallis's house only last night, those heavy endless breaths of a sleeper who could never wake. He was breathing like the house itself, like everything that had chilled and frightened us in the gloomy and ancient rooms, and it seemed as if the hospital room itself went deathly cold with every breath.

"My God! *What is it?*" Dr. Jarvis gasped.

TWO

One of the worst things you can ever discover in life is that some of us have it and some of us don't. I guess it's just as well, in a way. If every young boy had the talent to fly airplanes, or drive racing cars, or make love to twenty women in one night, there wouldn't be many volunteers for clearing out backed-up sewers on Folsom. But it's still tough when you discover that it's *you* who doesn't have it, and that instead of living a luxurious life of fun and profit in Beverly Hills, you're going to have to take a nine-to-five job in public works and cook on a hot plate.

I was born of reasonably well-shod parents in Westchester, New York, but when my father suffered a stroke, I left my mother with her house and her insurance money, and I headed West. I think I wanted to be a TV anchorman, or something grandiose like that, but as it turned out I was lucky to eat. I married a woman who was seven years older than me, mainly because she reminded me of my mother, and I was fortunately broke when she discovered me in bed with a waitress from the Fox commissary and sued me for divorce. My affair broke up, too, which left me high and dry and stranded, and having to look for the first time in my life at myself, at my own identity, and having to come to terms with what I could achieve and what I couldn't.

My name's John Hyatt, which is one of those names that people think they recall but in actuality don't. I'm thirty-one, and quite tall, with a taste for subdued, well-cut sport coats and widish 1950s-style pants in gray. I live alone on the top floor of an apartment block on Townsend Street, with my stereo and my house plants and my collection of paperbacks with broken spines. I guess I'm happy and content in my work, but haven't you ever gone out at night, someplace quiet maybe, and looked over the Bay at the lights twinkling all across America, and thought, well, surely there's more to life than this?

Don't think I'm lonesome, though. I'm not. I date girls and I have quite a few friends, and I even get invited to pool parties and barbecues. Right at the time we went up to Seymour Wallis's house, though, I was going through a kind of a stale period, not sure what I wanted out of life or what life wanted out of me. But I guess a lot of people felt like that when President Carter was elected. At least with Nixon you knew which side you were on.

Maybe what happened to Dan Machin helped me get myself together. It was something so weird and so frightening that you couldn't think about anything else. Even after he closed his big eyes, just a few seconds after we burst into the room, and sank back against his pillow, I was still shivering with shock and fright, and I could feel a prickling sensation of fear across the palms of my hands.

The nurse said, "He . . . he . . ."

Dr. Jarvis stepped cautiously up to Dan Machin's bed, lifted his wrist, and checked his pulse. Then he took a deep breath and raised Dan's eyelid. I felt myself flinching away, in case the eye was still that fiery red color, but it wasn't. It had returned to its normal pale gray, and it was plain that Dan was in another state of coma.

"Nurse, I want full diagnostic equipment brought up here right away. And page Dr. Foley."

The nurse nodded, and left the room, obviously glad to have something distracting to do. I walked up to Dan's bedside and looked at his pale, fevered face. He didn't look so much like the scientific hick from Kansas anymore. The lines around his mouth were too deep, and his pallor was too white. But at least he was breathing normally.

I glanced up at Dr. Jarvis. The doctor was jotting notes down on his clipboard, his expression intense and anxious.

"Do you know what it was?" I asked quietly.

He didn't look up, didn't answer.

"Those red eyes," I said. "Do you know what could possibly cause that?"

He stopped writing and stared at me.

"I want to know just what this breathing business you were involved in last night was all about. Are you absolutely sure it wasn't drugs?"

"Look, I'd tell you if it was. It had to do with a house on Pilarcitos."

"A house?"

"That's right. We both work for the sanitation department, and the owner invited us to come up to his house to listen to this breathing. He said the house made a breathing noise, and he didn't know what it was."

Dr. Jarvis made another check of Dan's pulse.

"Did you find out what caused it?" he asked. "The breathing?"

I shook my head. "All I know is that Dan's been breathing just like it. It's almost as if the breathing in the house has gone into him. As if he's possessed."

Dr. Jarvis set down his clipboard next to Dan Machin's bowl of grapes.

"Are you a full-fledged member of the nuts club or just an associate member?" he asked.

This time I didn't take offense. "I know it's difficult to understand," I said. "I don't understand it myself. But possession is just what it seems like. I heard the house breathing, and I heard Dan breathing just now, when his eyes were all red. It sounded to me like one and the same."

Dr. Jarvis looked down at Dan and shook his head. "It's obviously psychosomatic," he said. "He heard this breathing noise last night, and it frightened him so much that he began to identify with it and breathe in sympathy."

"Well, maybe. But what made his eyes go like that?"

Dr. Jarvis took a deep breath. "A trick of the light," he said evenly.

"A trick of the light? Now, wait a minute!"

Dr. Jarvis stared at me, hard. "You heard me," he snapped. "A trick of the light."

"I saw him myself! So did you!"

"I didn't see anything. At least, I didn't see anything that was medically possible. And I think we'd both better remember that before we go shouting our mouths off to anyone else."

"But the nurse—"

Dr. Jarvis waved his hand in deprecation. "In this hospital, nurses are regarded as housemaids in fancy uniforms."

I leaned over Dan and examined his waxy face and the way his lips moved and whispered as he slept.

"Doctor, this guy is more than just sick," I told him. "This guy has something really, really wrong. Now, what are we going to do about it?"

"There's only one thing we can do. Diagnose his problem and give him recognized medical treatment. We don't undertake exorcisms here, I'm afraid. In any event, I don't believe this is any worse than an advanced case of hypersuggestibility. Your friend here went up to the house and became hysterical when he thought he heard breathing. It was probably his own."

"But I heard it, too," I argued.

"Maybe you did," said Dr. Jarvis offhandedly.

"Doctor," I said, angry. But Dr. Jarvis turned on me before I could tell him how I felt.

"Before you start censuring me for lack of imagination, just remember that I work here," he snapped. "Everything I do has to be justified to the hospital board, and if I start raving about demonic possession and eyes that glow red in the dark, I'll suddenly find that my promotion has been shelved for a while and that I only get half the facilities and finance I need."

He came around the bed and faced me directly. In a low, urgent voice, he said, "I saw Mr. Machin's eyes go red, and so did you. But if we want to do anything about it, anything effective, we'd better keep it quiet. Do you understand?"

I looked at him curiously. "Are you trying to tell me that you believe he's really possessed?"

"I'm not trying to tell you anything. I don't believe in demons and I don't believe in possession. But I do believe that there's something wrong here that we need to work out for ourselves, without the knowledge of the hospital."

At that moment, Dan stirred and groaned. I felt the hair on the back of my neck prickle upright in alarm, but when he spoke, he was obviously back to some kind of normal.

"John . . ." he murmured. *"John . . ."*

I leaned over him. His eyes were only open in slits, and his lips were cracked.

"I'm here, Dan. What's wrong? How do you feel?"

"John . . ." he whispered. *"Don't let me go . . ."*

I glanced across at Dr. Jarvis. "It's okay, Dan. Nobody's going to let you go."

Dan weakly raised one of his hands. "Don't let me go, John. It's the heart, John. *Don't let me go.*"

Dr. Jarvis came close. "Your heart? Is your heart feeling

bad? Do you have any constriction? Any pain?"

Dan shook his head, just a fraction of an inch each way. "It's the heart," he said, in a voice almost too faint to hear. "It beats and it beats and it beats. It's still beating. It's the heart, John, it's still beating! *Still beating!*"

"Dan," I whispered urgently. "Dan, you mustn't work yourself up like this! Dan, for Christ's sake!"

But Dr. Jarvis held me back. Dan was already settling back on to his pillow, and his eyes were closing. His breathing became slow and regular again, slow and painful and heavy, and even though it still reminded me of the breathing we'd heard at Seymour Wallis's house, he seemed at last to be catching some rest. I stood up straight, and I felt shaken and tired.

"He should be okay now. At least for an hour or two," Dr. Jarvis said quietly. "These attacks seem to come at regular ninety-minute intervals."

"Can you think of any reason for that?" I asked him.

He shrugged. "There could be any number of reasons. But ninety minutes is the time cycle of REM sleep, the kind of sleep in which people have their most vivid dreams."

I looked down at Dan's drawn and haggard face. "He mentioned dreams to me earlier on," I said. "He had dreams about doorknockers coming to life, and statues moving. That kind of thing. It was all to do with that house we visited last night."

"Are you going back there? To the house?" Dr. Jarvis asked.

"I was planning a trip up there this evening. One of my engineering people thinks that what we heard could have been an unusual kind of downdraft. Why?"

Dr. Jarvis kept his eyes fixed on Dan. "I'd like to come with you, that's why. There's something happening here that

I don't understand, and I want to understand it."

I raised an eyebrow. "All of a sudden you're not so sure of yourself?"

He grunted. "Okay. I deserved that. But I'd still like to tag along."

I took one last look at Dan, young and pale as a corpse on his hospital bed, and I said, very softly, "All right. It's 1551 Pilarcitos. Nine o'clock sharp."

Dr. Jarvis took out a ballpen and made a note of the address. Then, before I left, he said: "Listen, I'm sorry about the way I spoke to you earlier on. You have to realize that we get a whole lot of friends and relatives who watch too much 'General Hospital' and think they know it all. I mean, I guess we're kind of defensive."

I paused, and then nodded. "Okay. I got you. See you at nine."

That afternoon, a gray and gloomy line of ragged clouds blew in from the ocean and threatened rain. I sat at my desk fidgeting and doodling until half after two, then I took my golf umbrella and went for a walk. My immediate superior, retired Naval Lieutenant Douglas P. Sharp, would probably choose this very afternoon for a snap inspection, but right now I couldn't have cared less. I was too edgy, too nervous, and too concerned about what was happening to Dan.

As I crossed Bryant Street, a few spots of rain the size of dimes speckled the sidewalk, and there was a tense, magnetic feeling in the air.

I guess I knew where I was headed all the time. I turned into Brannan Street, and there it was, The Head Bookstore, a tiny purple-painted shop lit from within by a couple of bare bulbs, and crammed with second-hand paperbacks, *Whole Earth Catalog*s, posters, and junk. I stepped in and jangled the bell, and the bearded young guy behind the counter looked up and said, “Hi. Looking for anything special?”

“Jane Torresino?”

“Oh, sure. She’s out back, unpacking some Castaneda.”

I shuffled past the shelves of Marx, Seale, and Indian incense, and ducked my head through the small door that led to the stockroom. Sure enough, Jane was there, squatting on the floor and arranging Yaqui wisdom into neat stacks.

She didn’t look up at first, and I leaned against the doorway and watched her. She was one of those girls who managed to look pretty and bright, no matter how scruffy she dressed. Today she was wearing tight white jeans and a blue T-shirt with a smiling Cheshire cat printed on it. She was skinny, with very long mid-blond hair that was crimped into those long crinkly waves that always remind me of Botticelli, and she had a sharp, well-boned face and eyes like saucers.

I had first met her at a party out at Daly City to welcome the Second Coming of Christ, as predicted by an 18th-century philosopher. The principal guest of honor, not altogether surprisingly, didn’t show. Either the predicted date was wrong, or Christ didn’t choose to come again in Daly City. I wouldn’t have blamed Him. But whatever went wrong with the Second Coming, a lot went right between me and Jane. We met, talked, drank too much Tokay, and went back to my apartment for lovemaking. I remember sitting up in bed afterward, drinking the intensely black coffee she had made me, and feeling pleased with what life had dropped so bountifully in my lap.

However, it didn’t work out that way. That night, Second Coming night, was the first and only time. After that, Jane insisted we were just good friends, and even though we went out for meals together, and took in movies together, the lovelight that shone over the *spaghetti bolognaise* was mine alone, and eventually I accepted our friendship for what it was, and switched the lovelight off.

What had developed, though, was an easy-going relationship that was intimate but never demanding. Sometimes we saw each other three times in one week. Other times, we didn't touch bases for months. Today, when I dropped by with my golf umbrella and my anxieties about Dan Machin, it was the first visit for six or seven weeks.

"The sanitation department sends you its greetings and hopes that your plumbing is in full operational order."

She looked up over her big pink-tinted reading glasses and smiled. "John, I haven't seen you in weeks!"

She stood up, and tippy-toed carefully toward me through the piles of books. We kissed, a chaste kiss, and then she said, "You look tired. I hope you're not sleeping with too many women."

I grinned. "That should be a problem? I'd rather stay tired."

"Come outside," she said. "We just got a new shipment of books in this morning, and we're pretty cramped. Do you have time for coffee?"

"Sure. I've given myself the afternoon off, for good behavior."

We left the bookstore, and went across the street to Prokic's Deli, where I ordered us cappuccino and alfalfa sandwiches. For some reason, I had a craze for alfalfa sandwiches. Dan Machin (God preserve him) had said that I was probably metamorphosing into a horse. I was trying to graduate from manure disposal (he said) to manure production.

Jane took a seat by the window, and we watched the rain spatter the street outside. I lit a cigarette and stirred my coffee, and all the time she watched me without saying a word, as if she knew that I had something to tell her.

"You're looking good," I told her. "Time passes, and you grow tastier with each hour."

She sipped her cappuccino. "You didn't come around to flatter me."

"No, I didn't. But I don't like to miss an opportunity."

"You look worried."

"Does it show?"

"Blatantly."

I sat back on my rush-seated chair, and blew out smoke. Up above Jane's head, on the wall, was a poster demanding the legalization of pot, but judging from the underlying aroma in Prokic's Deli, nobody was that impressed by the laws anyway. You could have gone in there for nothing more than a glass of milk and a salami sandwich, and come out high.

"Did you ever in your whole life come across something so consistently weird that you didn't know how to understand it?" I asked.

"What do you mean, *consistently* weird?"

"Well, sometimes weird things happen, right? You see someone in the street you thought was dead, or something like that. Just an isolated incident. But when I say *consistently* weird, I mean a situation that starts off weird and keeps on getting weirder."

She brushed back her hair with her hand. "Is that what's bugging you?"

"Jane," I said, in a husky voice, "it's not bugging me. It's scaring me stupid."

"Do you want to talk about it?"

"It sounds pretty ridiculous."

She shook her head. "Tell me, all the same. I like pretty ridiculous stories."

Slowly, with a lot of interruptions and explanations, I told her what had happened at Seymour Wallis's house. The breathing, the burst of energy, the way that Dan Machin had been knocked out. Then I described the incident at the hospital, and Dan's eerie luminous eyes. I also told her about his strange whispered words: *"It's the heart, John, it's still beating!"*

Jane listened to all this with a serious expression. Then she laid one of her long-fingered hands over mine. "Can I ask you just one thing? You won't be offended?"

I could guess what she was going to say. "If you think I'm shooting a line, trying to get us involved again, you're wrong. Everything I just told you happened, and it didn't happen last month or last year. It happened here in San Francisco last night, and it happened here in San Francisco this morning. It's real, Jane, I swear it."

She reached over and took one of my cigarettes. I held out my own and she lit it from the glowing tip. "It sounds like this thing, this ghost or whatever it is, actually possessed him. It's like *The Exorcist* or something."

"That's what I thought. But I felt so dumb trying to suggest it. I mean, for Christ's sake, these things just don't happen."

"Maybe they do. Just because they never happened to anyone we know, that doesn't mean they don't happen."

I crushed out my cigarette and sighed. "I saw it with my own eyes, and I still don't believe it. He was sitting up there in bed, and I tell you, Jane, his eyes were alight. He's just an ordinary young guy who works for the city and still wears crew cuts, and he looked like a devil."

"What can I do?" Jane asked.

I looked out of the deli window at the shoppers sheltering from the rain. The sky was a curious gun-metal green, and the clouds were moving fast across the rooftops of Brannan

Street. Early that morning, before I went to see Dan, I had telephoned Seymour Wallis to make an appointment to view the house again, and he had asked me that very same question. *"What can I do? For land's sakes, tell me, what can I do?"*

"I don't really know," I told Jane. "But maybe you could come along tonight when we look over the house. You know something about the occult, don't you? Spirits and ghosts and all that kind of thing? I'd like you to take a look at old man Wallis's front doorknocker, and some of the stuff inside. Maybe there's some kind of clue there. I don't know."

"Why me?" she asked calmly. "Surely there are better occult experts than me. I only sell books about it."

"You read them as well as sell them, don't you?"

"Sure, but—"

I held her hand. "Please, Jane, just do me a favor and come along. It's nine o'clock tonight, on Pilarcitos Street. I don't know why I need you along, but I feel that I do. I really feel it. Will you come?"

Jane touched her face with her fingertips as if gently reassuring herself that she existed, and that she was still twenty-six years old, and that she hadn't changed into anyone else overnight. "All right, John, if you really want me to. As long as it's not a line."

I shook my head. "Can you imagine a couple called John and Jane? It would never work out."

She smiled. "Just be thankful your name isn't Doe."

I went around a little early to Pilarcitos Street that night. Because of the overcast weather, it had grown dark much sooner than usual, and the heavy-browed house was clotted with shadows and draped with rain. As I stood in the street outside, I heard its gutters gurgling with water, and I could see the scaly shine of its wet roof. In this kind of weather, in this kind of gloom, number 1551 seemed to draw in on itself, brooding and uncomfortable in the rainswept city.

I had called briefly at the hospital again, but the nurse had told me that Dan was still sleeping, and that there was no change. Dr. Jarvis had been away on a break, so I hadn't been able to discuss Dan's progress with him any further. Still, with any luck, he would turn up tonight, and see what had happened for himself.

Across the Bay, lightning walked on awkward stilts, and I could hear the faraway mumbling of thunder. The way the wind was blowing, the storm would move across the city in a half hour, and pass right overhead.

I opened the gate and climbed the steps to the front door. In the dense shadows, I could just make out the shape of the doorknocker, with its grinning wolfish face. Maybe I was just nervous, and thinking too much about Dan Machin's dream, but that doorknocker almost seemed to open its eyes and watch me as I came nearer. I was half expecting it to start talking and whispering, the way Dan had imagined it.

Reluctantly, I put my hand out to touch the knocker and bang on the door. The moment I grasped it I recoiled, because for one split second, one irrational lurching instant, it *seemed as if I had touched bristles instead of bronze.* But I held it again, and I knew that I was imagining things. The doorknocker was grotesque, its face was wild and malevolent, but it was nothing but cast metal, and when I banged on the door, it made a loud, heavy knock that echoed flatly inside the house.

I waited, listening to the soft rustle of the rain, and the swish of passing cars on Mission Street. Thunder grumbled again, and there was more lightning, closer this time. Inside the house, I heard a door open and shut, and footsteps coming up to the door.

The bolts and the chains rattled, and Seymour Wallis looked around the gap. "It's you," he said. "You're early."

"I wanted to talk before the others arrived. Can I come in?"

"Very well," he said, and opened the solid, groaning door. I stepped into the musty hall. It was just as ancient and suffocating as it had felt yesterday, and even though their frames had been cracked and broken by last night's burst of power, the doleful pictures of Mount Taylor and Cabezon Peak still hung on the dingy wallpaper.

I went across to the strange figure of the bear that stood on the newel post of the banister. I hadn't looked at it particularly closely last night, but now I could see that the woman's face on it was quite beautiful, serene and composed, with her eyes closed. I said, "This is a real odd piece of sculpture."

Wallis was busy bolting the door. He looked older and stiffer tonight, in a loose, gray cardigan with unraveled sleeves, and baggy gray pants. He smelled of whisky.

He watched me run my hand down the bear's bronze back.

"I found it," he said. "That was years ago, when I was working over at Fremont. We were building a traffic bridge for the park, and we dug it up. I've had it with me ever since. It didn't come with the house."

"Dan Machin had a dream about it this morning," I told him.

"Really? I can't think of any special reason why he should. It's just an old piece of sculpture, I don't even know how old. What would you think? A hundred, two hundred years?"

I peered closely at the bear-lady's passive face. I don't know why, but the whole idea of a bear with a woman's face made me feel uneasy and creepy. I guess it was just the whole atmosphere of Wallis's house. But who had sculpted such an odd figure? Did it mean anything? Was it symbolic?

The only certainty was that it hadn't been modeled on life. At least, I damned well hoped not.

I shook my head. "I'm not an expert. All I know is sanitation."

"Is your friend coming? The engineer?" asked Wallis, leading me through to his study.

"He said so. And there's a doctor, too, if you don't mind, and a friend of mine who runs an occult bookstore on Brannan."

"A doctor?"

"Yes, the one who's treating Dan. We had a bit of an incident there today."

Wallis went across to his desk and unsteadily poured two large glasses of Scotch. "Incident?" he asked, with his back turned.

"It's hard to describe. But I get the feeling that whatever we heard in here last night has really got Dan upset. He's even been breathing in a similar kind of way. The doctor thought he had asthma at first."

Wallis turned around, a glass of amber Scotch in each hand, and his face in the green-shaded light of his desklamp was strained and almost ghastly. "Do you mean to tell me that your friend has been breathing the same way as *my* breathing here?"

He was so intense that I almost felt embarrassed. "Well, that's right. Dr. Jarvis thought it might be psychosomatic. You know, self-induced. It sometimes happens after a heavy concussion."

Seymour Wallis gave me my whisky and then sat down. He looked so troubled and thoughtful that I couldn't help asking, "What's wrong? You look like you lost a dollar and found a nickel."

"It's the breathing," he said. "It's *gone*."

"Gone? How do you know?"

"I don't know. Not exactly. Not for sure. But I didn't hear it all last night, and I haven't heard it at all today. Apart from that, well, I sense it's gone."

I sat on the edge of his desk and sipped my Scotch. The whisky was nine years old, and it tasted mature and mellow, but it didn't mix too well with half-digested alfalfa sandwich, and I began to think that I ought to have had something solid to eat before I went out ghost hunting. I burped quietly into my fist while Wallis fidgeted and twitched and looked even more unhappy.

"You think that the breathing might have somehow transferred itself out of the house and into Dan?" I asked him.

He didn't look up, but he shrugged, and twitched some more. "It's the kind of thing that enters your mind, isn't it? I mean, if ghosts are really capable of haunting a place, why shouldn't they haunt a person? Who's to say what they can do and what they can't do? I don't know, Mr. Hyatt. The whole damned thing's a mystery to me, and I'm tired of it."

For a while, we sat in silence. Seymour Wallis's study was as close and airless as ever, and I almost felt as if we were sitting in some small dingy cavern at the bottom of a mine, buried under countless tons of rock. The house on Pilarcitos gave you that kind of a sensation, as if it was bearing down on you with the weary weight of a hundred years of suffering and patience. It wasn't a feeling I particularly cared for. In fact, it made me feel depressed and edgy.

"You said something about the park," I reminded him. "When you first came to see me, you mentioned the park. I didn't know what you meant."

"The park? Did I?"

"Well, it sounded like it."

"I expect I did. Ever since I worked on that damned park

I've had one lousy piece of luck after another."

"That was the park at Fremont? Where you found the bear-lady?"

He nodded. "It should have been the easiest piece of cantilever bridging ever. It was only a pedestrian walkover, nothing fancy. I must have built twenty or thirty of them for various city facilities all the way down the coast. But this one was a real bitch. The foundations collapsed six or seven times. Three wetbacks got themselves seriously hurt. One was blinded. And nobody could ever agree on how to site the bridge or handle it. The arguments I had with city hall were insane. It took four months to put up a bridge that should have been up in four days, and of course it didn't do my reputation any good. I can tell you something, Mr. Hyatt, ever since Fremont I've felt dogged."

I lifted my whisky glass and circled it around to take in the study and the house. "And this," I said. "All this breathing and everything, you thought it could have been part of your bad luck?"

He sighed. "I don't know. It was just a thought. Sometimes I wonder if I'm going crazy."

Just then, the doorknocker banged twice. "I'll answer it," I said, and I went out into the shadowy hallway to open the front door. As I pulled back the bolts and the chains, I couldn't help glancing over at the bear-lady on the banister. In the dark, she seemed larger than she had with the light on, and shaggier, as if the shadows that clung around her had grown into hair. And around me, on every wall, were these dim and inspiring views of Mount Taylor and Cabezon engravings and etchings and aquatints, but apparently executed in the dullest weather. All I knew about either mountain was that they were in sunny New Mexico, which made it strange that every one of these dozens of views should have drawn on overcast days.

The doorknocker banged again. "All right! All right!" I snapped. "I can hear you!"

I pulled the door open, and there was Dr. Jarvis standing on the porch with Jane. It was still raining and thundering out, but after being shut in Seymour Wallis's study, the night air was cool and refreshing. Across the street, I could see Bryan Corder, his head bent against the sloping rain, his shoulders hunched as he walked quickly toward us.

"You two seem to have met," I said to Jane and Dr. Jarvis as I ushered them inside.

"It was just one of those chance encounters across a gloomy porch," said Jane.

Bryan came running up the steps, shaking rain from his hair like a wet dog. He was a solid, bluff man of almost forty, with a broad, dependable face that always reminded me of a worldly Pat Boone, if such a person could exist. He gripped my arm. "Hi, John. Almost couldn't make it. How's things?"

"Spooky," I said, and meant it. And before I closed the front door, I couldn't stop myself from taking a quick look at the doorknocker, just to see if it was still bronze, still inanimate, and still as fiercely ugly as ever.

I led everyone to Seymour Wallis's study and introduced them. Wallis was polite but distracted, as if we were nothing more unusual than realtors who had come to value his property. He shook hands and offered whisky, and pulled up chairs, but then he sat back at his desk and stared at the threadbare carpet and said almost nothing.

Dr. Jarvis looked less medical in a navy blue sport coat and slacks. He was sharp, short, and gingery, and I was beginning to like him. He took a swallow of whisky, coughed, and then said, "Your friend hasn't made much improvement, I'm afraid. He hasn't had any more of those attacks, but he still has respiration problems, and we can't wake him out of his coma. We're running some EKGs and EEGs later tonight to see if there's any sign of brain damage."

"Brain damage? But all he did was fall off a chair."

"I've known people to die from falling off chairs."

"Do you still think it's a concussion?" Jane said. "What about his eyes?"

Dr. Jarvis turned in his seat. "If I thought it was a concussion and nothing else, I wouldn't be here. But it seems like there's something else involved, and right now I don't have a dog's idea what."

"Was this the room where it happened? The breathing and everything?" Bryan asked.

"Sure."

Bryan stood up and walked around the perimeter of the study, touching the walls here and there and peering into the fireplace. Every now and then he tapped the plaster with his knuckles to feel how solid it was. After a while he stood in the center of the room, and he looked puzzled.

"The door was closed?" he asked me.

"Door and windows."

He shook his head slowly. "That's real strange."

"What's strange?"

"Well, normally, when you get any kind of pressure build-up because of drafts or air currents, the fireplace is free and the chimney is unblocked. But you can put your hand here in the fireplace and feel for yourself. There's no downdraft here. The chimney is all blocked up."

I went across and knelt on the faded Indian carpet in front of the fire. It was one of those narrow Victorian study fires, with a decorated steel hood and a fireclay grate. I craned my head around and stared up into the cold, soot-scented darkness. Bryan was right, there was no draft, no breath of wind.

Usually, when you look up a chimney stack, you can hear the sounds of the night echoing down the shaft, but this chimney was silent.

"Mr. Wallis," said Bryan, "do you know for certain that this chimney is blocked? Did someone have it bricked up?"

Wallis was watching us with a frown on his face. "That chimney isn't blocked. I had a fire in there just a few days ago. I was burning some old papers I wanted to get rid of."

Bryan took another look up the chimney. "Well, Mr. Wallis, even if it wasn't blocked then, it's sure blocked now. It's possible that the blockage may have had something to do with the noises you heard. Do you mind if I take a look upstairs?"

"Be my guest," said Wallis. "I'll stay here, if you don't mind. I've had enough of this for one day."

The four of us trooped out into the hallway and switched on the dim light that illuminated the stairs. It was dim because of its olive-and-yellow glass shade, which was thick with dust and spiderwebs. Everything in the house seemed to be musty and faded and covered with dust, but then I suppose that's what Wallis called character. I was beginning to feel like a dedicated supporter of Formica and plastic and tacky modern building.

As Bryan mounted the first stair, Jane suddenly noticed the bronze statuette of the bear-lady.

"*That's* unusual," she said. "Did it come with the house?"

"No. Seymour Wallis dug it up in Fremont someplace when he was working on a bridge. He builds bridges, or at least he used to."

Jane touched the serene face of the statuette as if she expected it to open its eyes at any moment.

"It reminds me of something," she said softly. "It gives me the strangest feeling. It's almost like I've seen it before, but I couldn't have."

She paused for a second or two, her hand touching the statuette's head, and then she looked up. "I can't remember. Perhaps I'll think of it later. Shall we get on?"

With Bryan leading the way, we trod as quietly we could up the old, squeaking staircase. There were two flights of about ten stairs each, and we found ourselves on a long landing, illumined by another dingy glass shade, and carpeted in dusty red. It didn't look as if the house had been decorated for twenty or thirty years, and all around was that pervasive silence and that moldering smell of damp.

"The study chimney must come up through this," said Bryan, and led us across to a bedroom door that was set at an angle on the opposite side of the landing. He turned the brass handle and opened it up.

The bedroom was small and cold. It had a window that overlooked the yard, where dark wet trees rose and fell in the wind and the rain. There was pale blue wallpaper on the walls, stained brown with damp, and the only furniture was a cheap varnished wardrobe and a shabby iron bed. The floor was covered with old-fashioned linoleum that must have been green many years ago.

Bryan went across to the fireplace, which was similar to the fireplace in Seymour Wallis's study, except that someone had painted it cream. He knelt down beside it, and listened, and the rest of us stood there and watched him.

"What can you hear?" I asked him. "Is it still blocked?"

"I think so," he said, straining his eyes to see up into the darkness. "I just need to see round the ledge and I might be able to . . ."

He shifted himself nearer and cautiously poked his head up under the hood of the fireplace.

Dr. Jarvis laughed, but it was a nervous kind of a laugh.

"Can you see anything?" he asked.

"I'm not sure," Bryan answered in a muffled voice. "There's a different kind of resonance here. Some sort of thudding noise. I'm not sure if it's echoing down the chimney or if it's vibrating through the whole house."

"We can't hear anything out here," I told him.

"Hang on," he said, and shifted himself so that his whole head disappeared up the chimney.

"I hope you don't mind washing your hair before you come back to civilization," said Jane.

"Oh, I've done worse than this," said Bryan. "Sewers are worse than chimneys any day of the week."

"Can you hear anything now?" I asked him, kneeling down on the floor next to the fireplace.

"Ssshh!" ordered Bryan. "There's some kind of noise building up now. The same kind of thudding."

"I still don't hear it," I told him.

"It's quite clear inside here. There it goes. *Thud-thud-thud-thud-thud.* It's almost like a heart beating. *Thud-thud-thud*—why don't you time it? Do you have a second hand on your watch?"

"I'll time it," put in Dr. Jarvis. "If it's a pulse, then it's my line of country."

"Okay," said Bryan, with a cough. "I'm starting now."

He kept his head right up inside the hood of the chimney, and groped his hand around until he could touch Dr. Jarvis's knee. Then as whatever he could hear began to thud in his ears, he beat out the time, and Dr. Jarvis checked it on his watch.

"It's not a pulse," commented Dr. Jarvis, after a couple of minutes. "Not a human pulse, anyway."

"Do you have enough?" coughed Bryan. "I'm getting kind of claustrophobic up here."

"More like Santa Claustrophobic," joked Jane. "Will you bring a sack of toys out with you?"

"Ah, nuts," said Bryan, and started to shift himself out.

Abruptly, horribly, he screamed. I'd never heard a man scream like that before, and for a second I couldn't think what it was. But then he shouted, "Get me out! Get me out! For God's sake, get me out!" and I knew something terrible was happening, and it was happening to him.

Dr. Jarvis seized one of Bryan's legs, and yelled, "Pull! Pull him out of there!"

Freezing with fear, I grabbed hold of the other leg, and together we tried to tug him out. But, even though it was only his head that was up inside the chimney, he seemed to be stuck fast, and he was shrieking and crying and his whole body was jerking in agonized spasms.

"Get me out! Get me out! Oh, God, oh God, get me out!"

Dr. Jarvis let go of Bryan's leg and tried to see what was happening up inside the chimney hood. But Bryan was flailing around and shrieking so much that it was impossible to understand what was going on. Dr. Jarvis snapped, "Bryan! Bryan, listen! Don't panic! Keep still or you'll hurt yourself!"

He turned to me. "He must have gotten his head caught somehow. For Christ's sake, try to hold him still."

We both got a grip on the fireplace hood and tried to wrench it away from the tiles, but it was cemented by years of dust and rust and there was no getting it loose. Bryan was still screaming, but then suddenly he stopped, and his body slumped in the fireplace.

"Oh God," said Dr. Jarvis. "Look."

From under the fireplace hood, soaking Bryan's collar and tie, came a slow stain of bright red blood. Jane, standing right behind us, retched. There was far too much blood for a minor cut or a graze. It dripped down Bryan's shirt and over our hands, and then it began to creep along the cracks in between the tiles on the fireplace floor.

"Carefully now," instructed Dr. Jarvis. "Pull him down carefully."

Little by little, we shifted Bryan's body downward. It seemed as if his head was still firmly caught at first, but then there was a sickening give of flesh, and he came completely out of the chimney, collapsing in the grate.

I stared at his head in rising horror. I could hardly bear to look but then I couldn't look away, either. His whole head had been stripped of flesh, and all that was left was his bare skull, with only a few raw shreds of meat and a few sparse tufts of hair remaining. Even his eyes had gone from their sockets, leaving nothing but glutinous bone.

Jane, her voice trembling with nausea, said, "Oh, John. Oh, my God, what's happened?"

Dr. Jarvis carefully laid Bryan's body down.

The skull made a sickening bonelike sound on the tiles. Dr. Jarvis's face was as white and shocked as mine must have been.

"I've never seen anything like it," he whispered. "Never."

I looked up toward the dark maw of the old Victorian fireplace. "What I want to know is what *did* it. For Christ's sake, Doctor, what's up there?"

Dr. Jarvis shook his head mutely. Neither of us was prepared to take a look. Whatever it was that had ripped the flesh off Bryan's head, whether it was a freak accident or some kind of malevolent animal, neither of us wanted to face it.

"Jane," Dr. Jarvis said, taking a card out of his breast pocket, "this is the number of the Elmwood Foundation Hospital where I work. Call Dr. Speedwell and tell him what's happened. Tell him I'm here. And ask him to get an ambulance around here as fast as he can."

"What about the police?" I said. "We can't just—"

Dr. Jarvis glanced cautiously across at the fireplacc. "I don't know. Do you think they'll believe us?"

"For Christ's sake, if there's anything up that chimney that rips people apart, I'm not going to go up there and look for myself. And neither are you."

Dr. Jarvis nodded. "Okay," he said to Jane. "Dial the police as well."

Jane was just about to leave the room when there was a soft knock at the door. Seymour Wallis's voice said, "Are you all right in there? I thought I heard shouting."

I went across to the door and opened it. Wallis stood there pale and anxious, and he must have seen from the look on my face that something had gone wrong.

"There's been an accident," I told him. "It's probably better if you don't come in."

"Is someone hurt?" he asked, trying to look around my shoulder.

"Yes. Bryan is badly injured. But please, I suggest you don't look. It's pretty awful."

Wallis pushed me aside. "It's my house, Mr. Hyatt. I want to know what goes on here."

Well, I guess he was right. But when he walked into the bedroom and saw Bryan's body lying there, its skull grinning up at the ceiling, he froze, and he could neither speak nor move.

Dr. Jarvis looked up. "Get that ambulance," he told Jane tersely. "The sooner we find out what happened here the better."

Wallis sat down heavily on the narrow bed, his hands in his lap, and stared at Bryan in unabating horror.

"I'm sorry, Mr. Wallis," said Dr. Jarvis. "He thought he

heard some kind of noise in the chimney, and he poked his head up there to see what it was."

Wallis opened his mouth, said nothing, then closed it again.

"We had the feeling that something or someone attacked him," I explained. "When his head was up there and we were trying to tug him out, it was just like someone equally powerful was pulling him back."

Almost furtively, Wallis turned his eyes toward the dark and empty fireplace. "I don't understand," he said hoarsely. "What are you trying to say?"

Dr. Jarvis stood up. There was nothing more he could do for Bryan now, except try to discover what had killed him. He said seriously, "Either he got his head caught in some kind of freak accident, Mr. Wallis, or else there's a creature up there, or a man, who tore the flesh off Bryan Corder's head in some sort of psychopathic attack."

"Up the chimney? Up the chimney of my house?"

"I'm afraid it looks that way."

"But this is insane! What the hell lives up a chimney, and tears people apart like that?"

Dr. Jarvis glanced down at Bryan's body, then back at Seymour Wallis. "That, Mr. Wallis, is exactly what we have to find out!"

Wallis thought about this for a while, then he rubbed his face in his hands. "It makes no sense, any of this. First breathing and now this. You realize I'll have to sell this place."

"You shouldn't lose your money," I said, trying to be helpful. "These old mansions are pretty much top-of-the-market these days."

He shook his head tiredly. "It's not the money I'm worried about. I just want someplace to live where things like this don't happen. I want some peace, for Christ's sake. That poor man."

"Well, as long as the ghost doesn't follow you, I guess that moving away might turn out to be the best solution," I told him.

Wallis stared at me in shock and annoyance. "It's up the damned chimney!" he snapped. "It just killed your colleague, and you're trying to talk about it like it isn't even important. It's up there, and it's hiding, and who are you to say that it won't come out at night and strangle me when I'm lying in bed?"

"Mr. Wallis," I said, "I'm not Rod Serling."

"I suppose you called the police," retorted Mr. Wallis, without even looking at me.

Dr. Jarvis nodded. "They should be here soon."

At that moment, Jane came back upstairs and said, "Two or three minutes. They had a car in the neighborhood. I called the hospital, too, and they're sending an ambulance right down."

"Thanks, Jane," I told her.

"I have a gun, you know," Wallis said. "It's only my old wartime Colt. We could fire it up the chimney, and then whatever it was wouldn't stand a chance."

Dr. Jarvis came over. "Do you mind if I borrow a pillow slip?" he asked. "I just want something to cover Mr. Corder's head."

"Sure. Take it off that pillow right there. It's a pretty gruesome sight. Can you think what the hell did it? Is there any kind of bird that does that? Maybe some kind of raven got trapped down the chimney, or maybe a chimpanzee."

"A chimpanzee?" I queried.

Dr. Jarvis said, "It's not so farfetched. There's an Edgar Allan Poe story about an ape who murders a girl and stuffs her up the chimney."

"Sure, but whatever did this is real fierce. It looks more

like a cat or a rat to me. Maybe it's starved from being trapped up the chimney stack so long."

Wallis got up off the bed. "I'm getting my gun," he said. "If that thing comes out, I'm not standing here unprotected."

Outside in the street, a siren wailed. Jane squeezed my arm. "They're here. Thank God for that."

There was a heavy knocking at the front door, and Wallis went down to answer it. We heard feet clattering up the stairs and two cops in rain-speckled shirts and caps came into the small bedroom. They knelt down by the body of Bryan without looking at any of the rest of us, as if Bryan was their habitually drunken brother they were coming to take home.

"What's this pillow slip over his head?" asked one of the cops, a gum-chewing Italian with a drooping moustache. He didn't make any attempt to touch the pillow slip or move the body. Like most West Coast cops, he had a sense of suspicion that was highly attuned, and one of the first rules he'd ever had to learn was *don't touch anything until you know what it is.*

I said, "We were surveying the house. There were some noises here that Mr. Wallis found a nuisance. My name's John Hyatt and I work for the sanitation department. This is Jane Torresino and this is Dr. Jarvis from Elmwood."

The cop glanced over at his buddy, a young Irishman with pale gray eyes and a freckly face that was almost more freckle than face. "How come the sanitation department is working so late?"

"Well," I said, "this came outside the usual type of sanitary investigation. This is what you might call personal."

"How about you, Doctor?"

Dr. Jarvis gave a brief, twitchy smile. "It's the same for me. I'm moonlighting, I guess."

"So what happened?"

I coughed, and explained. "This gentlemen, Bryan

Corder, he's an engineer from the same department as me. He's a specialist in house structure and he usually works on slum clearance, that kind of thing. We brought him along because he knows about odd noises, and drafts, and everything to do with dry rot."

The policeman continued to stare at me placidly, but still made no move to lift the pillow slip from Bryan's head.

"He thought he heard a thudding noise in the chimney," I said, almost whispering. "He put his head up there to hear it better, and well, that's the result. Something seemed to attack him. We didn't see what."

The cop looked at his buddy, shrugged, and lifted off the pillow slip.

A white-and-gold Cadillac ambulance whooped away through the easing rain, bearing Bryan Corder's body off to the Elmwood Foundation Hospital. I stood on the front step of 1551 and watched it go. Beside me, the police lieutenant who had arrived to deal with the case lit up a cigarette. He was a tall, laconic man with a wet hat and a hawkish nose, and a manner of questioning that was courteous and quiet. He had introduced himself as Lieutenant Stroud and produced his badge like a conjurer producing a paper flower out of thin air.

"Well," he said gently, blowing out smoke. "This hasn't been your evening, Mr. Hyatt."

I coughed. "You can say that again."

Lieutenant Stroud smoked for a while. "Did you know Mr. Corder well?"

"We worked in the same department. I went 'round to his place for supper one night. Moira's a real hand at pecan cookies."

"Pecan cookies, huh? Yes, they're a weakness of mine. I

expect Mrs. Corder will take this very hard."

"I'm sure she will. She's a nice woman."

An upstairs window rattled open, and one of the policemen leaned his head out. "Lieutenant?"

Stroud stepped back a pace, looked upward. "What is it, officer? Have you found anything?"

"We've had half of that goddamned chimney out, sir, and there's no sign of nothing. Just dried blood."

"No signs of rats or birds? No secret passages?"

"Not a thing, sir. Do you want us to keep on searching?"

"Just for a while, officer."

The window rattled shut, and Lieutenant Stroud turned back to the street. The clouds had all passed overhead now, and stars were beginning to sparkle in the clear night sky. Down on Mission, the traffic booped and beeped, and out of an upper window across the street came the sounds of the *Hallelujah Chorus.*

"You a religious man, Mr. Hyatt?" asked Lieutenant Stroud.

"On and off," I said cautiously. "More off than on. I think I'm more superstitious than religious."

"Then what you said about breathing and heartbeats in the house . . . you really believe it?"

I looked at him carefully across the porch. His eyes were glistening and perceptive. I shook my head, "Uh-huh."

"What I have to consider is a number of alternatives," Lieutenant Stroud said. "Either Mr. Corder died in a particularly bizarre and unlikely accident; or else he was attacked by an animal or bird that was trapped in the chimney; or else he was attacked by an unknown man or woman who somehow hid him or herself in the chimney; or else he was attacked and killed by you and your friends."

I stared down at the wet sidewalk and nodded. "I realize that."

"Of course, there is the possibility that some supernatural event occurred somehow connected with your occult investigations here."

I glanced up. "You consider that as a possibility?"

Lieutenant Stroud smiled. "Just because I'm a detective, that doesn't mean I'm totally impervious to what goes on in this world. And out of this world, too. One of my hobbies is science fiction."

I didn't know what to say for a while. Maybe this tall, polite man was trying to win my confidence, trying to inveigle me into saying that Dr. Jarvis and Jane and I had sacrificed Bryan at some illicit black magic ceremony. His face, though, gave nothing away. It was intelligent but impassive. He was the first cultured-sounding policeman I'd ever met, and I wasn't sure I liked the experience.

I turned back to the door and indicated the wolfish door-knocker with a nod of my head.

"What do you make of that?" I asked him.

He raised an eyebrow. "I noticed it when I came in. It does look a little sinister, doesn't it?"

"My friend thought it looked like a werewolf."

Lieutenant Stroud stopped back. "Well, I wouldn't know about that, Mr. Hyatt. I might like science fiction, but I'm not an expert on vampires and demons and all that kind of thing. And in any case, my superiors prefer flesh-and-blood killers they can lock in cages. I always look for the natural answer before I think of the supernatural one."

"Well, you're a policeman."

The front door opened and Dr. Jarvis stepped out. He was pale and he looked as if he'd spent the evening giving blood. "John, can I just have a private word with you?"

Lieutenant Stroud nodded his assent. Dr. Jarvis led me into the hallway, and next to the statue of the bear-lady he turned around and faced me with an expression that was even more shocked and grave than before.

I said, "What's wrong? You look awful."

He took out his handkerchief and patted the sweat from his forehead. "I couldn't tell the lieutenant about this. He's going to find out sooner or later in any case. But I'd rather he heard it from someone else, someone who's actually there."

Just then, Jane came down the stairs. She said, "They've almost demolished the whole bedroom and they haven't found anything. John, can we leave now? I'd give my gold lame tights for a gin-and-orange juice."

"Jane," Dr. Jarvis said, "you might as well hear this, too. You were there when it happened. At least you'll believe it."

Jane asked, frowning, "What is it? Is anything wrong?"

I took the opportunity of putting my arm around her, and giving her a protective, masculine squeeze. It's strange how a man's sexual instincts go on working, even in moments of crisis and horror. But my ardor wasn't exactly firing on all eight. And when Dr. Jarvis told us his news, my hand dropped to my side and I stood there, frightened and wooden and coldly convinced that what was happening in Seymour Wallis's house was growing darker and more powerful and more malevolent with every hour that passed.

"I had a call from Elmwood. They took your friend Bryan Corder straight into the morgue, and began a postmortem."

"Did they find out how he died?" asked Jane.

Dr. Jarvis swallowed uncomfortably. "They didn't find out because they couldn't. In spite of what happened to his head, he's still clinically alive."

My mouth fell open like an idiot. "Still alive? He can't be!"

"I'm afraid that he is. At least, the surgeons believe he is. You see, his heart's still beating. They listened to his chest, and it's beating loud and clear at twenty-four beats to the minute."

"Twenty-four?" asked Jane. "That's not—"

"Not human," put in Dr. Jarvis. "Not human at all. But the fact remains that his heart's beating and while it's beating they're going to try *to keep* it beating."

It was right then that I was sure I heard someone or something whispering. It may have been one of the policemen upstairs. It may have been an automobile's tires on the wet street. But when I turned around instinctively to see who it was, I realized I was standing nearer to that damned hideous doorknocker than anything else, that doorknocker that said: *"Return."*

THREE

I tossed and turned on my sweaty, wrinkled bed for a couple of hours, and then at five in the morning I got up and made myself a mug of strong black coffee and topped it up with Calvados. It's what the old men of Normandy drink to brace themselves on cold December days. I stood by the window looking down over the wan early morning street, and I felt as if the whole course of my life had subtly and strangely changed, like taking a wrong turn in a city you think you know, and finding yourself in an unfamiliar neighborhood where the buildings are dark and tatty, and the people unfriendly and unsociable.

By six I couldn't restrain my curiosity any longer, and I called Elmwood Foundation Hospital to see if Dr. Jarvis was there. A bland receptionist told me that Dr. Jarvis was taking no calls, but she made a note of my number and promised to have him call me back.

I sat back on my floral sofa and sipped more coffee. I'd been thinking all night about everything that had happened at 1551 Pilarcitos, and yet I still couldn't understand what was going on.

One thing was certain, though. Whatever force or influence was haunting that house, it wasn't anything friendly. I really hesitated to use the word "ghost" even when I was thinking about it in the privacy of my own apartment, but what the hell else could it be?

There were so many odd sides to this situation, and none of them seemed to have anything to do with anything else. I had the feeling that Seymour Wallis himself was more important than he knew. After all, it was his house, and he'd been the first to hear all that breathing, and he'd said himself that bad luck had been dogging him around ever since he worked at that park on Fremont. He still had that odd souvenir of Fremont, too, the bear-lady on the banister.

Above everything, though, I had the strongest feeling that whatever was going on wasn't erratic or accidental. It was like the opening of a chess game, when the moves appear casual and unrelated, but are all part of a deliberate stratagem. The question was whose stratagem? And why?

How Bryan Corder's terrible accident and Dan Machin's eerie concussion could possibly be connected, though, I couldn't understand. I didn't want to think about it too deeply, either, because I kept getting ghastly mental pictures of Bryan's fleshless head, and the thought that he might still be alive made the creeps twenty times creepier. I didn't have a strong stomach at the best of times. I was always the squeamish person who couldn't eat the squid in the seafood platter and ordered his eggs wellboiled.

The telephone rang and gave me a chill prickly feeling up

the back of my scalp. I picked it up and said, "John Hyatt here. Who is this?"

"John? It's Jane."

I took a mouthful of coffee. "You're up early," I remarked. "Couldn't you sleep?"

"Could you?"

"Well, not exactly. I kept thinking about Bryan. I called the hospital a little while ago, but they don't have any news yet. I almost hope he's dead."

"I know what you mean."

I carried the telephone over to the sofa and stretched out. Right now I was beginning to feel tired. Maybe it was just the relief of having someone friendly to talk to. I finished my coffee and accidentally took a mouthful of grounds, and I spent the rest of the conversation trying to pick them off my tongue.

"The reason I called you was something I found out," Jane said.

"Something to do with Bryan?"

"Not exactly. But something to do with Seymour Wallis's house. You know all those pictures of Mount Taylor and Cabezon Peak?"

"Sure. I was wondering about those."

"Well, I went and looked them up in some of my books back at the store. Mount Taylor's in the San Mateo Mountains, elevation eleven thousand, three hundred eighty-nine feet, and Cabezon Peak is way off to the northeast in San Doval County, elevation eight thousand three hundred feet."

I spat grounds. "That's in New Mexico, right?"

"That's right. Real Indian country. And there are dozens of legends connected with those two mountains, mostly Navaho stories about Big Monster."

"Big Monster? Who the hell is Big Monster?"

"Big Monster was a giant who was supposed to terrorize the southwest centuries and centuries ago. He made his home on Mount Taylor. He had a blue-and black-striped face, and a suit of armor made out of flints, woven together with the intestines of all the people and animals he'd slaughtered."

"He doesn't sound like the John Weitz of the ancient world."

"He wasn't," said Jane. "He was one of the fiercest giants in any legend in any culture. I have an 18th-century book right here that says he was in charge of all man-destroying demons, and that no mortal could destroy him. He was slain, though, by a pair of brave gods called the Twins, who deflected his arrows with a rainbow, and then knocked off his head with a bolt of lightning. They threw his head off to the northeast, and it became Cabezon Peak."

I coughed. "That's a very pretty story. But what does it have to do with Seymour Wallis's house? Apart from all the etchings of Mount Taylor and Cabezon Peak, of course."

"Well, I'm not sure, exactly," said Jane. "But there's a reference here to the First One to Use Words for Force, which I don't really understand. Whatever or whoever the First One to Use Words for Force was, it was apparently powerful enough to have cut off Big Monster's golden hair, and make a mockery out of him, and there's something else, too. The First One to Use Words for Force was eternal and immortal, and his motto to all the gods and humans who tried to dispose of him was a Navaho word which I can't pronounce but which means 'to come back by the path of many pieces.' "

"Jane, honey, you're not making much sense."

"John, darling, there's another word for 'come back,' in case you've forgotten. *'Return.'* "

I swung my legs off the sofa and set up straight. "Jane," I said, "you're clutching at totally improbable straws. Now, I don't know why Seymour Wallis has all of those pictures of Mount Taylor and Cabezon Peak in his house. I guess they were there when he moved in. But you could take any mountain in the whole of the southwest and find some kind of Indian legend connected with it. It's no big deal, really. I mean, maybe we're dealing with some kind of supernatural power. Some latent force that has suddenly been released as a kinetic force. But we're not dealing with Navaho monsters. I mean, there's no way!"

Jane wasn't abashed. "I still think we ought to look into it further," she said. "The trouble with you is, you're too rational."

"Rational? I work for the sanitation department and you think I'm rational?"

"Yes, I do. John Hyatt, the national rational. You're so rational they even named a hotel chain after you."

I couldn't help laughing. "Listen, will you do me a favor? Will you call the office for me? Speak to Douglas P. Sharp and tell him I'm sick. I want to get around to Elmwood Hospital this morning and see Dr. Jarvis."

"Shall I meet you for lunch?"

"Why not? I'll come by the bookstore and pick you up."

"Will you call me when you find out how Bryan is? I'd appreciate it."

"Sure."

I laid down the phone. I thought about what Jane had said for a while and then I shook my head and smiled. She liked ghosts and magic and monsters. She had once dragged me off to see all the old original horror pictures, like Bela Lugosi's *Dracula*, and Boris Karloff's *Frankenstein*. Somehow, the idea that Jane believed in ghouls and monsters 'round at 1551 Pilarcitos was reassuring. It brought out the hearty patronizing male chauvinist in me. Perhaps that's why I'd asked her along there in the first place. If Jane believed it, then it *couldn't* be true.

The telephone rang again just as I was shaving. With my chin liberally lathered with hot mint foam, I picked it up like Father Christmas taking an order for next winter's toys.

"John? This is James Jarvis. You left me a message to call."

"Oh, hi. I was just wondering how Bryan Corder was."

There was a pause. "His heart's still beating."

"You don't think he's going to live?"

"It's hard to say. I wouldn't like him to. In any case, he could never go out into the world again. He'd have to spend the rest of his life in a sanitized oxygen tent. The whole brain is exposed, and any infection would kill him straight away."

I wiped foam away from my mouth with the back of my hand. "Couldn't you pull the plug out and let him die anyway? I think I know Bryan well enough to say that he wouldn't want to go on living like *that.*"

"Well," said Dr. Jarvis, "we have."

"You have what?"

"We've taken him off life-support systems. He's getting no plasma, no blood, no intravenous nutrition or sedation, no adrenalin, no electronic heart pacing, no nothing. Medically, he should have died hours ago."

He paused again, and I heard someone come into his office, and say something indistinct. Then Dr. Jarvis said, "The trouble is, John, his heart's still beating and it won't stop. However serious his injuries, I can't certify that he's dead until it does."

"What about euthanasia?"

"It's illegal, that's what. And no matter how bad Bryan's injuries are, I can't do it. I'm taking enough of a risk as it is, depriving him of life-support systems. I could lose my license."

"Has his wife, Moira, seen him?"

"She knows he's had an accident, but that's all. We're obviously doing everything we can to keep her away."

"How about Dan Machin? Any improvement?"

"He's still comatose. But why don't you come up to the hospital and see for yourself? I could do with some moral support. I haven't been able to talk about last night with anyone here. They're all so goddamned sane, they'll think I belong to a coven or something."

"Okay. Give me a half hour."

I shaved, dressed in my off-white denim suit and a red shirt, and splashed myself with Brut. It's surprising what a change of clothes can do for your morale. Then I made my bed, rinsed up my coffee cup, blew a kiss to the picture of Dolly Parton that hung in my bijou hallway, and went downstairs to the street.

It was one of those bright mornings that make you screw your eyes up. The blue skies and the torn white clouds did a lot to reassure me that life was still capable of being ordinary, and that last night's accident could have been an isolated and unpleasant freak of nature. I walked down to the corner and hailed a taxi. I used to own a car, but keeping the payments up on a sanitation officer's salary was like trying to clear up a blocked-up sewer with a toothbrush. The repossessors had arrived one foggy morning, and driven away my metallic blue Monte Carlo into the swirling pea-souper. It was only after they'd gone that I realized I'd left my Evel Knievel sunglasses in the glove box.

As we drove up Fulton Street toward the hospital, which was one of those multi-leveled teak-and-concrete structures overlooking the ocean, the taxi driver said, "Look at them damn birds. You ever see anything like that before?"

I glanced up from my *Examiner*. I'd been trying to find any mention of Bryan Corder's accident. We were turning between neatly clipped hedges into the hospital's wide forecourt now, and to my fascination and disquiet, the building's rooftops were thick with gray birds. It wasn't just a flock that had decided to settle. There were thousands of them, all along the skyline of the main building, and sitting on every outbuilding and clinic and garage.

"Now that's what I call weird," said the taxi driver, circling the cab around the forecourt and pulling up by the main door. "Weird with a capital W."

I climbed out of the car and stood there for a moment or two, looking along the fluttering ranks of gray. I didn't know what species of bird they were. They were big birds, like pigeons, but they were gray as a thundery sky, gray as the sea on a restless day. What's worse, they were silent. They didn't chirrup or sing. They sat on the hospital roof, their dark feathers ruffled in the warm Pacific breeze, patient and quiet as birds on a granite gravestone.

"You see that Hitchcock movie?" asked the taxi driver. "The one where the birds go crazy?"

I coughed. "I don't need reminding of that, thanks."

"Well, maybe this is it," said the taxi driver. "Maybe this is where the birds take over. Mind you, I'd like to see a bird trying to drive this hack. The fan belt slipped off twice this morning. I'd like to see a bird put a fan belt back on."

I paid the driver and walked through the automatic doors into the cool precincts of the hospital. It was all very tasteful in there. Italian tiles on the floor, paintings by David Hockney, palm trees, and soft music. You didn't come to Elmwood Foundation Hospital unless your medical insurance was well paid up.

The receptionist was a buxom girl in a tight white dress who must have tipped the balance for many a touch-and-go coronary patient. She had bouffant black hair, in which her nurses cap nestled like a neatly laid egg, and enough teeth for herself and three others like her. Not that there could have been three others like her, or even one.

"Hi," she said. "I'm Karen."

"Hi, Karen, I'm John. What are you doing tonight?"

She smiled. "This is Wednesday. My hair wash night."

I looked up at her beehive. "You mean you wash that thing? I thought you just had it revarnished."

She went huffy after that, and prodded a button to page Dr. Jarvis. "Some of us still believe in the old values," she said tartly.

"You mean like stiletto heels and cars with fins?"

"What's wrong with stiletto heels and cars with fins?"

"Don't ask me, ask Claes Oldenburg."

The receptionist blinked sooty eyelashes. "Claes Oldenburg? Is he an intern?"

Dr. Jarvis mercifully appeared from the elevator, and came across with his hand out.

"John! Am I glad to see you!"

I nodded meaningfully toward the brunette receptionist. "The feeling could be mutual," I told him. "I think your front-desk lady keeps her brains in her bottom drawer."

Dr. Jarvis ushered me over to the elevator, and we rose up to the fifth floor. Gentle Muzak played "Moon River" which (unless you had any taste in music) was supposed to be soothing.

We emerged in a shiny corridor that was lit by dim fluorescent tubes and hung with mediocre lithographs of Mill Valley and Sausalito. Dr. Jarvis led the way down to a pair of wide mahogany doors and pushed them open. I followed obediently and found myself in an observation room with one glass wall that looked into the murky, blue-lit depths of an intensive-care unit. Dr. Jarvis said, "Go ahead," and I walked across the tiled floor and peered through the glass.

The sight of Bryan in that livid blue room, lying on a bed with his naked skull resting on a pillow, and his full-fleshed body in a green medical gown was eerie and frightening. Even though I'd seen him before, and actually had the shock of trying to drag him out of the chimney, this grinning skeletal vision was almost too much for me. But what was worse was the electrical screen monitor beside his bed, which showed his heartbeats coming slow but regular, tiny traveling blips of light that meant: I am still alive.

"I don't believe it," I whispered. "I can see it with my own eyes, but I just don't believe it."

Dr. Jarvis came up and stood next to me. He was very white, and there were mauve smudges of tiredness under his eyes, "Nor do I. But there it is. His heartbeat is very slow, but it's regular and strong. If we killed him now, there would be no doubt at all that we would technically be committing a homicide."

A young intern standing next to us said, "He can't hold out very much longer, sir. He's real sick."

Dr. Jarvis shrugged. "He's not just sick, Perring. He's dead. Or at least he should be."

I stared at Bryan's white and glistening head for four or five minutes. The vacant eye sockets looked like dark mocking eyes, and the jaws were bared in a bony grin. Beside me, Dr. Jarvis said nothing, but I could see his hands out of the corner of my eye, twisting a ball-point pen around and around his fingers in nervous tension.

And in the depths of that blue-lit room, the heartbeat went on and on, the blips coursing ceaselessly across the screen, keeping Bryan Corder alive in a hideous aquamarine hell that he could never see nor understand.

“I have some kind of a theory. Do you want to hear it?” Dr. Jarvis said hoarsely.

I was glad to turn away from that glass inspection panel, and keep my eyes and my mind off that living skull. “Sure. Go ahead. Jane’s got herself some theories, too, although I have to tell you that they’re pretty wild.”

“I don’t suppose mine are any less wild than hers.”

I took his arm. “Is there any way of getting a drink around here? I could sure use one.”

“I have an icebox in my office.”

We left the observation room thankfully, and walked along the corridor to Dr. Jarvis’s office. It was pretty cramped, with just space enough for a desk and a tiny icebox and a narrow settee, and the view was only impressive if you liked staring at the backs of buildings. Apart from a cheap desk lamp and a stack of medical journals, and a photograph of Dr. Jarvis standing on a rustic bridge with a freckly young girl—“my daughter by my ex-wife, God bless her”—the room was undecorated and bare.

“I call this the broom closet,” explained Dr. Jarvis, with a wry grin. “The best offices are all along the west wall, overlooking the ocean, but you have to work here for at least a century before you get one.”

He took a bottle of gin from his desk drawer and produced tonic and ice from his diminutive fridge. He mixed us a couple of g-and-t’s, and then sat back and propped his feet on his desk. One of his shoes was worn through to the cardboard lining.

“Jane thinks that what’s happening at Wallis’s house is something to do with Red Indian legends,” I said. “Apparently Mount Taylor used to be the home of some giant dude called Big Monster, and Cabezon Peak is his head. He had it knocked off by lightning.”

Dr. Jarvis lit a cigarette and passed me one. I didn't smoke very much these days, but right then I felt like smoking the whole pack. There was a pool of nausea someplace down in my stomach, and every time I thought of Bryan Corder's sightless eyes, it stirred itself around and around.

"Well, I don't know about legends," said Dr. Jarvis, "but there seems to be some kind of connection between what happened to Machin and what happened to Corder. When you think about it, both of them were investigating some kind of noise at 1551 Pilarcitos, and both of them came away from that investigation actually producing the sound that they'd heard. Machin is breathing like the breathing he heard in Seymour Wallis's study, and Corder's heart is beating just like the beat he heard up Wallis's chimney."

I sipped my gin-and-tonic. "So what's the theory?"

Dr. Jarvis pulled a face. "That's it. That's the whole theory. The theory is that whatever influence or power is dominating that house, it's kind of smuggling itself out of there in bits and pieces."

"Oh, sure," I said laconically. "What do we get next? Legs and arms? Noses and ears?"

But right at the very moment I was saying those words with my lips, my mind was saying something else. Reminding me of what Jane had said on the telephone only an hour or two ago. *A Navaho word which I can't pronounce which means "to come back by the path of many pieces."*

And on the doorknocker, it said: *"Return."*

"What's the matter?" asked Dr. Jarvis. "You look sick."

"I don't know. Maybe I am. But something that Jane said about her Indian legend kind of ties up with something that you said. There was a demon or something that was capable of besting this Big Monster, even though Big Monster was almost indestructible by humans and demons and almost everyone else. This demon was called the First One to Use Words for Force, something like that."

Dr. Jarvis finished his gin-and-tonic and poured himself another. "I don't see the connection," he said.

"The connection is that this demon's motto was some Indian word that means coming back by the path of many pieces."

Dr. Jarvis frowned. "So?"

"So everything! So what *you* said was that whatever power was possessing Wallis's house, it's smuggling itself out of there in bits and *pieces!* First its breathing and now its heartbeat."

Dr. Jarvis looked at me long and level, and didn't even lift his drink from the table. I said, almost embarrassed, "It's a thought, anyway. It just seemed like too much of a coincidence."

"What you're trying to suggest is that these noises in Wallis's house are something to do with a demon who's gradually taking people over? Bit by bit?"

"Isn't that what you're suggesting?"

Dr. Jarvis sighed, and rubbed his eyes. "I don't exactly know *what* I'm suggesting. Maybe we ought to call at the house again, and ask Mr. Wallis if the heartbeat's vanished, too."

"I'm game if you are. I haven't heard from him all day."

"He left a message that he telephoned here," said Dr. Jarvis. "He was probably asking about Corder."

Dr. Jarvis found the message on the pad and punched out Wallis's number. It rang and rang and rang. In the end he put the receiver back and said, "No reply. Guess he did the wise thing and went out."

I finished my drink. "Would *you* stay there? I wouldn't. But I'll call around there later this afternoon. I decided to take the day off work."

"Won't San Francisco miss its most talented sanitation officer?"

I crushed out my cigarette. "I was thinking of a change anyway. Maybe I'll go into medicine. It seems like an idle kind of a life."

He laughed.

I drank some more. "Did you see the birds?"

"Birds? What birds? I've been shut up with Corder all night."

"I'm surprised nobody mentioned it. Your whole damned hospital looks like a bird sanctuary."

Dr. Jarvis raised an eyebrow. "What kind of birds?"

"I don't know. I'm not Audubon the Second. They're big and kind of gray. You should go out and take a look. They're pretty sinister. If I didn't have better taste, I'd say they were buzzards, waiting for Elmwood's rich and unfortunate patients to pass away."

"Are there many?"

"Thousands. Count 'em."

Just then Dr. Jarvis's telephone bleeped. He picked it up and said, "Jarvis."

He listened for a moment, then said, "Okay. I'm right there," and clapped the phone down.

"Anything wrong?" I asked him.

"It's Corder. I don't know how the hell he's been doing it, but Dr. Crane says he's been trying to sit up."

"Sit up? You have to be kidding. The guy's almost a corpse!"

We left our drinks and went quickly back down the corridor to the observation room. Dr. Crane was there, along with the bearded pathologist Dr. Nightingale, and a nicely proportioned black lady who was introduced to me as Dr. Weston, a specialist in brain damage. Nicely proportioned though she was, she spoke and behaved like a specialist in brain damage, and so I left well enough alone. One day, she'd find herself a good-looking neurologist and settle down.

It was what was happening behind the window, in the blue depths of the intensive-care unit that really stunned me. I had the same desperate breathless sensation you get when you step into a swimming pool that's ten degrees too cold.

Bryan Corder had turned his head away from us, and all we could see was the back of his skull and the exposed muscles at the back of his neck, red and stringy and laced with veins. He was moving, though, actually moving. His arm kept reaching out, as if it was trying to grasp something or push something away, and his legs stirred under the covers.

Dr. Jarvis said, "My God, can't we stop him?"

Dr. Crane, a bespectacled specialist with a head that seemed to be two sizes too large for his body, said, "We've already tried sedation. It doesn't appear to have any effect."

"Then we'll have to strap him down. We can't have him moving around. It's bizarre!"

Dr. Weston, the black lady, interrupted him. "It may be bizarre, Dr. Jarvis, but it's quite unprecedented. Maybe we should just let him do what he wants. He's not going to survive, anyway."

"For Christ's sake!" snapped Dr. Jarvis. "The whole thing's inhuman!"

Just how inhuman it really was, none of us really understood, not until Bryan suddenly lifted himself on one elbow, and slowly swung himself out of his bed.

Dr. Jarvis took one look at that stocky figure in its green robes, with its ghastly skull perched on its shoulders, standing alone and unaided in a light as blue as lightning, as blue as death, and he shouted to his intern, *"Get him back on that bed! Come on, help me!"*

The intern stayed where he was, white and terrified, but Dr. Jarvis pushed open the door between the observation room and the intensive-care unit, and I went in behind him.

There was a strange, cold smell in there. It was like a mixture between ethyl alcohol and something sweet. Bryan Corder—what was left of Bryan—stood only four or five feet away from us, silent and impassive, his skull fixed in the empty, ravenous look of death.

"John," said Dr. Jarvis quietly.

"Yes?"

"I want you to take his left arm and lead him back to the couch. Force him to walk backward, so that when he reaches the couch, we can push against him and he'll have to sit back. Then all we have to do is swing his legs across, and we'll have him lying flat again. See those straps under the couch? As soon as we get him down, we buckle him up. You got me?"

"Right."

"You frightened?"

"You bet your ass."

Dr. Jarvis licked his lips in nervous anticipation. "Okay, John, let's do it."

Bryan's heartbeat, monitored in steady blips through the wires that still trailed from his chest, was still at a slow twenty-four beats to the minute. But right then, my own heartbeat felt even slower. My mouth was dry with fear, and my legs were the bent wobbly legs of someone who wades into clear water.

Dr. Jarvis and I both inched closer, our hands raised, our eyes fixed on Bryan's skull. For some reason I felt that Bryan could still see, even though his eye-sockets were empty. He took a shuffling step toward us, and the raw muscle that held his jaw in place started to twitch.

"My God," whispered Dr. Jarvis, *"he's trying say something!"*

For a moment I thought that I probably wasn't going to have the nerve to grab hold of Bryan's arm and force him back on the bed. Supposing he fought back? Supposing I had to touch that naked, living skull? But then Dr. Jarvis snapped, *"Now!"* and I went forward awkward and clumsy with my courage as weak as a girl's. I think I even shrieked out loud. I'm not ashamed it. At least I tried.

Bryan collapsed in our arms. Instead of forcing him back, we had to drag him, and we heaved him up on to the couch like a sack of meal. Dr. Jarvis held the back of his skull to prevent any injury, and we laid him carefully down with his arms by his sides and strapped him tight with restraining bands. Then we stood and looked at each other across his supine body, and all we could do was smirk with suppressed fear.

Dr. Jarvis checked Bryan's heartbeat and vital signs, and they were still the same. Twenty-four beats a minute and continuing strong. Respiration slow but steady. I took a deep breath and wiped my forehead with the back of my hand. I was sweating and shaking, and I could hardly speak.

Dr. Jarvis said, "This beats everything. This guy is supposed to be dead. Every rule in the book says he's dead. But here he is living and breathing and even walking about."

At that moment Dr. Weston came in. She looked down at Bryan Corder and said, "Maybe it's a miracle."

"Well, maybe it is," said Dr. Jarvis. "But maybe it's a damned evil piece of black magic, too."

"Black magic, Dr. Jarvis?" said Dr. Weston. "I didn't think you white folks believed in that."

"I don't know what to believe," he muttered. "This whole thing is totally insane."

"Insane or not, I have my tests to run," she said. "Thank you for restraining him so well. And thank you, too, Mr. Hyatt."

I coughed. "I won't say it's been a pleasure."

We left Dr. Weston and her interns to run through their brain-damage tests on Bryan Corder's exposed skull, and we went out into the corridor. Dr. Jarvis stood for a long time by the window, staring out across the hospital parking lot. Then he reached into the pocket of his white coat and took out a pack of cigarettes.

I stood a little ways away, watching him and keeping quiet. I guessed he wanted to be alone then. He was suddenly faced with something that turned his most basic ideas about medicine upside down, and he was trying to rationalize a bizarre horror that, so far, could only be explained by superstition.

He lit his cigarette. "You were right about the birds."

"Still up there?"

"Thousands of them, all along the roof."

I stepped up to the window and looked out. They were there, all right, ragged and fluttering in the Pacific wind.

"They're like some kind of goddamned omen," he said. "What's the matter with them? They don't even *sing.*"

"They look like they're waiting for something," I said. "I just hope that it's nothing more portentous than a packet of birdseed."

"Let's go take a look at Machin. I could use some light relief," Dr. Jarvis suggested.

"You call what happened to Dan light relief?"

He took a last drag at his cigarette and nipped it out between his finger and thumb. "After what happened just now, a funeral would be light relief."

We walked along the corridor until we came to Dan's room. Dr. Jarvis looked through the small circular window in the door and then opened it.

Dan was still in a coma. There was a nurse by his bedside, and his pulse and respiration and blood pressure were being closely observed. Dr. Jarvis went across and examined him, lifting his eyelids to see if there was any response. Dan's face was white and spectral, and he was still breathing in that same deep, dreamless rhythm that had characterized the breathing in Seymour Wallis's house.

As Dr. Jarvis was checking Dan's body temperature, I said, "Supposing—"

"Supposing what?" he said, preoccupied.

I came closer to Dan's bedside. The young boy from Middle America was so still and pallid he might have been dead, except for his hollow, regular breathing.

"Supposing Bryan was trying to get here, to see Dan."

Dr. Jarvis looked around. "Why should he want to do that?"

"Well, each of them has one of the sounds that used to haunt Seymour Wallis's house. Maybe the two of them have enough in common that they want to get together. All that Indian stuff that Jane was talking about, you know, returning by the path of many pieces, well maybe that means some kind of reincarnation by numbers."

"I don't follow."

"It's pretty simple. If this power or influence or whatever it is that's haunting Seymour Wallis's house was all kind of split up, you know, breathing in one place and heartbeat in another, then maybe it might try to get itself back together."

"John, you're raving."

"You've seen Bryan walking around with no skin on his skull and you tell me I'm raving?"

Jarvis made a note of Dan's temperature on his chart and then stood up straight. "There's no point in trying to find far-fetched answers," he said. "Whatever's going on, there has to be a simple explanation."

"Like what? One man goes crazy and another man loses

the skin off his head, and we have to look for a simple explanation? James, there's something planned and deliberate going on here. Somebody wants all this to happen. It's as if it's all been worked out."

"There's no evidence in favor of that," he said, "and I'd rather you called me Jim."

I sighed. "All right, if you want to take it the logical, medical way, I don't suppose I blame you. But right now I feel like talking to Jane and Seymour Wallis. Jane has a theory that's worth listening to, and I'll bet you two Baby Ruths to six bottles of Chivas Regal that our Wallis knows more than he's told us."

"I don't drink Chivas Regal."

"Well, that's okay. I don't eat Baby Ruths."

I took a taxi down to The Head Bookstore just after noon. As I was driving away from the hospital I couldn't help looking back at the birds on the roof. From a distance they looked like a gray scaly encrustation, as if the building itself was suffering from some unhealthy skin condition.

I asked the taxi driver if he knew what species of bird they were, but he didn't even know what "species" meant.

Surprisingly, Jane wasn't there when I called at the purple-painted shop on Brannan. Her young, bearded assistant said, "I don't know, man. She just upped and went out, round about a half hour ago. She didn't even say *ciao*."

"You don't know where she went? I was supposed to meet her for lunch."

"She didn't say a word, man. But she went that way." He pointed toward The Embarcadero.

I went out into the street. Slices of sunlight were falling across the sidewalk, and I was jostled and bumped by the lunchtime crowds. I looked around, but I couldn't see Jane anywhere. Even if I walked along to The Embarcadero, I'd probably miss her. I went back into the bookstore and told the boy to have Jane call me at home, and then I hailed another taxi and asked the driver to take me to Pilarcitos Street.

I was annoyed, but I was also worried. The way things had been going these past couple of days, with Dan Machin and Bryan Corder both in the hospital, I didn't like to lose touch with anybody. In the back of my mind I still had this unsettling notion that whatever was happening was part of some preconceived scheme, as if Dan had been *meant* to go to 1551 Pilarcitos, and as if Bryan had been deliberately maneuvered into going there, too. And don't think I didn't wonder if something equally horrific was going to happen to me.

The taxi stopped on Pilarcitos, and I paid the driver. The house looked shabby in the sunlight, and as gray as the birds on the hospital roof. I swung the wrought-iron gate open and went up the steps. The doorknocker grinned at me wolfishly, but today, in the clear light of noon, it didn't play any tricks on me. It was heavy cast bronze and that was all.

I knocked three times, loudly. Then I waited on the porch, whistling "Moon River." I hated that damn tune, and now it was stuck on my mind.

I knocked again, but there was still no answer. Maybe Seymour Wallis had taken himself off for a walk. I waited for another few moments, gave one final bang on the knocker, then turned around to go home.

But just as I went back down the steps, I heard a creaking sound. I looked around and the front door had opened a little way. My last knock must have pushed it ajar. It obviously wasn't locked, or even closed on the catch.

Now considering how many bolts and chains and safety locks Wallis had installed on that door, it seemed pretty much out of character for him to leave it completely unlocked. I stood by the gate staring at the door wondering *what's wrong?* For some reason I couldn't even begin to describe, I felt chilled and frightened. Worst of all, I knew that I couldn't leave the door open like that and just walk away. I was going to have to go into the house, that ancient house of breathing and heartbeats, and see what was up.

Slowly, I remounted the front steps. I stood by the half-open door for almost a minute, trying to distinguish shapes and shadows in the few inches of darkness that I could see. The doorknocker was now looking away from me, up the street, but its smile was as smug and vicious as ever.

I looked at the doorknocker and said, "Okay, smartass. What particular nasty traps have you set up this time?"

The doorknocker grinned and said nothing. I hadn't really expected it to, and I think I would have jumped out of my skin if it had, but it was one of those creepy situations where you just like to make sure that if the spooks are spooks, and not just doorknockers or shadows or hat stands, then they don't got the idea that they're fooling you.

I reached out like a man reaching across a bottomless pit, and pushed the door open a ways. It groaned a little more and shuddered. Inside, the hallway was swirling in dust and darkness, and that musty closed-up smell was still as strong as ever.

Swallowing hard, I stepped inside. I called, "Mr. Wallis? Seymour Wallis?"

There was no reply. Once I entered the hallway, all the sounds from the street outside were muffled and suppressed, and I stood there and heard nothing but my own taut breathing.

"Mr. Wallis?" I called again.

I walked across to the foot of the stairs. The bear-lady, eyes closed, still reared on the banister post. I squinted up into the stale darkness of the second floor, but I couldn't make anything out at all. To tell you the God's honest truth, I didn't feel particularly inclined to go up there. I decided to take a quick look in Seymour Wallis's study, and if he wasn't at home, to get the hell out of there.

As quietly as I could, I tippy-toed along the worn-out carpet of the corridor to the door under the stag's head. The study was closed, but the key was in the lock. I turned it slowly, and I heard the lock mechanism click in that impenetrable silence, disturbing that breathless air that seemed to have hung around the house for all the years that it had stood here.

I put my hand on the brass doorknob and turned it. The study door opened. It was gloomy in there, and the drapes were still drawn, so I reached around the lintel to find the light switch. My fingers groped along the damp wallpaper, and I clicked the switch down, but nothing happened. The bulb must have burned out.

Nervously, I pushed the door wider and stepped inside. I took a quick, almost panicky look behind the door to make sure nothing and nobody was hiding there, and I had a half second of shock when I saw Seymour Wallis's bathrobe hanging there. Then I strained my eyes, and stared across at the dark shape of Seymour Wallis's desk and chair.

For a while, I couldn't see if there was anyone there or not. But then my eyes grew gradually accustomed to the darkness, and something began to take shape. "Oh, Christ." The words came out like strangled puppies.

Some enormous inflated man was sitting in Seymour Wallis's chair. His head was blackened and puffy, and his arms and legs were swollen twice their normal size. His face was so congested that his eyes were tiny slits, and his fingers came out of the sleeves of his shirt like fat purple slugs.

I could never have recognized him except by the clothes. It was Seymour Wallis. A distended, swelled-up, grotesque caricature of Seymour Wallis.

I could hardly get the words out. "Mr. W-Wallis?"

The creature didn't stir.

"Mr. Wallis, are you alive?"

The telephone was on his desk. I had to call Dr. Jarvis right away, and maybe Lieutenant Stroud, too, but that meant reaching across this inflated body. I circled the study cautiously, peering more and more closely at him, trying to make up my mind if he was dead. I guessed he must be. He wasn't moving, and he looked as if every vein and artery in his whole body had hemorrhaged.

"Mr. Wallis?"

I stepped up real close, and bent my knees a little so that I could look right into his purplish, blown-up face. He didn't seem to be breathing. I swallowed again, in an effort to get my heart back down in my chest where it belonged, and then I slowly and nervously leaned forward to pick up the telephone.

I dialed Elmwood Foundation Hospital. The phone seemed to ring for centuries before I heard the receptionist's voice say, "Elmwood. Can I help you?"

"Can you get Dr. Jarvis for me?" I whispered. "It's an emergency."

"Will you speak up, please? I can't hear you."

"Dr. Jarvis!" I said hoarsely. "Tell him it's urgent!"

"Just a moment, please."

The receptionist put me on hold, and I had to listen to some schmaltzy music while she paged Dr. Jarvis. I kept glancing anxiously down at Seymour Wallis's bloated face, and I was hoping and praying that he wasn't going to jump up suddenly and catch me.

The music stopped, and the receptionist said, "I'm afraid Dr. Jarvis is out at lunch right now, and we don't know where he is. Would you like to speak to another doctor?"

"No thank you. I'll come right up there."

"In that case please use the south entrance. We're having the city sanitation people around to clear away some birds."

"The birds are still there?"

"You bet. The whole place is covered."

I set down the telephone and backed respectfully away from Seymour Wallis. I was only two or three paces toward the door, though, when his revolving chair suddenly twisted around, and his huge body dropped sideways on to the carpet, face first, and lay there prone. The shock was so great that I stood paralyzed, unable to run, unable to think. But then I realized he was either dead or helpless, and I went over and knelt down beside him.

"Mr. Wallis?" I said, although I have to admit that I didn't hold out any hopes of an answer.

He stayed where he was, swollen up like a man who has floated around in the sea for weeks.

I stood up again. On his desk was a cheap shorthand notebook, in which be had obviously been writing. I picked it up, and flicked back some of the pages. It was written in a heavy, rounded hand, like the hand of a dogged, backward child. It looked as if Seymour Wallis had been struggling to complete his notes before the swelling made it impossible for him to write any further.

I angled the notebook sideways so that the dusty light from outside strained across the pages. The notebook read: "I know now that all those disastrous events at Fremont were merely the catalyst for some far more terrible occurrence. What we discovered was not the thing itself, but the one talisman that could stir the thing into life. Perhaps there was always a predestined date for its return. Perhaps all these ill-starred happenings have been coincidental. But I realize one thing for sure. From the day I discovered the talisman at Fremont, I had no choice but to buy the house at 1551. The ancient influences were far too strong for someone as weak and as unaware of their domineering power as me to resist."

That was how it ended. I couldn't figure it out at all. Maybe Seymour Wallis thought that his bad luck on the Fremont job had caught up with him at last, and judging by his condition, I couldn't say that I blamed him. But right then, the first thing I wanted to do was get out of that house and contact Dr. Jarvis. I definitely had the feeling that 1551 was harboring some hostile, brooding malice, and if three people had already suffered so hideously while trying to discover what that malice was, I was pretty sure that I could easily be the fourth.

I went out through the hallway, casting a quick backward glance up the stairs just in case something horrible was standing up there, then I dodged past the doorknocker and out on to the porch. As I turned to close the door, though, I saw something that made me feel more unsettled and frightened than almost anything that had happened before.

The banister post was missing its statuette. Bear-lady had gone.

Outside the hospital, the vermin crew from the sanitation department were trying to scare the gray birds off with blank gunshots. I recognized one of them, Innocenti, and I went across to ask him how they were getting on.

Innocenti jerked a disgusted thumb at the serried ranks of silent birds still perched on the rooftops, undisturbed by the crackling racket of gunfire.

"I never seen birds like 'em. They just sits there.

"You shout and they sits. You yell and they sits. We sent Henriques up on the roof with a clapper, and what do they do, sits. Maybe they're hard of hearing. Maybe they don't give a damn. They sits, and they don't even shits."

"Have you found out what they are?" I asked.

Innocenti shrugged. "Pigeons, ravens, ducks, who knows from birds? I ain't no ornithologist."

"Maybe they have some special characteristic."

"Sure. They're so fuckin' bone idle they won't even fly away."

"No, but maybe they're a special type of bird."

Innocenti was unimpressed. "Listen, Mr. Hyatt, they could be fuckin' ostriches for all I care. All I know is that I have to get 'em off the roof, and until I get 'em off the roof, I have to stay here and miss my dinner. Do you know what's for dinner?"

I gave him a friendly wave of my hand and walked across to the hospital entrance.

"Osso bucco!" he yelled after me. "That's what's for dinner!"

I went into the hospital and walked straight across the Italian-tile foyer to the elevators. The elegant stainless-steel clock on the wall said seven o'clock. It was four hours now since I'd telephoned Dr. Jarvis from the booth on the corner of Mission and Pilarcitos. Four hours since the ambulance crew had arrived to collect Seymour Wallis's distended body under a green blanket that any casual bystander could have seen was bulging grossly, bulging far too much for a natural corpse. Four hours since Dr. Jarvis and Dr. Crane had been carrying out a detailed post mortem.

I took the elevator to the fifth floor, and walked along the corridor to James Jarvis's office. I let myself in, and raided his desk for his gin bottle and his icebox for his tonic. Then I sat back and took a stiff, refreshing drink, and by Saint Anthony and Saint Theresa, I needed it.

I'd been trying all afternoon to locate Jane. I'd called every mutual friend and acquaintance I could think of, until I'd finally run out of dimes and energy. I'd revivified myself on a McDonald's cheeseburger and a cup of black coffee, and then made my way up to Elmwood. I felt helpless, lost, frustrated, and frightened.

I was just pouring my second gin-and-tonic when Dr. Jarvis came in and flung his coat across his chair.

"Hi," he said, a little tersely.

I lifted my glass. "I made myself at home. I hope you don't mind."

"Why should I? Fix me one while you're at it," he asked.

I clunked ice into another glass. "Did you finish Wallis's postmortem?" I asked.

He sat down heavily, and rubbed his face with his hand. "Oh, sure, we finished the postmortem."

"And?"

He looked up through his fingers; his eyes were red with fatigue and concentration. "You really want to know? You really want to get involved in this thing? You don't have to, you know. You're only a sanitation officer."

"Well, maybe I am, but I'm involved, already. Come on, Jim, Dan Machin and Bryan Corder were friends of mine. And now Seymour Wallis. I feel responsible."

Dr. Jarvis reached in his pocket for his cigarettes. He lit one unsteadily, and then tossed the pack across to me. I left it lying there. Before I sat back and relaxed, I wanted to know what was going on.

He sighed, and looked up at the ceiling, as if there was a

kind of TelePrompTer up there that might give him a clue what to say. "We tried every possibility. I mean, everything. But that bodily distension was caused by one factor and one factor only, and no matter what we hypothesized, we always came back to the same conclusion."

I sipped gin. I didn't interrupt. He was going to tell me, no matter what.

"I guess the cause of death will officially go down as blood disorder. That's a kind of a white lie, but it's also completely true. Seymour Wallis *was* suffering from a severe blood disorder. His blood wasn't lacking in red corpuscles, and it didn't show any signs of disease or anemia. But the simple fact was that he had too much of it."

"Too much of it?"

He nodded. "The normal human being has nine pints of blood circulating through his body. We emptied the blood from Seymour Wallis's body and measured it. His arteries and veins and capillaries were swollen because he had twenty-two pints of blood in him."

I could hardly believe it. "Twenty-two pints?"

Dr. Jarvis blew out smoke. "I know it sounds crazy, but that's the way it is. Believe me, if I thought I could sweep this whole business under the rug, I'd empty that extra blood down the sink."

He sat there for a while, staring at his untidy desk. I guessed that with all the weird ramifications of Seymour Wallis and his malevolent house, that he hadn't had much time for his paperwork.

"Have the police been around?" I asked.

"They've been informed."

"And what did they say?"

"They're waiting for the postmortem. The trouble is, I don't know what to tell them."

I finished my drink. "Why not? Just tell them he died of natural causes."

Jarvis grunted sardonically. "Natural causes? With nearly three gallons of blood in him? And, anyway, it's worse than that."

"Worse?"

He didn't look my way, but I could tell how confused and anxious he was. "We analyzed the blood, of course, and put it through the centrifuge. Dr. Crane is one of the finest pathologists in the business. At least, he gets paid as if he is. He says that without a shadow of a doubt, the blood we found inside Seymour Wallis was not human."

There was a pause. Dr. Jarvis lit another cigarette from the butt of the first.

"There isn't any question that all twenty-two pints were the blood of some species of dog. Whatever happened to Seymour Wallis, the blood he died with wasn't his own."

FOUR

Jane called. She was sorry she hadn't been around at lunchtime and she hoped I hadn't been anxious. I glanced across at Dr. Jarvis and said, "Anxious? Do you know what's happened?"

"I saw it on television. Seymour Wallis died."

"Well, it's worse than that. He died with more blood in his system than Sam Peckinpah gets through in a whole movie. Twenty-two pints. And what's more, Jim here says the blood wasn't even his own. They analyzed it and it turned out to be some kind of dog's blood."

"You're kidding."

"Jane, if you think I'm in a mood for kidding—"

"I didn't mean that," she said quickly. "What I meant was, it all ties in."

"Ties in? Ties in with what?"

"That's what I've been trying to tell you," she said. "I went out at lunchtime to Sausalito. You know all that Indian stuff I was telling you about? Well, I have friends out at Sausalito who know quite a few Indians, and they're all into Indian culture. They'd heard about this demon they call the First One to Use Words for Force, and they think I ought to go up to Round Valley and talk to one of the medicine men."

I sighed and said nothing. Jane asked, "John? Did you hear me?"

"Yes," I said. "I heard you."

"But you don't think it's a good idea?"

"Just wait a moment."

I put my hand over the receiver and said to Jim Jarvis, "Jane is convinced that everything that's been happening round at Seymour Wallis's house has been connected with some Red Indian legend. Now she wants to talk to some medicine man upstate. What do you think?"

He shrugged. "I don't know. Maybe it's a good idea. Any theory is better than no theory."

I took my hand off the phone. "Okay, Jane. Dr. Jarvis says let's try it."

"You couldn't have stopped me anyway," she answered tartly.

"Jane," I said, irritated, "I spent the whole damned afternoon trying to find out where you were. We've had two people injured and one man dead. Right now, the least advisable thing for any of us to do is to go wandering off on our own."

"I didn't know you cared," retorted Jane.

"You know damned well I do."

"Well, if you care that much, you'd better come to Round Valley with me. I'm borrowing Bill Thorogood's car."

I put down the phone. At least it was Saturday tomorrow, and I wouldn't have to keep on inventing excuses for my boss, Douglas P. Sharp. I said to Dr. Jarvis, "It looks like I've roped myself in. I just hope it's worthwhile."

He crushed out his second cigarette and shrugged. "There are times when you come up against things in medicine that make you feel excited. Real challenges, like difficult cases of poisoning, or unusual compound fractures. At times like that, you feel everything about being a doctor is worthwhile. The hospital politics, the squabbles over financial allocations, the whole bit."

He looked up, and added, "There are other times though, like now, when you just don't understand what the hell is happening, and you're powerless. I can spend the rest of the day *schlepping* around from Dan Machin to Bryan Corder to Seymour Wallis, and I won't be able to do a damned thing to help any of them."

He reached for the cigarettes. "In other words, John, go on up to Round Valley and consider yourself lucky that you're doing *something.* Because I can't."

I looked at him for a while. "I didn't know doctors got down in the dumps. I thought that only happened on television."

He coughed. "And I thought that what's happening right now only happened in nightmares."

Saturday morning was clean and clear and we sped across the Golden Gate with the ocean sparkling beneath us, the sun flickering through the bridge's wires and uprights in a bright stroboscopic blur. Jane sat back in her seat, dressed in a red silk blouse and white Levis, with huge sunglasses perched on her nose and a red scarf around her hair. Bill Thorogood was lucky enough to own a white Jaguar XJ 12, and profligate enough to lend it out, so I sat behind the wheel and pretended I was some minor movie star on a day trip to someplace private and expensive, instead of a sanitation official on a one-hundred-and-sixty-mile flog up to Round Valley.

We burned up 101 through Marin and Sonoma counties, through Cloverdale, Preston, and Hopland, and we stopped at Ukiah for lunch, with the sun high and brassy up in the sky and the wind blowing off Lake Mendocino. Sitting on a low breezeblock wall outside a roadside diner, we ate chiliburgers and watched as a father tried to cram his five kids into the back of his station wagon, along with fishing tackle, inflatable rafts, and pup tents. Every time he managed to get all of the gear inside, one of the kids would climb out, and then he'd have to get around to the back of the wagon again and rearrange everything.

"The futility of life," remarked Jane. "As fast as you do something, it gets itself undone again."

"I don't think that life's futile."

Jane swallowed Coca-Cola from the can. "You don't think that someone's using us as playthings? Like now?"

"I don't know. I think it's more serious than that. But I believe we have to try to fight it, whatever it is."

She reached over and touched my hand. "That's what I like about you, John. You're always ready to fight."

We climbed back in the car and I drove it out of the parking lot with a squeal of tires. Then we headed north again, speeding on 101 until we reached Longvale, then turning off into the hills to Dos Rios and the Eel River, and up into Round Valley Reservation.

The medicine man we had arranged to see was George

Thousand Names. All that Jane knew about him was that he was one of the oldest and most respected of southwestern medicine men, and that he spent more time in San Francisco and Los Angeles than he did upstate, working for Indian investment corporations and protecting Indian rights. Right now, though, he was back home at Round Valley with his family, and anybody that wanted to consult him had to make the trek.

The Jaguar bounced slowly across the grass and rutted tracks that led up the valley between tall pines and undulating hills to George Thousand Names's home. He kept himself apart from most of the trailers and houses where the Round Valley Indians lived, up on a woodsy ridge overlooking the Eel River. As we made our way up the bumpy trail, his chalet-style house gradually came into view, a split-level architect-designed home with a balcony and wide sliding windows.

"Some tepee," remarked Jane.

I stopped the Jaguar at the foot of the wooden stairs that led up to the house. Then I climbed out and squinted against the sun, looking for any signs of life. I blew the car horn a couple of times, and then one of the sliding windows opened and a small man in a plaid shirt and well-pressed slacks came out on to the balcony.

"Excuse me," I called. "Are you Mr. Thousand Names?"

"I'm George Thousand Names. Who are you?"

"John Hyatt. And this is Jane Torresino. Ms. Torresino made an appointment with you?"

"I'm not a dentist," said George Thousand Names. "You don't have to make appointments. But I remember. Come on up."

We climbed the stairs that led up to the balcony, and George Thousand Names came up and shook hands. Up here, he looked even smaller, a delicate and diminutive old man with a face as creased and crinkled as a cabbage leaf. He stood very straight, though, and he had an inner dignity about him that immediately made me feel he was someone extremely special. Around his neck hung amulets and necklaces that looked ancient and potent and mysterious, but he wore them as naturally as if they were nothing more than decoration. On his wrist was a Cartier wristwatch, solid gold, with a tiger's-eye face.

"Your friends from Sausalito briefly mentioned that you were worried about some of our legends," said George Thousand Names, leading us into the house. It was a calm, elegant place, built of polished pine, with Indian rugs and cushions all around. Through a half-open sliding door I could see a modernistic kitchen with a ceramic range and microwave oven.

Jane gave George Thousand Names a pottery jar of tobacco she had bought that morning in Healdsburg. "I've heard it's kind of traditional," she said. "I hope you like Klompen Kloggen."

George Thousand Names smiled. "I don't know why white people are always so apologetic in the face of tradition," he said. "Sure, that's a fine brand. Won't you sit down? How about some coffee?"

We sat around on comfortable cushions on the floor while a young Indian girl who was presumably George Thousand Names's maid percolated coffee for us. Just behind George Thousand Names's shoulder, the sun slid in through the wide window like a lance, and gave his aged head a brilliant halo of light.

"There is something in both of your minds that is troubling you greatly," he began. "You fear that you have no comprehension of what it might be, and that you will both be swallowed up by it."

"How did you know that?" I asked him.

"Very easy, Mr. Hyatt. It shows on your faces. In any case, white people don't usually consult Indian medicine men unless they feel they have exhausted every possible explanation that their own culture can offer."

"We're not at all sure that this has anything to do with Indian legends, Mr. Thousand Names," Jane said. "It was just a guess. But the more we find out about it, the more things that happen, the more it seems to point this way."

"Tell me about it. From the beginning."

I explained about my job at the sanitation department, and how Seymour Willis had come in to see me about the breathing in his house. Then I described what had happened to Dan Machin, and next to Bryan Corder, and finally to Seymour Wallis himself. I talked about the pictures of Mount Taylor and Cabezon Peak, and about the bear-lady who was missing, and about the doorknocker with the hideous face.

George Thousand Names listened to all this calmly and impassively. When I'd finally gotten through, he lifted his head. "Do you have any idea what you're describing to me?"

I shook my head.

Jane said, "The whole reason we've come up here is because we can't understand it. I work in a bookstore, and I looked up Mount Taylor and found there were all these stories about Big Monster connected with it, and the First One to Use Words for Force. I wouldn't have thought much about it, except that the First One to Use Words for Force was supposed to come back by the path of many pieces or something like that, and it somehow seemed to click. I can't even explain why."

The Indian girl brought us coffee in pottery mugs and fresh pecan cookies. Shc must have had a psychic sensitivity to my innermost thoughts, like George Thousand Names.

Being served up with a plateful of fresh pecan cookies almost made up for having "Moon River" on the brain.

George Thousand Namcs said softly, "Every Indian demon has a common name and a ritual name, like many European demons. There were, for instance, the Eye Killers, who were said to have been created by a chief's daughter abusing herself with a prong from a sour cactus. Then, as you say, there was Big Monster, whose real name was quite different, and the First One to Use Words for Force."

The medicine man seemed to be choosing his words carefully. He bit into a pecan cookie with immaculate dentistry, and chewed for a while before he continued.

"The First One to Use Words for Force was the most terrible and implacable of all Indian demons. He was wily and cunning and vicious, his chief enjoyments were causing hatred and confusion, and satisfying his lust on women. The reason we call him the First One to Use Words for Force is because his tricks and his savagery created in the hearts of men their first feelings of fury and revenge.

"As you may know, there are benevolent Indian gods and evil Indian gods. At the great council of the deities, the evil gods sat facing the north and the good gods sat facing the south. The First One to Use Words for Force, however, was so treacherous and malevolent that he was accepted by neither side, and he sat alone by the door. He was the demon of chaos and disorder, and the Indians sometimes say that when he was asked in ancient days to help to place the stars, he tossed his own handful of stars up into the night sky at random and created the Milky Way."

George Thousand Names sipped his coffee. "Is this what we're up against? This First One to Use Words for Force?" I asked.

The Indian's face gave nothing away. He replaced his

coffee mug on its saucer, and delicately patted his lips with a clean handkerchief.

"From what you have told me, Mr. Hyatt, it seems more than likely."

I didn't know whether he was trying to put me on or not. Knowing the dry sense of humor that Indians have, I guessed he could have been pulling our legs. I could just imagine him retelling the story of how the dumb white folks had come all the way up to Round Valley to ask his advice, and how he'd solemnly told them about a demon who threw stars up in the air, and how the white folks had gone away convinced they were up against some ancient redskin spirit, and the whole damned tribe would be busting their sides.

"Likely?" I asked him cautiously. "What's likely about a demon?"

He smiled. "I sense your suspicion," he said. "But I assure you absolutely that I am not playing with you."

I couldn't help coloring up a little. In front of this medicine man, I felt as if I had a television screen in my forehead, giving a late late show on everything I was thinking. Whatever his sense of humor was like, he was a real astute guy.

"The First One to Use Words for Force was the only Indian demon to conquer death. He died many times, sometimes as false proof of his love for a woman, sometimes as the consequence of a punishment meted out by the other gods. But each time, before he went to the underworld, he made sure that he hid in the upper world the essential ingredients he needed to come back to life again. His breath, his heart, his blood, and the hair he cut from Big Monster's head."

The sun had now dropped behind George Thousand Names's back, and I could hardly make out his face in the darkness. I said, appalled, *"His breath, his heart, and his blood?"*

He nodded. "That's why you were right to come up here, Mr. Hyatt. From what you have said this afternoon, it seems that the First One to Use Words for Force has decided to return to life, through the medium of your unfortunate friends."

"But I don't understand," Jane said. "How could a demon's breath and blood and everything be *there,* inside a house?"

"It's quite easy. The First One to Use Words for Force was banished to the underworld many centuries ago, long before any white man discovered this continent. In those days, medicine men were almost gods in their own right, and even if they weren't actually able to slay the First One to Use Words for Force, they would certainly be capable of sending him temporarily back to the underworld. From what you say, I expect that the demon hid his vital parts in a forest or in the ground, and when this house was constructed, it was unwittingly built out of trees or out of stones in which the First One to Use Words for Force had instilled his many pieces."

"But what about all those pictures of Mount Taylor? The demon couldn't have put those up. And what about the doorknocker?"

George Thousand Names raised his hand. "Of course the demon himself didn't put those artifacts there. But I expect that his influence in the house has been strong for centuries. Those people who have been unfortunate enough to live there have probably done many things, quite unconsciously, to prepare the way for the demon's eventual return to life. I expect that the doorknocker you talk about is a likeness of the demon's face."

"And the pictures?"

"Well, who knows?" he asked. "But remember that the ancient Indians used to draw pictures of prominent landmarks from a whole variety of different angles so that they could locate hidden hoards of weapons or supplies or underground springs. All those prints of Mount Taylor and Cabezon Peak could be a very sophisticated form of pictography, and if you put them all together, you may find that they lead you to some spot where the First One to Use Words for Force has secreted something important."

"Like what?" asked Jane. "I mean, whatever it is, it must be very important."

George Thousand Names smiled at her benevolently. "I don't usually like to hypothesize, my dear, but my guess would be that those pictures lead the way to the shorn-off hair of Big Monster. The First One to Use Words for Force cut off Big Monster's hair because it had magical properties that made the wearer invulnerable to human and supernatural weapons. It was said to be as gray as iron, this hair, and as strong as a whip. From what I recall of the legend, the First One to Use Words for Force hid the hair in the New Mexico lands of the Acoma and Canoncito Indians, so that the twin gods who killed Big Monster would never find it. But it was discovered, and spirited away, and nobody knows where. Without that hair, the demon would be open to attack and would never have the stamina he needed to remain in the world of men and living spirits."

I sat back on my cushion. George Thousand Names was so calm, so self-possessed, that I could no longer consider he was joking. But what he was saying needed such an enormous stretch of imagination to believe that I wasn't sure I could accept it even now, no matter how sincerely he had said it. If it hadn't have been for Dan and Bryan and Seymour Wallis, I would have politely finished my coffee and left. But two of them were sick and the third was lying dead in the morgue, and what he had told us was the only explanation anyone had given us so far.

"If the First One to Use Words for Force is the demon's ritual name, what's his common name?" Jane asked.

George Thousand Names raised an eyebrow. "You've probably heard it," he said. "The demon is usually called Coyote. The dogs of the desert were named after him. It's a name that means cunning and cajolery and vicious trickery."

I coughed. "Is there any way we can tell if he's really around? Is there any sign, any giveaway mark?"

"Like poltergeists, which are frightened of fire? Or vampires?" Jane suggested.

"Coyote comes in many guises, but you can always recognize him. He has the face of a demonic wolf, and he is always accompanied by signs of bad luck," he described.

"Like what?"

"Like thunderstorms, or sickness, or certain birds or animals."

I felt that familiar freezing sensation around my scalp. "Gray birds?" I asked the medicine man. "Gray birds that sit there and never sing?"

George Thousand Names nodded. "The gray birds are Coyote's most constant companions. He uses their feathers to fletch his arrows, which is something no Indian warrior would ever have done. The gray birds are the birds of disaster and panic."

"I've seen them."

For the first time, George Thousand Names leaned forward, his face intent and pale. "You've *seen* them?"

"Thousands of them, literally thousands. They're all perched on the roof of the hospital where Dan Machin and Bryan Corder and Seymour Wallis were taken. My own sanitation department was around there yesterday, trying to get rid of them, but they wouldn't leave."

"They're actually there?" he asked, as if he couldn't believe what I was saying. "You saw them with your own eyes?"

I nodded.

George Thousand Names looked away. His eyes, gleaming and bright in the folded wrinkles of his skin, seemed to be searching into some invisible faraway distance. He whispered, more to himself than to Jane and me, "*Coyote* . . . so it's come to pass."

I licked my lips uncertainly. "Mr. Thousand Names," I said, trying not to sound too much like a white tourist bartering for Indian blankets, "is there anything we can do? Or is there anything you can do to help us?"

He jerked his head toward me and stared at me as if I was losing my bananas. "I? What can I do in the face of a demon like Coyote?"

"Well, I don't exactly know. But if you can't do anything, what the hell can we do?"

George Thousand Names stood up and walked across to the open window. It was around five o'clock now, and the sun was only a couple of hours above the treeline. He stepped out on to the balcony, and Jane and I glanced worriedly at each other as he stood there, gazing out over the hills and the rivers of Round Valley. I stood up, too, and followed him out into the open air. There was a fresh smell of pine and woodsmoke in the air, and from far away came the echo of someone chopping logs.

"Someone has set this ancient evil working again," he said hoarsely. "Somehow, Coyote has come together again."

"I don't follow."

The medicine man turned and looked at me. "The way the gods and the medicine men dismissed Coyote to the underworld was to make sure that he was split up into parts, and that he had no means of recovering those parts. The first four times he died, he hid a flint on his body, so that he could dig up his breath and his blood and his heartbeat all over again. The last time he died, the gods made sure that he had no flint, and no ax. All that could possibly have conjured him up again was the Bear Maiden."

"Mr. Thousand Names," I said. "I don't like to seem ignorant, but these legends are pretty much beyond me. I mean, I find them all a little hard to swallow."

He turned away. "Of course you do," he said, in a flat voice that was neither irritated nor indulgent. "How do you think I felt when I first heard about Jesus Christ walking on water?"

Jane, who was standing by the open window, said, "Tell us about the Bear Maiden. Please."

George Thousand Names tiredly pinched the bridge of his nose between finger and thumb.

"The Bear Maiden was a beautiful girl whom Coyote lusted after. He tried dozens of times to seduce her, but every time she resisted him. It was she who sent him off to the underworld the first few times, to make him prove that he would gladly die for her. In the end, however, she succumbed to his sexual advances, and he gave her a night of love that won her over completely.

"From that moment on, Coyote filled her mind with evil thoughts, and gradually she changed from a woman into a bear. Her teeth grew long, her nails grew sharp, and dark hair grew down her back. Her greatest pleasure from then on was snapping men's necks with her powerful jaws."

"Not your fun Saturday-night escort, in other words," I remarked.

George Thousand Names gave me a down-home look that meant he was a long way away from flippant jokes. "It's quite possible that this man Wallis's statuette, the one he found at Fremont, was enough to provoke Coyote into life. It could have been invested with magic, like a small totem. Did he mention any problems or difficulties at Fremont? Any sickness or argument or inexplicable events?"

"Yes. They were building a pedestrian bridge in a park and apparently the whole damned thing was confusion from beginning to end."

"Then that's it," he said. "The statuette of Bear Maiden was more than just an antique curiosity. It was the original magical totem that could give Coyote the strength and the will to wake from his sleep in the underworld. And Seymour Wallis brought it into the house."

"Do you think that was accidental?" asked Jane. "I mean, it seems like a tremendous coincidence, him buying that one particular house."

George Thousand Names shook his head.

"From the moment Seymour Wallis dug up that statuette, Coyote was working his influence on him. He told you he felt dogged by bad luck, right? It wasn't bad luck at all. It was the demands of Coyote, drawing him nearer and nearer to Pilarcitos Street. I'll bet you something else, too."

"What's that?"

"Pilarcitos Street is the first turning after Fifth Street off Mission."

I nodded. "That's right."

He held up the fingers of both hands. "Five plus one is six. Then you have the number 1551. One plus five is six, and five plus one is six. Three sixes—666. The number of the greatest of demons, no matter what culture you're talking about. The mark of the beast."

Out there on the balcony, I suddenly felt cold. Jane, in the doorway, shivered. "What are we going to do?" I asked.

George Thousand Names scratched the back of his neck. "Two practical steps to begin with. First call up your friend at Elmwood Hospital and have him separate all three of Coyote's victims into different clinics or hospitals. That's vital. Second, get hold of those pictures of Mount Taylor and Cabezon Peak and see if you can work out where that shorn-off hair is located. If you can keep *that* away from Coyote, you might have half a chance. Third, and this is more difficult, keep any nurses or female doctors or any women at all away from Coyote's different parts. Coyote has a hunger for women's flesh, and that's what he's probably after right now."

I took a deep breath. However strange and farfetched all this legendary stuff seemed to be, I knew that for my own peace of mind I was going to have to call Dr. Jarvis and tell him. He was intelligent, Jim Jarvis, and he was open to suggestion, but I wondered just what he was going to say when I passed on George Thousand Names's instructions.

"Mr. Thousand Names, do you mind if I use your phone?" I asked.

"Be my guest. Would you care for some firewater?"

"I sure would. How about Russian firewater and tonic?"

I walked across the polished wooden floor and picked up the phone. Meanwhile, George Thousand Names came back inside and told his maid to bring us some drinks. Then he sat down cross-legged on his Indian-patterned settee and opened up his jar of tobacco. There was a pipe rack on the coffee table next to him, and none of them looked much like a pipe of peace. There were a couple of expensive meerschaums and three English briars.

The Round Valley Reservation operator put me through to San Francisco, and San Francisco put me through to Elmwood Foundation Hospital. Dr. Jarvis, for once, was free.

"Jim?" I said. "This is John Hyatt. I'm calling from Round Valley."

"Thank God, I've been trying to get you. It's all hell down here."

"What's wrong?"

"The whole place is going berserk. Your friend Dan Machin woke out of his coma and he's locked himself in with Bryan Corder. We've tried breaking the door down, but no luck so far. Dr. Crane has just called the police for cutting equipment."

Again, the surge of fear.

"He's locked himself in? You mean, they're *together?*"

"That's right. I don't know what the—"

The connection suddenly broke off. I rattled the phone, but the line was completely dead. George Thousand Names said, "Sorry, that sometimes happens. Is anything wrong?"

I laid down the useless receiver. "I think there is. Dan Machin has shut himself up with Bryan Corder. The hospital staff can't get in there."

George Thousand Names steadily packed his pipe with tobacco and reached for his matches. "It sounds as though it's started," he said. "Perhaps we'd better get down there."

"We?"

The Indian girl brought the drinks, and George Thousand Names lifted his glass of bourbon.

"You don't think I'm going to let white men have the greatest Indian demon all to themselves, do you? This is something that red men are going to talk about for generations to come. Now let's drink to the confusion of our enemies."

I raised my vodka. "I don't know about the confusion of our enemies," I said dryly, "but I know damn well that *I'm* confused as hell."

★★★★★

We drove back down to San Francisco that night at over ninety miles an hour, with bugs pelting our windshield, and our faces strained in the green glow from the Jaguar's instrument panel. Tires squealing, we took the curves down the mountains, and then we hit 101 and snaked southward through Willits, Ukiah, Cloverdale, and back down into Sonoma County. It was just after midnight when we crossed into Marin County, and it was only when I saw the glitter of San Francisco sprinkled across the darkness of the bay that I eased my foot off the gas and cruised across the Golden Gate at forty.

George Thousand Names had been snoring fitfully in the back seat but he woke up with a start as we turned off Presidio Drive and made our way up toward the hospital. He stretched and said, "The trouble with English cars, they expect you to sit upright all the damned time. What do they think I am, a country squire?"

"You didn't have to come," I reminded him, as we took the Elmwood turn-off and bounced down the drive into the hospital forecourt.

"That's like trying to tell Custer not to go to the Little Big Horn," he retorted.

"Are you that pessimistic?" asked Jane.

George Thousand Names blew his nose very loudly. "Pessimism isn't a particularly Indian characteristic. I consulted the day's omens before I left, and they seem okay, although I have to admit that there's a cloud on the horizon, no bigger than a man's fist."

"There are the birds," I said, pointing. "It looks like the sanitation department gave up trying to get rid of them."

Our headlights, as we swung down the driveway, flashed across the ruffled gray ranks of birds. Then I pulled the Jaguar up, and we climbed out, and George Thousand

Names stood in the breezy darkness, staring up at the silent feathery witnesses to Coyote's rebirth.

"Well?" I asked.

He nodded. "There is no doubt at all. These are the rare birds we call Gray Sadness. They were seen gathering at Wounded Knee, and at the funeral of Sitting Bull, and when Rain-in-the-Face died. They are the birds of mourning and bad luck."

Jane reached over and held my hand. Her own hand was very cold. "Do they really mean that Coyote is here?"

George Thousand Names lifted his head as if he were sniffing the wind. "Can you smell something?" he asked us.

I sniffed. "Not much. I have a sinus condition."

Jane said, "It's like . . . I don't quite know what it's like. It's like dogs. Dogs, when they get wet."

He nodded and didn't say anything more. I took Jane's arm and led her into the hospital doors, and he followed, glancing up now and again at the birds, the Gray Sadness, with his eyes as wary and fearful as those of a man who is brought into a mortuary to view his father's body.

There were two uniformed policemen from the SFPD standing guard by the elevators. One of them came across the tiled lobby as we walked in and raised his hand.

"I'm sorry, sir. Nobody allowed inside right now."

"I've come to see Dr. Jarvis. He's expecting us."

The policeman examined us suspiciously. "That's too bad. I got strict orders that no one goes up."

"What do you mean?" I demanded. "Dr. Jarvis telephoned me three or four hours ago, and we've come all the way from Round Valley."

"Mister," said the policeman patiently, "I don't care if you've come from the planet Mars. My orders are nobody goes up."

The second policeman came across and said, "That's right. Those are the orders."

"Now hold on a goddamned minute—" I said, but George Thousand Names interrupted me.

"We have authority," he told the cop quietly. "Do you wish to examine it?"

The policemen looked across at him with mistrust. But George Thousand Names reached into his red windbreaker and raised one of the golden amulets that hung around his neck.

"What's that?" asked one of the cops.

"Look at it," insisted George Thousand Names. "Examine it."

Somehow he caught the light in the lobby with his amulet and flashed it into the policemen's eyes. The policemen appeared to blink, and stare, and took a step back as if someone had elbowed them out of the way. I looked at George Thousand Names, and then I looked at Jane, but all Jane could do was shrug.

"We have authority to pass," said George Thousand Names loudly. "Do you understand?"

The policemen nodded. One of them, like a sleepwalker, turned around and opened the elevator doors for us, and we stepped inside. George Thousand Names told me, "It's all yours, Mr. Hyatt," and I pressed the button for 5.

"Is that a kind of hypnosis?" I asked him as we rose smoothly upward. "The way you used that amulet?"

The medicine man tucked it back into his windbreaker. "We call it The Way of Kindly Conquest. It is a kind of hypnosis, yes, but it has the advantage of inducing an obedient trance for just a few moments at a time, a few moments that the victim never recalls. You can't make it work on people who are openly aggressive, or on people who are determined to resist hypnosis. But it does work quite well on ordinary people whose minds are fairly relaxed."

"But won't those policemen come after us?" asked Jane.

George Thousand Names shook his head. "It's very doubtful. Right this minute they're probably standing downstairs shaking their heads, absolutely sure that something's gone wrong, but totally unsure what it could have been."

We reached the fifth floor, and the elevator doors slid open. George Thousand Names courteously ushered Jane out into the corridor, and I stepped after them, looking for signs of the terrible panic that Jim had called me about.

The corridor was silent. I listened for a while, but I couldn't even hear the normal sounds of a busy private hospital, like trolleys, and conversation, and intercoms calling for doctors. There was nothing but the *click-hum* of the elevator as its doors closed behind us and it rose to higher floors.

"I guess we'd better try Dr. Jarvis's office first," I suggested. "If he's not there, he'll be down at intensive care."

"Lead on," said George Thousand Names. "The sooner we get to grips with this monster, the better!"

Jane laughed nervously. "You're making this sound like a Frankenstein movie."

George Thousand Names stuck his hands in his jeans pockets and made a moue. "It's worse than that," he said pragmatically.

We walked along the soft red carpet until we reached Jim's office. I held my breath and rapped on the door. We waited, but there was no reply. George Thousand Names, his eyes as patient as a lizard's in his leathery face, said, "I hope you told this doctor what he was up against."

I opened Dr. Jarvis's door and quickly checked his tiny room. It was neat and orderly, and there was even a polystyrene cup of coffee on the desk, left abandoned like the last lunch on the *Marie Celeste*. A cigarette butt smoldered in the crowded ashtray. The bottle of gin, almost empty, stood on the filing cabinet.

"Spooky," said Jane.

"They must be down at intensive care," I said. "It's just along here, on the left."

We began to hurry as we turned the corner and made our way toward the intensive-care unit. I don't know why. The silence gave us a sense of urgency somehow, as if the longer it stayed silent, the more terrifying everything was going to get. All we could hear was our own breathing and the rustle of our clothes as we walked quickly along.

I didn't bother to knock on the double doors of the unit. I just pushed my way into the gloom and the shadows and the blue twilight world where Bryan Corder was living out his unnatural life.

Dr. Jarvis was there, and so were Dr. Crane and Dr. Weston and Lieutenant Stroud from the police department, and two baffled and burly cops. Jim turned as we came in. "You made it. I was afraid you wouldn't."

"What's going on?" I asked him. "What's happening in there?"

Jim took my arm and led me forward to the glass panel, which looked into the depths of the unit itself. It was still illuminated with blue light, but somehow the light seemed dimmer and more restless, like the cold phosphorescence that crawls across the sea at night, or the uncanny glow of decaying fish. I could make out the shape of the couch, and around the couch I could still see the chromium stands with saline drips and plasma. I thought I could see the bone-white curve of Bryan Corder's skull, too, but on the couch itself there was an indefinable lump of twisted limbs and flesh, and it was too dark to understand what it could possibly be.

"Dan Machin's in there?" I asked. "I don't see where."

"Can't you get in?" Jane asked.

Lieutenant Stroud, tall and urbane as usual, answered, "Lady, we're not standing out here for our health. We've tried six or seven times to get inside and each time we've been repulsed."

"Repulsed?" I queried. "What do you mean, 'repulsed'?"

"Try it for yourself," suggested Lieutenant Stroud. "The door's right here."

I stepped forward, but George Thousand Names said, very softly, "Don't, Mr. Hyatt. It's not worth it."

Lieutenant Stroud said, "What do you know?"

George Thousand Names glanced at me through the gloom, and I could see that he was trying to suppress a smile.

"This is George Thousand Names, Lieutenant," I said. "I brought him down tonight from the Round Valley Reservation."

"You're still gibbering about this Red Indian stuff?"

"You can call it gibbering," I put in quietly. "But so far it's the only reasonable explanation. George Thousand Names believes that what we're witnessing here is the rebirth of an Indian demon from way back in time."

Lieutenant Stroud looked at Dr. Jarvis, then at the other doctors, then at his two flatfoots. Then he turned to George Thousand Names with a sarcastic, beatific smile. "A Red Indian demon from way back in time? Is that right?"

George Thousand Names was too old and self-possessed to be fazed by sarcasm. He simply nodded. "That's right. The demon's name is Coyote, sometimes called the First One to Use Words for Force. He is generally understood to be the demon of confusion, anger, and argument, apart from his insatiable lust for women."

Lieutenant Stroud laughed, short and harsh. "The demon rapist?"

George Thousand Names smiled, but kept his cool. "That's just about right, Lieutenant. The demon rapist. There's an old Navajo song that tells how Coyote met a young woman on a mountain pass, and how he tricked her into lifting her dress for him. It's a charming song, in its way. But what it omits is that Coyote was the most fierce and fearsome looking of all demons anywhere, and that once he'd seduced a woman he'd generally behave like less than a gentleman."

"What do you mean, 'less than a gentleman'?" asked Lieutenant Stroud coldly.

"There are ladies present," George Thousand Names said.

"None of the ladies here are going to worry about anatomical details, if that's what you're thinking."

"It's not that," he replied. "It's just that if this demon does manage to bring himself back to life, then no woman in San Francisco will be safe, and I'd hate to frighten these ladies unnecessarily."

"Spit it out, will you?" demanded Lieutenant Stroud. "If there's something going on here, I want to know what it is!"

"Very well," said George Thousand Names. "Coyote first seduces his women, then he treats them to what the Navaho used to call the Ordeal of Three."

Jane said, "My God. I've heard of that."

George Thousand Names touched her arm. "It was the strangest of all ancient tortures, and its history goes back far beyond the civilization of the North American tribes. It is said by many of our wise men that it was Coyote's personal invention, but who can say?"

Jim frowned. "I've never heard of the Ordeal of Three. What the hell is it?"

George Thousand Names touched one of the amulets around his neck. He said in a toneless voice, "The Ordeal of Three involved cutting open a woman's stomach and sewing up into her stomach a live reptile, like a Gila monster, then cutting open a horse or a cow and disemboweling it, then sewing up the woman inside the horse. The art of the torture was to keep all three victims, lizard, woman, and horse, alive as long as possible."

Dr. Weston said, "Oh, come on. You're just making that up."

George Thousand Names shook his head. "Check with your own anthropologists if you have to. The skeletons of a lizard, a woman, and a horse, one inside the other like a Chinese puzzle, were dug up at Lake Winnemucca, in Nevada, not six years ago, by Professor Forrester of the University of Colorado."

Lieutenant Stroud pulled at his lower lip. "Okay, Mr. Thousand Names. If you know what goes on around here, what do you suggest is going on *there?*"

He pointed through the glass panel to the dim shadowy forms on the care-unit couch. Something was moving in there, some shape, bulky and dark, moving and twitching with that jerky, unpleasant twitching that characterizes the first movements of insects as they work their way out of their chrysalis.

George Thousand Names said, "The Gray Sadness was enough to show me. What you're seeing here is the coming together of Coyote, the foulest of Red Indian demons. When he was banished to the underworld, he concealed his breath and his blood and his heartbeat, and now he's managed to bring them all back together again in one place. He's coming to life, whether you like it or not."

Lieutenant Stroud stared at George Thousand Names for quite a while, his eyes glistening attentively in the darkness. "So you really believe it. You really believe that's happening."

"It's not belief, Lieutenant. It's not an act of faith. I *know* what's happening. It's as plain to me as a flat tire on an automobile is to you. It's a fact," George Thousand Names insisted.

"Then what, then what's going on here?" Jim asked.

"Go get a flashlight and you'll see," said George Thousand Names, rather too calmly for my liking. "The breath and the heartbeat are joining together. Soon, all Coyote will need is his blood and his terrible face."

"Jane," I said, leaning over and speaking quietly in her ear. "The doorknocker at Pilarcitos Street. Can you go get it? Knock it off the door with a hammer if you have to."

Jane held my arm. "I don't want to leave you, John. Not now."

I took out a ten-dollar bill and folded it into her hand. "You won't be away for long. Take a taxi. But just get ahold of that doorknocker before anyone else does."

Jane looked up at me with those wide china-blue eyes, then she put her arm around my neck and kissed me. "Maybe we should have stayed together, you and I," she whispered, and then she slipped out of the room and made her way off to 1551.

Lieutenant Stroud was saying: "We've tried flashlights. It's the angle of the glass or something, but they won't penetrate."

George Thousand Names turned from Lieutenant Stroud to Dr. Jarvis and back again. "In that case," he said, "the great Coyote has gained more strength than I thought. He is powerful enough to absorb your light completely."

Dr. Weston said, "Absorb? What are you talking about?" She clearly didn't think much of George Thousand Names's ethnic folklore. She had enough ethnic folklore of her own.

"You haven't been reading your *Scientific American* lately," George Thousand Names said. "When an object has sufficient density, it can actually prevent light from reflecting away from it. It attracts the light back to itself by its intense gravitational pull. That's what's happening here. Coyote is a beast of the underworld. If you like, he's a living black hole."

"You mean, he's going to be completely invisible?" Jim asked.

George Thousand Names shook his head. "Only when he desires it."

"What about his blood?" Dr. Crane put in. "If his heart-beat and his breath are getting together here, shouldn't we try to isolate Mr. Wallis? He's the vessel for this demon's blood, I presume."

"Yes," answered the medicine man. "Try to get him away. But be careful of the birds, and be careful of any magical tricks that Coyote might try to pull to prevent you doing it."

"Magical tricks?" asked Lieutenant Stroud skeptically. "Like what?"

"Lieutenant, this may seem like a joke but it's not. When I say magical tricks, I'm not talking about lifting rabbits out of a hat or sawing ladies in half. I'm talking about death and injury and illusions like you've never seen," the medicine man claimed.

I put in, "It makes sense, Lieutenant. Everything that George has said so far, it makes sense."

"Who asked you?" snapped Lieutenant Stroud.

Dr. Jarvis said, "There's no point in arguing, Lieutenant. None of us has a better idea."

"You don't think so?" said Lieutenant Stroud, turning around. "Well, maybe I've got myself a better idea. Maybe this whole damned thing is a hoax."

"A hoax?" I said. "You think we'd take the flesh off a man's skull for a hoax?"

"Well, all this damn stupid stuff about Indian demons—"

"Stuff!" said George Thousand Names, bristling. "You call our demons stuff! Are you crazy? Do you know what Coyote can do? Do you have any idea?"

Lieutenant Stroud was taken aback by George Thousand Names's ferocity. "Well, you mentioned the Ordeal of Three . . ."

"That's *nothing!*" he retorted. "That's what he does with the women he's played with and thrown aside! Coyote has powers beyond all human comprehension. Powers that made it almost impossible for all the good and evil gods combined to destroy him. And that's without the added powers he stole from other demons like Big Monster and the Loogaroos."

"The Loogaroos?" said Lieutenant Stroud, in disbelief.

"That's what the French colonists called them, when they first came to America. It's a corruption of *loups-garous,* which means 'werewolves.' Coyote took powers from all of them. He covers his back with the hide of a werewolf and wears on his head the scalp of Big Monster, and with those he is almost indestructible."

Lieutenant Stroud listened to this outburst, and then stood there silent for a long moment, while all of us watched his face, wondering how the hell he was going to respond. I thought at first he was going to dismiss everything that George Thousand Names had said as garbage, but then I saw his expression soften and the lines around his mouth deepen, and I knew that the medicine man's conviction had almost convinced him.

"I want to know what's going on in there, inside that room. I want you to explain it to me," he said finally.

George Thousand Names stepped forward. The blue light that irradiated from the intensive-care unit made his eyes glisten and painted the lines and creases of his face in ultramarine. He raised one shriveled hand, his fingers decorated with silver rings and his wrist hung with bead bracelets, and pressed it against the glass, as if he could feel vibrations from the dark and twisted mass that was Dan, or Bryan, or both of them, or neither.

With his other hand holding his golden amulet, he said softly, "It is almost time for Coyote to make himself live once more, to model himself out of the clay of human flesh. He needs blood but he can rise without blood. He is molding himself from the bodies of those who possess his heartbeat and his breath. *Look!*"

All the time that George Thousand Names had his hand pressed to the window, he must have been mentally struggling against the powers of Coyote. Because when he said, *"Look!"* the blue light rose and brightened, and in that brief and horrifying brightness we actually saw what it was that he had been trying to explain to us. We saw the beginnings of Coyote, the demon, the rapist and traitor, the First One to Use Words for Force.

On the couch, we saw limbs rising and falling. At first they looked like the arms and legs of people drowning in a lake of darkness, but then the contorted mass of flesh seemed to rise up and stand almost upright, and all I could do was stare at what it was and feel a horrifying shudder all the way down my back.

In some unspeakable way, Dan Machin and Bryan Corder had been twisted together as one creature. It was almost eight feet tall, rearing blindly off the couch with Bryan's fleshless skull as its head, but with both men's arms and legs reaching out toward us. Their torsos were combined in a shapeless double torso of knotted muscle, and Dan Machin's ghastly face appeared momentarily from inside the beast's stomach, pressed against the translucent skin with his mouth wide open in a hellish howl.

Jim said, "It's impossible!" and Dr. Weston moaned as if she was hurt. But then the blue light dimmed again, and all we could see was the murky outline of that monstrous creature, and the white reflection of the emergency lamps from what had once been Bryan's head.

Lieutenant Stroud, his voice dry, said, "All right, Mr. Thousand Names, what is it?"

George Thousand Names lifted himself wearily away from the window. "It's Coyote," he said simply. "He takes on many forms, but this one more than most. It could have been a woman, or a deer, or even a fish. He is said once to have molded his earthly manifestation out of a girl and a tarantula. But tonight he's lucky. He has two strong young men for his reincarnation, and downstairs in the morgue you have Seymour Wallis's blood."

"Did you give orders to get rid of that blood?" demanded Lieutenant Stroud.

"Dr. Crane's taken care of it," Dr. Jarvis said. "Seymour Wallis's body should be halfway to Redwood City by now."

"Redwood City?" asked the lieutenant. "What's at Redwood City?"

"Elmwood Foundation finances a cryogenic research center at Redwood. We can put him on ice for as long as we like."

"What are we going to do about *that?*" I pointed toward the bulky shape in the intensive-care unit. "We can't just leave it the way it is."

Lieutenant Stroud gave me an impatient glance, as if to

tell me to mind my own goddamned business, but he went up to Jim and laid his hand confidingly on his shoulder.

"Doctor," he said. "Is that thing a threat to human life? To the lives of your staff?"

Jim licked his lips. "I don't have any evidence of that. So far I've seen nothing more than extreme physiological abnormality. It hasn't threatened us in any way at all."

George Thousand Names butted in. "Coyote's very existence is a threat! Once he has his blood running through his veins again, he'll tear us to pieces!"

"You have some proof?" asked Lieutenant Stroud. "I'm not doubting your word, sir, but that thing in there is kind of human, and I'm not authorized to shoot human beings unless I have reasonable grounds to believe that they may be threatening life or property."

George Thousand Names stood stiff as the spine on a porcupine, his eyes blazing. He pointed with a rigid arm toward the intensive-care unit. "That, Lieutenant, is Coyote, returned from the underworld! What more can I tell you? That's Coyote!"

Lieutenant Stroud looked across at his two officers, and one of them raised his eyebrows as if to suggest that George Thousand Names may not have all of his marbles.

"What do you think, Doctor?" the lieutenant asked Dr. Weston. "Is that a Red Indian demon or not? Or is it just a medical freak?"

Dr. Weston, although she was shaken by what she had seen in the intensive-care unit, replied, "It's a freak. It has to be. I've never seen anything like it, but we can't kill it."

"Supposing—" Dr. Jarvis began.

"Supposing nothing!" interrupted Dr. Weston. "Jim, this thing is thc strangest medical event we've ever seen. It's like Siamese twins being created in front of our eyes. We can't destroy it now. There's no way!"

"Dr. Weston," I put in, "you didn't see Bryan Corder hurt. You didn't see Dan Machin when his eyes lit up like a devil's. You can't say that. Whatever it is in there, whether it's a demon or not, we've got to make sure it doesn't kill anyone else!"

Dr. Weston was about to answer, but she never had the chance. What happened next was like a freeway accident, it blurred past my eyes so fast that it was hard to comprehend. I do remember one or two vivid and horrifying things, though, and I guess they're going to stay in my mind forever.

Jim suddenly said, "It's coming this way!" and just as we turned to look at the intensive-care unit there was a blast of shattering glass and thousands of fragments of the observation panel sprayed across the room in a razor-sharp hail. One of the cops dropped to his knees at once, his face like chopped liver, and the other one turned away with his hands over his eyes and blood running down his fingers. My own cheeks were slashed in the glittering, tumbling burst of glass, but it wasn't the glass that frightened me, it was the apparition of Coyote, rearing like a huge, pale praying mantis, his skull grinning fixedly on top of its shapeless trunk, his four arms smashing the remains of the window aside without hesitation.

And there was the heat. The appalling, scorching heat. It must have been two hundred degrees inside that intensive-care unit, and now a dry, roasting wind moaned and howled as it surged out of the broken window.

Lieutenant Stroud plucked his police special from his pants and fired twice at the monstrous Coyote. But the demon waved one arm toward him, and he was hurtled away across the room, cracking his back against the wall, his gun skidding off into the slush of broken glass.

Dr. Jarvis shrieked, "John! Hold him!" But I knew that there was no way we were going to hold this thing back, and I wrenched open the door, shouting, "Forget it! For Christ's sake, get out of here!"

George Thousand Names, his hands lifted to protect his head, scrambled out of the room as quickly as he could. Dr. Weston followed him, and then me, and then Jim. The cop with the bleeding eyes was trying to help Lieutenant Stroud, but the demon waved his arm again, and the cop shrieked, and staggered helplessly toward the door.

"I'm burning!" he yelled. "Put me out! For God's sake! I'm *burning!*"

Jim ran toward him, but then the cop opened his mouth, and a fierce gout of flame gushed out from between his lips. *He was blazing inside,* his stomach and his lungs were on fire, and every time he tried to cry for help, a monstrous funnel of superheated flames bellowed out. "John! A blanket! Get me a blanket!" Dr. Jarvis hollered, but it was too late. The cop rolled against the side of the corridor and slid to his knees, leaving a trail of fiercely burning blood on the wall. Then he collapsed and lay still, and in front of our eyes, to our overwhelming horror, the flames that were burning inside him gradually broke out, singeing and then setting fire to his uniform from inside, and then engulfing his whole body until he lay on the carpet blazing like a ritual suicide.

There was another moan of hot air from inside the room and we heard something like a grumble and a roar, the sound of a devilish beast that was determined to destroy us. Then, miraculously, Lieutenant Stroud came diving out of the doorway, rolling sideways toward us, and gasping for air like an athlete who's testing his threshold of pain.

George Thousand Names and Dr. Jarvis knelt down

beside him. "I'm okay, I'm okay," he told them, trying to stand up. "My back's bruised but I think I'm okay. For God's sake, let's get out of here. That thing's gone crazy."

"Not crazy. That's his natural behavior," George Thousand Names said. "He's going to destroy and devour us and there's nothing we can do."

Lieutenant Stroud painfully climbed to his feet, his eyes fixed on the dark doorway where Coyote was hiding.

"Well, maybe there's nothing that you can do, medicine man, but I know what I'm going to do. That—that *thing* in there has declared war, and if it's war he wants, he's damned well going to get it!"

George Thousand Names reached out and held the lieutenant's arm. "Please, Lieutenant you're not dealing with the Creature from the Black Lagoon. Bombs and tear gas could never hurt Coyote. All you can do is to—"

His words were drowned in a roar that shook the whole building. Pieces of broken door, ribbons of shredded carpet, fragments of plaster, and a dry fierce heat that stank of animals and death came blasting over us. It was Coyote, coming out in search of his blood, coming out in search of his face, and coming out to slaughter us. It was Coyote, the demon of wrath and fear!

FIVE

I was hardly conscious. A chunk of door jamb had struck me on the left side of the head, and my legs had given way beneath me. I was lying against the side of the corridor, shrouded in tattered carpet, and it seemed that the whole world was coming down around me. The hot hurricane howled and shrieked, and pieces of debris tumbled and flew down the corridor. Over it all, as Coyote approached us, I heard a noise like someone screaming down an endless echoing pipe; a hopeless dreary screaming that frightened me more than almost anything else.

Screwing up my eyes against the scorching wind, I tried to look up. I could see George Thousand Names sprawled against the opposite wall, and Lieutenant Stroud huddled beside him. Jim was further away, his hands clutched over his gingery hair, but I couldn't see Dr. Weston at all.

Then the very air itself seemed to darken, and out of the darkness came something that wasn't much to do with Bryan Corder and Dan Machin anymore. It was a spectral manifestation, a ghost made of eerie density, and contorted flesh. It had a kind of negative glow to it, the glow of deep shadows or gloomy rooms, and it glided darkly down the corridor, the skull with its hideous grin, and behind it a rippling and loathsome cloak of half-substantial flesh. The screaming grew drearier and louder as Coyote went by, but there was yet another sound that accompanied his passing. It was *the flap of dead skin,* like flaccid tarpaulin on a deserted warehouse roof. It was almost more than I could bear.

The noise and the wind seemed to drone on forever, but suddenly I raised my head again and I became aware that Coyote had passed us by without harming us. I looked up a little more and turned around to check behind me, and the demon had vanished.

George Thousand Names whispered dryly, "I think it's all right now, at least for a while. He's gone to search for his blood."

"How do you know that?" asked Lieutenant Stroud.

"Because he would have killed us otherwise, and taken great pleasure in raping Dr. Weston. He needs his blood to stay alive, and if he doesn't get it in one moon's rising and descending, he'll be banished back to the underworld."

Lieutenant Stroud, clutching his back, stood up against the wall. "Well, that's the first piece of good news I've heard all day. All we have to do is keep Coyote away from innocent bystanders for twenty-four hours, and that's the end of that."

George Thousand Names brushed off his windbreaker. "I'm afraid not, Lieutenant. Whatever you do, Coyote will make sure that he finds his blood."

"What about his face?" I said. "His face was on the doorknocker."

"He'll go searching for that too."

"But I just sent Jane off to get that."

George Thousand Names stared at me, and his face was totally grave. "You sent Jane to get the doorknocker? You mean that?"

I felt panicky. "Well, sure, I just thought that if he didn't have his face—"

George Thousand Names said, "Great Spirit, preserve us. If Coyote catches her with that thing, she won't stand a chance."

Lieutenant Stroud came forward and he looked impatient. "I'm sorry to interrupt the ominous warnings, but what did you mean about the blood? That blood should be locked up at Redwood City by now, isn't that right, Doctor? How's Coyote going to find it, let alone get hold of it?"

"Oh, come on, Lieutenant," I said, equally testy. "Coyote just burst his way through three inches of toughened glass."

"I didn't ask you," retorted Lieutenant Stroud sharply. "I was asking our resident expert."

"Well, the answer to your question is that Coyote is a dog monster of sorts," said George Thousand Names. "He has a supernatural ear and a supernatural sense of smell. The old legends said that when Bear Maiden was hiding in a cave, Coyote was able to smell her through ten spear-lengths of solid rock, and he destroyed the cave and half the mountain to find her. That was supposed to have happened on Nacimiento Peak, more years ago than even the Navahos can remember."

Lieutenant Stroud looked grim. "Thanks for the optimistic forecast."

"What are you going to do now?" I asked him.

"The first damned thing I'm going to do is call in the SWAT squad. We're going to find that thing, whatever it is, and give it a dose of what it just handed out to us."

"Lieutenant," put in George Thousand Names. "I thought you were a sophisticated man. At least, more sophisticated than most policemen."

"What's that supposed to imply?"

The old Indian looked at the detective cold and level. "Your massive firepower is useless. Would you hunt a fox with a tank, or try to kill a mosquito with a machine gun? Coyote is too cunning for you, Lieutenant, too powerful, too elusive. What you must do is track him down in the way that the ancient gods used to, by appealing to his lust and his vanity and by coaxing him into engineering his own destruction."

"Are you kidding?" said Lieutenant Stroud. "When I have to make my report about this, I'm going to have to say what immediate and decisive action I took. I can just think what the commissioner's going to say when he reads that I appealed to the fugitive's lust and vanity and coaxed him into engineering his own destruction. Now, if you'll excuse me."

The lieutenant went across to an office close by and picked up the telephone. He rattled the receiver a few times, and eventually got through. As he called reinforcements, George

Thousand Names looked at Jim and me and shrugged. "You can never explain to white men," he said.

"What about Jane? Can we do something to help her?" I asked.

"Of course," replied the Indian. "In fact, the best plan for you and I right now is to go to this house on Pilarcitos Street and seal it off from Coyote with the strongest spells we can. If he hasn't got there already, he'll try to steal the doorknocker and he'll also try to get to those pictures of Mount Taylor and Cabezon Peak."

"Why's that?" Jim asked.

"Simple, he wants the hair that he cut from Big Monster. Once he finds it, his immortality will be assured. We will never be able to destroy or dismiss him then."

"All right," I said. "What are we waiting for?"

As we left the front door of the hospital, the first of the SWAT trucks and cars were arriving and the night was howling and warbling with sirens. We walked quickly across the parking lot to Dr. Jarvis's Monte Carlo, and Jim held the front seat forward so that I could climb awkwardly into the back. As he stood there, he glanced up at the roof of the hospital. "The birds, they're gone."

George Thousand Names seemed to take it all very calmly. As he eased himself into the front seat, he said, "Of course. They have followed Coyote. They hang over his head like a cloud of sorrow. Sometimes they seem to fill the air like heavy smoke; other times they are almost invisible. Birds are very magical and strange creatures, Dr. Jarvis. They have spirits of supernatural kind that men can rarely understand."

Jim started the motor and we drove out of the hospital gates and into the streets of midnight San Francisco. It was a warm, clogged night, and the city lights sparkled and rippled through air that was almost unbreathably humid. Although it was late, it was Saturday night, and there were still plenty of cars cruising around and couples walking down the sloping streets.

As we sped along Seventeenth Street as far as Delores Street, I glimpsed a girl in a red blouse and white jeans on the sidewalk. "Jim, that's Jane! I'm sure that's Jane! Pull over!"

He swung the car to the curb and backed up. I looked frantically through the tinted back window and Jane came into view. She was walking steadily and purposefully in the direction of Mission Street, and she hadn't even turned our way. Dr. Jarvis honked the horn, and it was only then that she stopped, frowning in a dazed kind of a way, and came over to the curb.

Jim climbed out of the car and I squeezed myself out after him. I went around the front of the car and took Jane by the arms and held her. She was pale, and her eyes had a moist, myopic look about them, but otherwise she seemed okay. "Jane, Jane, what's wrong?"

She smiled, but somehow she didn't seem to be concentrating. "There's nothing wrong," she whispered. "Nothing wrong at all."

"But why didn't you take a taxi? What are you doing here?"

"Here?" she said, raising her head and looking at me vaguely.

"This is Seventeenth. You were supposed to be going to Pilarcitos in a taxi."

Jane touched her forehead as if she was trying to remember. "Oh, yes. Pilarcitos Street."

Dr. Jarvis pushed me gently away, and examined Jane with swift professionalism. He raised one of her eyelids with his thumb and checked her pulse. While he was doing this, she stood there silent and passive, her only expression a faint frown, her eyes staring off into some private distance that I couldn't even guess at.

"Is she all right?" I asked him. "She seems like she's suffering from shock."

"It could be shock," he said. "On the other hand, it could be a form of hypnosis, or trance."

"Do you think Coyote—"

"John, I don't know what I'm supposed to think. But the main thing is that she's safe. Let's get her into the car and get up to Pilarcitos Street. Then your Indian friend here can do what he has to do to keep Coyote out of the house, and we can get Jane back to the hospital."

George Thousand Names stuck his bead out of the car window. "Are we going to be long?" he asked me. "The quicker we get to that house the better. If Coyote has gotten there already, we won't stand a chance."

Between us, Jim and I helped Jane to climb into the back seat of the ear, then we swerved off from the curb and made our way toward Mission Street and Pilarcitos.

As we came up the sloping street, the house at 1551 looked as dark and as brooding as before. The windows were like sunken eyes and the scabrous paintwork seemed to have flaked even more. Dr. Jarvis slowed the car as we came nearer, and as we stopped outside he switched off the motor and we sat there for a minute in silence.

"Do you think Coyote's in there?" I said, in an unsettled voice.

"It's impossible to say," answered George Thousand Names. "But if he is, we'll soon find out."

"How?"

"He'll kill us."

Jim wiped his mouth with the back of his hand. "But he

may not *be* there, right? He may still be looking for Seymour Wallis's blood?"

"Of course."

I looked at Jim and Jim looked at me. "Well," I said, wryly. "Here goes nothing."

We got out of the car and went around to help George Thousand Names. Jane stayed where she was, silent and presumably in shock. The three of us crossed the sidewalk and stood by the front gate of 1551, looking up at the gloomy porch and the scaly lintels.

"Is the doorknocker still there?" asked George Thousand Names. "I find it hard to see without my eyeglasses."

Jim and I peered into the shadows. At first I thought it had gone, but then I caught the dark gleam of bronze and I knew that Coyote was still off pursuing his blood. For the moment, we were safe.

We opened the creaking gate and went up the steps. George Thousand Names stood for a while looking at the evil grinning face on the doorknocker, then he slowly shook his head.

"If any Indian had ever walked past this house and seen this face, he would have known immediately what it was," he said quietly. "This is just as provocative as having an effigy of Satan on your door. Well, let's make sure that Coyote can never use it."

He reached into his windbreaker and lifted out an amulet. It was a small gold medallion with a strange pictograph scratched on it. He held it for a moment in the fingers of both hands, and touched it against his forehead. Then he stepped right up to the doorknocker and raised his hand.

"Evil Coyote, devilish one of the southwest," he muttered. "This likeness is forever bound by my spell, forever locked away from you. This likeness will burn you, this likeness will freeze you, this likeness will blow like the winds of the north against you. You may never touch this likeness, never use this likeness, without the wrath of the great spirits falling upon you forever."

There was silence. A truck banged and rumbled across a distant road junction.

Then, softly, I heard a hissing sound. It was like someone drawing breath. Someone about to speak.

A gentle, insidious voice said, *"Fools."*

I felt myself shaking. I knew it was stupid to tremble like that. But it was the doorknocker, the bronze doorknocker itself, that was speaking. Its wild eyes shone with a lurid light, and maybe it was my imagination working overtime, but I *knew* this time that it was bristling with hairs and that its teeth were as savage and sharp as any real wolf or dog.

George Thousand Names stood upright. It was clear that he was making a fierce mental effort to stay in control of the situation. He crossed his arms in front of his face, then made a sweeping, dismissive gesture with both hands.

"Coyote is a dog that runs in the night," he said. His voice was shaking with dignity and stern passion. "Coyote is a sneak and a liar. The gods hear this and the gods know this. They dismiss you, they dismiss you, they dismiss you."

There was a chilling laugh from the doorknocker.

"Silence!" shouted George Thousand Names. *"I command you to be silent!"*

Again, there was that hissing, and another hideous laugh.

"You have no power over me, you dotard," whispered the doorknocker. *"My master is coming soon, and then we will see."* It laughed again.

The front door of the house suddenly jerked open by itself and banged shut again.

But George Thousand Names hadn't given up. He raised his arms again. "The frost of the north will enclose you, the frost of the north will crack you. Coyote of the deserts will feel your chill and retreat like the hound he is."

I still can't really believe what I saw then, but I'd already seen so much that night that one more weirdness couldn't faze me all that much. George Thousand Names pointed directly at the doorknocker with a rigid index finger, and out of that finger came a visible spangling cloud of ice. The ice settled on the doorknocker, encrusting it with white crystals, and its hissing died away almost at once.

Still he kept his finger pointed at the knocker, and the ice grew thicker and thicker. I could feel the cold from where I was standing two or three feet away. Then, abruptly, the bronze head snapped and pieces of frozen metal clattered on to the floor of the porch.

George Thousand Names let his arm fall. He was sweating and breathing in agonized gasps. But he had enough spirit left to kick at the fragments of doorknocker with his foot and say, "A dotard, huh? You chunk of scrap."

Jim let out a long whistle. "That was amazing. I never saw anything like that. Mr. Thousand Names, you ought to get yourself a job in the frozen-food business."

I took George Thousand Names's arm. "You won one," I said. "You took Coyote on, and yon won one."

He shook his head. "We haven't finished yet, and my powers are not great. Dr. Jarvis, do you have space in your car for those pictures of Mount Taylor and Cabezon Peak?"

"Why, sure. But I thought you were just going to seal off the house with a couple of spells."

George Thousand Names wiped his forehead with his handkerchief. "I wish I could, Dr. Jarvis. But fighting that likeness of Coyote has made me realize that I haven't the strength. I'm too old, too weak. We're going to have to do it some other way."

I pushed open the heavy front door and we cautiously stepped inside. The pictures were still there. I said, "Right. Collect up as many as you can and stack them in the trunk. Then let's get going."

Working swiftly and silently, we unhooked the prints and drawings from the walls and carried them down to the trunk of Jim's car. There must have been sixty or seventy of them, and by the time we had finished, the whole back of the car was weighed down with picture frames.

Jane, who was still sitting in the rear seat, looked up. "Is everything all right? I feel very peculiar."

"Don't you worry," Jim said. "We'll take you right back to the hospital for a check-up."

"Oh, no," she said. "I'm fine, honestly. I think I'm just suffering from shock."

"All the same," said Jim, "a medical once-over might be a good idea."

He climbed into the car and started the motor. George Thousand Names said, "We ought to find someplace safe for these pictures. Someplace small, that I can easily protect with spells."

"How about my place?" I suggested. "I have a real small apartment, and if you stood behind the front door with a baseball bat, you could keep the barbarian hordes at bay for a week."

"That sounds good. Can you direct us there?"

We drove over to my apartment building, and Sam the Janitor eyed us with undisguised suspicion as we hefted all the pictures of Mount Taylor and Cabezon Peak into his elevator and took them upstairs. I unlocked my apartment door and between us we stacked all the pictures in my small hallway under the poster of Dolly Parton. I stood back and brushed the dust off of my hands. "Right. Now what about the spells?"

George Thousand Names said, "I'd like a drink first."

We went through to my diminutive sitting room and I opened up my black Formica cocktail cabinet with the gold spangles on it and poured out four Hiram Walkers. I didn't really approve of bourbon made in Illinois, but it was all I had. All four of us stood there, tired and shaken, and swallowed it down like patent medicine.

"I'm going to hang this on your door," George Thousand Names told me. He took a small bone necklace out of his windbreaker pocket and held it up. It didn't look like anything special. The bones were old and chipped and discolored, and even though there had once been red and green paint on them, it had now mostly worn off.

"This is the necklace worn by our ancient hero Broken Shield when he climbed Leech Lake Mountain and defied the thunder gods. Historically, it's beyond price. It may be three thousand years old. But it was made to be used and that's why I want you to have it tonight. Keeping Coyote away from Big Monster's scalp is far more important than any relic, no matter how much it means to us. Coyote will not dare to touch this. If he does, he will invoke the anger of Gitche Manitou the great spirit himself."

"I thought Coyote was the kind of demon who didn't mind defying anyone or anything," said Dr. Jarvis.

"He is," agreed George Thousand Names. "But like most vain and idle demons, he would rather live a quiet life, and the anger of Gitche Manitou would be quite enough to disturb his fun for the next five thousand years."

"Fun?" queried Jim, and shook his head in disbelief.

"Dr. Jarvis," said George Thousand Names. "Just remember that to some of the fiercer demons, devouring a human is nothing more diverting than eating a bag of roasted peanuts is for us."

George Thousand Names hung the necklace on the handle of my front door, and muttered a few incantatory words over it. Then he said, "I expect we're all tired, and we want to be fresh for tomorrow. I suggest that we all get some rest. I had my maid make a reservation for me at the Mark Hopkins. Do you think you could give me a ride that way, Doctor?"

"Sure," replied Jim. "How about you, Jane? Can I drop you off?"

Jane had been sitting by herself on my favorite wicker chair. She said in a flat voice, "No, that's all right. If John doesn't mind, I think I'll stay here."

"Mind?" I asked her. "You have to be joshing. I haven't had female company here since my Aunt Edith came up from Oxnard and brought me a cake!"

Jim squeezed my arm. "I'll believe you, John. Millions wouldn't."

George Thousand Names came over and shook my hand, too. He said, softly, "I want to thank you for having enough imagination to see what was really happening. At least we stand some kind of a chance."

They were about to leave when my telephone rang. I beckoned them back inside and picked it up.

"John Hyatt."

It was Lieutenant Stroud. "So you're back home, huh? I've been looking for you. Is that Indian with you?"

"George Thousand Names. Yes."

The detective coughed. "We've had a little trouble on the Bayshore Freeway just past Millbrae. The ambulance with Dr. Crane and Seymour Wallis's body was kind of ambushed."

"Ambushed? You mean by Coyote?"

Lieutenant Stroud let out a testy breath. "All right. If

that's what you want to call it. The ambulance driver said he was driving along real normal and suddenly this immense kind of a monster reared up in the roadway ahead of him. He was the only man to escape alive. Dr. Crane, I'm sorry to say, is dead. Burned out like my patrolman."

I put my hand over the telephone receiver and said to Dr. Jarvis, "I'm sorry, Jim. Dr. Crane is dead. Coyote got to the ambulance just past the airport."

George Thousand Names looked deadly serious. "The blood," he insisted. "Did he get the blood?"

"Mr. Thousand Names wants to know if Coyote got the blood," I asked the officer.

Lieutenant Stroud coughed. "Tell him that Seymour Wallis was found a half hour later in the Bay. He was so sucked out that the guy who hauled him out thought at first held found a dead shark."

All I could say was, "That's it then. What else can we do? Do you have any idea where Coyote is?"

"We have an APB out and the SWAT squad is checking every possible hideout. But if you ask me it's going to be hopeless," he said.

"Okay, Lieutenant," I told him, and laid down the phone.

In the first smeary light of early morning that seeped into my room, George Thousand Names looked tired and hunched. He ran his gnarled fingers through his white hair. "Let's hope we don't lose this one, friends. If Coyote gets loose, then I can't tell you what carnage there's going to be."

Jane suddenly looked up and smiled, and I can remember thinking how strange that smile was. What the hell could there be to smile about?

I made up a makeshift bed for Jane on the couch. I was too exhausted and shaken to think of seduction, and in any case

Jane was acting so withdrawn and remote that I could have yelled, "Let's ball!" at the top of my voice and all she would have said was, "Pardon?"

She wrapped herself in a blanket and fell asleep almost straight away. I went around the apartment turning off the lights and drawing the drapes, but somehow I didn't feel much like lying down and closing my eyes. I went out into the hallway and looked at some of the drawings of Mount Taylor. The glass in the frames was pretty dusty and stained, and most of the prints were badly foxed, but if you looked close you could see that someone had penciled under each one, *"Mount Taylor from Lookout Mountain,"* or *"Mount Taylor from San Mateo."* There were similar notations under the pictures of Cabezon Peak, like *"Cabezon Peak from San Luis."*

I tippy-toed across my sitting room and quietly took down my *Rand McNally Road Atlas.* Then I crept back into the kitchen, closed the door, and spread it out on the table, along with as many pictures of Mount Taylor and Cabezon Peak as I could crowd around. I laid a sheet of waxed paper over the map, took out my pen, and began to mark on the overlay the locations from which each of the views of the two mountains had been drawn.

To keep myself going, I smoked half a pack of cigarettes and made myself a big mug of black coffee, as the sunlight outside the kitchen window grew stronger and eight o'clock chimed from the pine clock on the sitting room wall.

By nine, I had almost every viewpoint plotted, and I lifted the sheet of waxed paper up and admired the pattern of tiny Xs that I had marked all over it. I couldn't imagine what the hell they all meant, and there didn't seem to be any pattern to them that I could make out, but I guessed that George Thousand Names would probably be able to enlighten me.

I tucked the paper in my pants pocket, then crossed the kitchen to put the percolator on for another mug of coffee. I switched on the small black-and-white television that my mother had given me last Christmas, and after a couple of messages for Sugar Frosties and some kind of dumb plastic catapult for shooting Action Man over your neighbor's hedge, I caught a news bulletin about the ambulance that Seymour Wallis had been abducted from.

The announcer said, "San Francisco's SWAT squad is still hunting for a ghoulish hijacker who ambushed an ambulance on its way to Redwood City Clinic from Elmwood Foundation Hospital and stole the cadaver of former city engineer Seymour Wallis. The hijacker, described by investigating detectives as 'armed and extremely violent,' inflicted fatal injuries on Dr. Kenneth Crane, who was accompanying the body on its trip along Bayshore Freeway, and on Miguel Corralitos, a twenty-seven-year-old hospital orderly. The body of Mr. Wallis was later found by an early-bird fisherman in the Bay off Millbrae. So far police have no clues to the hijacker's motives for purloining the corpse, but they promise fresh bulletins shortly."

After that, they went into some report about orange blight in a fruit farm downstate, and I switched the television off. So Coyote was still free, although I couldn't imagine what kind of form he had taken on now, or where he might be. What does a hideous demon do in the daytime? He can't very well roam the streets of San Francisco, especially with Lieutenant Stroud and the SWAT squad tracking him down. That's if he left any tracks.

My percolator started gurgling and popping and gave me quite a start. I lit another cigarette and looked out over the backs of the apartment buildings around me. It was Sunday, and a pregnant girl in a smock was sitting on a fire escape brushing her hair dry in the morning sunshine. I coughed and wished I could stop smoking. Right now though, there didn't seem much point. If cancer didn't get me, Coyote probably would.

The telephone rang. I lifted it up. "John Hyatt."

It was George Thousand Names calling from the Mark Hopkins. "Did you sleep okay?" he asked.

"I didn't sleep at all," I told him. "I spent the rest of the night charting those viewpoints of Mount Taylor and Cabezon Peak."

"Does it look like anything interesting?"

"Well, it could be. But I think it needs an interpreter. I came second to bottom in trigonometry, and that was only because I kept my pencils sharper than the guy who came bottom."

"Do you want to come over? As long as you leave that necklace on the door, your place will stay safe."

"You're sure?"

"Sure I'm sure. In any case, Coyote will probably be resting up right now, absorbing his blood into his system."

"I was wondering where demons go to in daytime."

"Demons are things of the dark," George Thousand Names told me. "In sunlight, their powers are weakened. So you can bet that Coyote is holed up in some abandoned house someplace, or down in some culvert, or maybe he's even made it to 1551."

"Isn't it worth trying to flush him out now that it's daylight?"

"John," he said, "when I say his powers are weakened, I don't mean that he doesn't *have* any powers. If we go near that creature, we're dead meat. I mean that."

"Thanks for the cheerful message. I'll come over in about one hour. I want to take a shower first. I smell like a pig."

"Okay," he said. "Don't forget to bring the chart you made."

I was just about to say "you bet," when the words died on my lips. The kitchen door had opened a small way and there was something standing outside watching me. I could see the glitter of dark eyes and an even darker shape. I felt as if the world had disappeared from under me and every nerve in my body tingled and crept with fright.

"Did you hear what I said?" said the tinny, distant voice of George Thousand Names.

"Wait. There's something outside my door. I don't know what it is. Wait."

"Which door?" he demanded.

"The kitchen door. The kitchen door, it's—"

The door slammed open so hard that splinters of wood and broken hinges flew across the room. I gave a high-pitched yelp, and pitched off my chair, scrabbling across the floor toward the sink.

I kept my knives there in a drawer, and what I needed right now was instant protection.

The beast came through that door like a tidal wave of black fur. It was a bear, a massive, full-grown grizzly, nearly four hundred pounds of hair and muscle and vicious curved claws. It collided heavily with the kitchen units, and the telephone and percolator and spice racks clattered and crashed to the floor. As the bear turned, it snarled viciously, and I wrenched open the kitchen drawer too quick and too hard letting out a shower of knives and forks and bean slicers and apple corers all over the floor.

I ducked down, caught hold of my biggest kitchen cleaver, and rolled as fast as I could toward the broken door. The bear paused, and snarled again, and it was only then that I really looked at it.

It was more than a huge beast of shaggy fur and dark animal smell. It had a pale white face, pale as a woman's but with yellowish teeth that were bared with every snarl and growl. I stared at it, trying to understand what it was, what it could possibly be. I was so shocked and horrified that I couldn't grasp it at first, just couldn't get my mind around the fact of this terrifying beast's existence.

It was Jane. Hard and ferocious though they were, those eyes were hers. That face was hers. The strange statuette on Seymour Wallis's banister post had come to life, and it was her.

I whispered, "Jane . . ."

She didn't answer, just snarled again and moved implacably toward me, her hard claws scratching on the kitchen floor. Saliva dripped from the points of her teeth, and there was nothing in her expression but blind animal hatred.

"Jane, listen," I said, in a croaky voice. All the time I was trying to back toward the door. I saw the muscles rippling under that coarse glossy fur, and I knew that she was going to run for me again, and this time she probably wouldn't miss.

On the floor, the telephone receiver kept saying: *"John? John? What's the matter, what's going on?"*

There was a brisk tattoo of sharp claws, and the Bear Maiden leaped toward me with the force of a huge black automobile. I know that I yelled out, but it was with aggressive desperation this time, the kind of banzai scream they teach you in the Army to pump your adrenalin up.

As the giant bear hurtled toward me, I swung back my arm and whammed it straight in the face with the meat cleaver. That didn't do very much to help me. The force of the Bear Maiden's leap banged me back against the wall, and we collided together on the floor in a ghastly embrace of blood and fur and claws. I think I was concussed for a moment, almost crushed, but then I managed to push some of the furry weight off my legs and hips, and roll her over.

I thought she was dead at first. The cleaver had struck her in the left side of the face, chopping a deep bloody V into her forehead, and damaging her left eye. The velocity of her own leap had done the most damage, because there was no way *I* could have hit anybody that hard. I knelt beside her, shaking and quaking, and almost heaving up my last few mugs of coffee.

She opened her right eye and looked at me. I twitched nervously and stood up, well away from those claws and those teeth. She smiled. A sort of sour, self-satisfied grin.

"My master will want you now," she whispered. *"He has waited so long for his beautiful Bear Maiden, and look what you have done. My master will track you down, and he will make sure that you die the worst death that anyone could ever imagine."*

I said thickly, "Jane?"

But even if the face looked like Jane, there was nothing in the creature's mind that remembered Jane or the way she used to feel about me. She lay there, panting and bleeding, but I knew that I hadn't killed her, and it was only a matter of time before she came after me again.

The telephone said, "Hello? Hello? John!"

I picked it up from the floor. "I'm here, George. I'm okay for now. The Bear Maiden's here. It's Jane. The Bear Maiden is Jane."

"Get out of there, quick. While you still have the chance."

"She's hurt. I hit her with the meat cleaver."

"That's not going to please Coyote. Listen, just get your maps and git."

"*Git?* I haven't heard anyone say that since Hopalong Cassidy."

"John, you're hysterical. Just get the hell out of there."

Still stumbling and staggering, I gathered up my *Rand McNally* and my wallet, and stepped over the Bear Maiden's twitching legs to the door. She rolled her eyeball up to watch me as I passed and whispered, "Coyote will get thee. Have no fear."

I went out of the front door, made sure the necklace was tightly fastened around the handle, and headed for the elevator with wobbly knees. It was only after I'd hailed a taxi in the street and we'd pulled away into the traffic that I felt the first surge of real nausea.

I tapped the driver on the shoulder.

"Yup?" she asked me.

"Excuse me," I said. "I think I'm going to puke."

She turned around and stared at me, a cigarette hanging from her lower lip.

"Mister," she said. "This ain't no goddamned airline. Sick bags ain't provided."

"What do you suggest I do?" I asked her, sweating.

She drove at forty miles an hour over a cross street, bouncing and jolting on the taxi's suspension. "Swallow it," she said, and that was the end of that discussion.

Maybe Red Indians are self-disciplined and ascetic, but George Thousand Names wasn't so self-disciplined that morning that he didn't take my hand in both of his when I walked through the door of his room at the Mark Hopkins, and he wasn't so ascetic that he didn't pour us both a large Jack Daniels.

"It's a nightmare. The whole damned thing is a nightmare," I said.

He was wearing a red satin bathrobe and slippers with beads sewn all over them. He looked as if he was starring in a cowboy movie financed by Liberace. "That's the worst mistake you can make, to think it's a nightmare. If you think that, you will close your eyes to whatever happens, and hope to wake up. But you *are* awake, John, and this is really happening."

"But how the hell can a girl I know, a girl I used to love damnit, a girl I still love, turn into a creature like that?"

The old Indian set his glass down on top of the television set. With the sound turned down, some golf star was mouthing the virtues of tooth polish.

"She was a *bear,* George," I said. "She had hair all over, and there was only her face. And she didn't even recognize me. I couldn't say anything. She came right across that kitchen at me like a locomotive, and she would have killed me if I'd given her half a chance."

George Thousand Names sat down on the edge of his bed. It didn't look slept in, but then I had heard that some well-trained Indians could sleep standing up. Maybe that was just an apocryphal story, but somehow I could just imagine George Thousand Names standing in the corner, arms crossed, snoring the night gently away.

"Between the time that you sent her to get the door-knocker, and the time that we found her on Seventeenth Street, Coyote must have assaulted her."

I took a fiery swallow of bourbon. "Assaulted? I don't understand."

George Thousand Names looked across at me with elderly concern. I was beginning to feel that if I could ever have had a choice of fathers, this man would have been it. He was compassionate, and understanding, but he was also cynical and wise, and you knew that whatever he said was God's honest truth. Or Gitche Manitou's honest truth.

"Coyote is the most lustful of demons. He probably raped her. There is an old Navaho song about how Coyote meets a maiden on a mountain pass. One day walking through a mountain pass, Coyote met a young woman. What have you in your pack? she asked. Fish eggs, answered Coyote. Can I have some? the maiden asked. Only if you close your eyes and hold up your dress. She did as she was told. Higher, said Coyote, and walked up to the woman. Stand still so I can reach the place. I can't, she said, there is something crawling between my legs. Don't worry, said Coyote, it's a scorpion, I'll catch it. The woman dropped her dress. You weren't fast enough, it stung me."

He had recited this song in a flat, monotonous voice. When he'd finished, he looked up at me. "You see? He is cunning as well as brutal. When I say assaulted, I mean seduced."

I couldn't believe it. "That thing, that thing we saw last night, that had sex with Jane?"

George Thousand Names nodded. "Very probably. According to the legends, it was only after Coyote had filled her mind with the most evil ideas of antiquity that Bear Maiden grew hair and claws. I'm sorry, John, but if we're going to lick this thing we've got to face the facts."

"Oh, sure." I felt bitter and upset. Of all people, why Jane? If I hadn't been dumb enough to send her on that fool's errand, she might have been safe.

George Thousand Names went to the window and looked out over downtown San Francisco through the hotel drapes. "John," he said, "I know you take this personally, but you must understand that we're struggling with a life-and-death situation."

I tried to smile. "It depends on whose life it is."

He shook his head. "Not *whose* life, but how many lives? There are people out there, John, thousands of them, and Coyote can turn this city into a dismal carnage. If he stays loose, these streets will look like a slaughter house before you know it. Coyote is a mad, random killer, John. A maniac beyond all maniacs. The only way to destroy him now is to outwit him and make absolutely sure that he can't find Big Monster's shorn-off hair."

"But all the pictures are at my apartment."

"You sealed the door with the necklace?"

"Of course."

"Then Bear Maiden can't get out and Coyote can't get in. At least, I hope not."

I took out a cigarette and lit it. It tasted like a Hungarian steelworker's instep, but I needed something to steady my nerves. "What do we do now?"

He rubbed his chin. "I think we ought to discover where Big Monster's hair might be," he suggested. "Then, we can go tackle Bear Maiden. She's ferocious enough, but I think I have spells that could hold her. After we've done that, we'll go looking for the big one. Coyote himself."

"Well, I just hope we live this day out."

George Thousand Names smiled. "The Costanoan Indians used to live here in San Francisco before the Spanish arrived. They had a prayer that began: 'When evening falls, give me the small darkness and not the great.' "

I laid my road atlas on the table and produced the crumpled grease-proof overlay that I had painstakingly marked out that morning. We arranged the overlay on the map, and George Thousand Names scrutinized it like a skeptical art expert. He sniffed a couple of times, and his lips moved in a silent whisper as he located places and villages and mountains. After a while, he sat back on the arm of the couch and frowned in deep concentration.

"Well?" I asked him. "What does it mean?"

He glanced back it. "I'm not sure. It's a very unusual arrangement of viewpoints, quite unlike the usual pictographs that Indians used to draw to locate waterholes. If you look here, you'll see that it's made of several symmetrical curves. Now, that just didn't happen when Navahos were making their charts of the desert areas. Time was too precious and the countryside was too inhospitable. You made your pictures where you could and didn't worry about symmetry."

"So, what does that prove? That it isn't genuine?"

George Thousand Names shook his head. "No. We're certainly pointed in the right direction. The very fact that there's a pattern here is meaningful. What we have to work out is what the pattern means."

"How can we do that?"

He held the piece of grease-proof paper up to the window. "Well, I have the feeling that what we're seeing here isn't a regular map. Those pictures of Mount Taylor and Cabezon Peak had a magical significance because they were the home of Big Monster, but I'm beginning to wonder if Big Monster's hair is hidden around that area or someplace else."

He crossed the room and opened his brown pigskin suitcase. Then he came back to the table with a small glass vial of something that looked like black dust.

"I hope the supernatural doesn't embarrass you," he said.

"Why should it?"

"Well . . . you're a white man. And it's a long time since white men understood the supernatural for what it really is."

Having taken a chance on Jane's one-off theory about Coyote and Big Monster, and having traveled through the night to bring George Thousand Names down to San Francisco, I felt slightly irked at the suggestion that I was just another white bigot. But all I said was, "One day, the Indians are going to find out that not all palefaces are mindless barbarians."

George Thousand Names raised an eyebrow. "Those Indians who are still left."

We left that particular argument where it was. With Coyote loose, this was no time to do a big Wounded Knee number. But I knew that one day, if we escaped this thing alive, George Thousand Names and I were going to have to sit down and do some pretty serious talking. What Coyote's gruesome reincarnation had made me realize for the first time in my life was that America wasn't our land, not white land, at all. The Spanish hadn't arrived in San Francisco until 1775, and before that, all those centuries before that, Indian lore and Indian magic had made this land what it was. There were demons and ghosts in them thar hills, but they weren't white, and they didn't take any heed of white man's effete magical powers.

While I watched, he opened his glass vial and sprinkled blue-gray dust on my grease-proof paper map. He blew on it gently and whispered a few words. Then, right in front of my eyes, the dust shifted across the paper just like iron filings drawn into patterns by a magnet. In a few seconds, it had marked out a pattern of curves that connected up the penciled crosses I had made from each of the original pictures.

He studied the pattern and then smiled. "Well, wonders will never cease."

"What does it mean?" I asked him.

He pointed to the pattern with a stubby finger.

"That is a very ancient symbol. When I say 'ancient,' I mean that it bears about as much relation to present-day Indian tongues as Middle English does to modern American speech. It is very difficult to express precisely, but what it means roughly is 'the place you will one day see from the north lodgepole of the tepee of the beast.' "

I blinked. "I don't think I'm any the wiser."

George Thousand Names looked at me carefully. "It's

really very clear. The tepee of the beast is 1551 Pilarcitos Street, you remember how it worked out as 666. The north lodgepole simply means the view from the top of the house facing northward. Whatever you see from that vantage point, that is where Big Monster's hair is hidden."

"Well, for Christ's sake," I said. "What are we waiting for? Let's get up there!"

"Give me three minutes to bathe and dress," George Thousand Names insisted. "Meanwhile, you might give Dr. Jarvis a call and tell him where we're going. If he has the time, he'll probably want to come along."

The old Indian went into the bathroom and ran the tub, while I sit down on the side of the bed and picked up the phone. I dialed Elmwood Foundation Hospital and asked to speak to Dr. Jarvis.

"I'm sorry sir," the receptionist said. "Dr. Jarvis isn't here right now."

"Is there any way I can reach him?"

"I don't think so. He left here about twenty minutes ago with a young lady."

I sighed. "Okay. Can you leave him a message? Tell him John Hyatt called."

"Oh, it's you, Mr. Hyatt. In that case you may know where he's gone. He left with a lady friend of yours."

"What did you say?"

"A pretty looking girl with long hair. Ms. Torresino."

For a moment, I couldn't think what to say or do. My mouth was very dry, and I felt distinctly bilious again, as if I'd been eating too many Japanese seaweed cocktail crackers. I put my hand over the phone and shouted, *"George!"*

The medicine man appeared in the bathroom doorway, wrapped in a towel.

"I just called the hospital. They told me that Jim left about twenty minutes ago with Jane."

"What?"

"That's what they told me."

He began to rub himself quickly dry. "In that case, we have to move really fast. If Jane's gotten herself out of your apartment, then Coyote must know where to look for Big Monster's hair. And the pictures were there, right?"

I said, "Thanks a million," into the phone, and laid it down. Then I asked him, "What happened? I thought the necklace was supposed to keep her locked up."

George Thousand Names stepped into a large pair of floral boxer shorts, and then sat down on the bed to put on freshly creased linen slacks.

"The necklace was no guarantee. She may have found a way to shake it loose, or maybe a cleaner removed it. Even Coyote could have come by and persuaded someone to take it off."

"But even so, George, she's a bear. How the hell can she walk the streets like a bear?"

He laced up his shoes and reached for a smart blue blazer. "She's a bear, and she isn't a bear. The hair and the teeth and the claws are the physical manifestations of the evil that Coyote has put into her mind. But they don't have to show themselves all the time. The Bear Maiden is a kind of Jekyll-and-Hyde creature. She changes to her needs."

"You mean she probably looks normal now, but she could change back into a bear at any time?"

He nodded.

I let out a long, frustrated breath. Then I put my arm around George Thousand Names's shoulder and said quietly, "Why don't we think about this, George? Think where they might have gone? Maybe Lieutenant Stroud knows."

"You heard the news," said George Thousand Names.

"The police are looking for a medical freak, not an Indian demon. Right now, Coyote is holed up someplace, waiting for nightfall, and laughing down his sleeve at all of us. Especially Lieutenant Stroud."

"Do you think Coyote's gone up to 1551?"

"It's possible. In fact, if he's really managed to work out where Big Monster's hair is, I'd say it's a certainty."

For quite a few moments, we sat and looked at each other, and both of us felt the fright and the burden of what we had elected to do. We didn't *have* to get involved. We could leave it all to Lieutenant Stroud and the SWAT squad, and take the next plane to Honolulu. But somehow we both felt that now Coyote had brought his evil into our lives, there was only one way to go. And that wasn't off to Hawaii.

"George," I said quietly. "Is there any way at all that we can wipe Coyote out? Is there any weakness anywhere that we can attack?"

George Thousand Names stared at the carpet. "I thought the necklace would work, but it obviously hasn't. Maybe Coyote's gained some new powers since he's been in hibernation. His only real soft spot, or so the legend says, was for Bear Maiden; and that isn't exactly a weakness because Bear Maiden was always so devoted to him."

"What about Big Monster's hair?"

"That's the greatest threat of all," he said. "Once he finds it, that will give him all the strength he needs, and immortality, too. If that happens, we might as well pack up our bags."

"Supposing we found it first?"

The Indian shrugged. "Even if we did, we couldn't do much with it."

"Couldn't we wear it ourselves? Would it give us strength?"

George Thousand Names looked at me as if I was totally bananas. "If a mortal man attempts to wear the scalp of a giant or a demon, he will be destroyed by what he sees. In other words, for as long as he could survive it, which wouldn't be long, he would become a demon himself, and his mind just couldn't take it. So the Hualapai Indians say, or at least they used to."

I reached for another cigarette. "Okay. We'd better get ourselves up to Pilarcitos. Doing anything is better than doing nothing."

SIX

Clouds had begun to drift across from the ocean, and by the time we reached Mission Street, the day, which had started off bright, was humid and dull. The taxi let us off at 1551, and with a feeling of dread we stood on the sloping sidewalk and looked up yet again at that dead and dilapidated house that just wouldn't let us go. George Thousand Names said, "Whatever happens now, I want you to trust my knowledge and my wisdom, such as it is, and do what I tell you. It could mean the difference between life and death."

I gave a nervous laugh. "You really have a way of putting things that uplifts the weariest heart."

He looked testy. "Just do what I say, right?"

"You're the boss."

We swung open that groaning gate, and went up the steps to the porch. The fragments of doorknocker had gone, although there was still a mark on the old gray paintwork where it had been, and blisters from the freezing cold that George

Thousand Names had used to break it. There was something else, too. The word *"Return"* had disappeared.

I pushed the door and it seemed to be locked.

"Maybe the police locked it," I said. "The SWAT squad could have been round here at some time."

I stepped back down the porch and stared up at the house. It looked grim and photographic under the gathering clouds. There was a feeling in the air that something dark and unpleasant was going to happen, and I couldn't resist a shiver.

For a second, something seemed to flicker in an upstairs window. It was pale, and it only appeared for a brief moment. But I clutched George Thousand Names's shoulder. "I saw something. They're in there. I swear it."

The old Indian turned, and there was an airplane thundering low across the sky toward SF International Airport. "It was just a reflection from the plane, you mustn't get yourself upset."

"George, there's something in that house."

He stared at me. There were forty years and two divided cultures between us, and I guessed nothing could really bridge that gap. But something was working between us, too, some kind of trust, and I was grateful for it.

We approached the door again, and George Thousand Names reached out for the lock. He muttered quickly under his breath, gestured three times with his left hand, and the door clicked and swung open. Inside, there was that same dusty, forbidding darkness, and I smelled again that stale smell that would remind me of 1551 Pilarcitos Street to the moment I went to my grave. The Indian said, "Come," and we stepped in.

First, we checked the downstairs rooms. Seymour Wallis's study, the dining room, the kitchen. In the sitting room, gloomy behind closed shutters, we looked over the spooky dust-sheeted furniture, the gold ormolu clock silent under its glass dome, and the oil paintings of grotesque hunts across nightmare landscapes that were so dark it was almost impossible to make out what they were. The house was so silent around us that we held our breath, and walked with as little noise as we possibly could.

In the hallway again, George Thousand Names stood and listened. He frowned. "Do you hear anything? Anything at all?"

I stood still and strained my ears.

"I don't think so."

"I feel that someone's watching," he said. "Whoever they are, whatever they are, they know that we're here."

We stayed silent for a few moments more looking around at the dingy wallpaper with all the marks where the pictures of Mount Taylor and Cabezon Peak had once hung, but the house stayed so quiet that I began to think we'd made a mistake. Perhaps it *was* empty, and all that I'd seen flitting across that window was a passing reflection. I sneezed a couple of times from the dust and blew my nose.

As I was putting my handkerchief away, I looked up the stairs and I went cold. *There was a small face watching me from the top step.* A face that was evil and hairy, with red-lighted eyes, and a grin so wolfish and vicious that I couldn't move, couldn't speak, couldn't even reach out for George's arm to warn him.

It was the doorknocker. The living doorknocker. Back in one piece again, and even more hideous and terrifying than it had been before.

George Thousand Names suddenly saw that I was gaping up the stairs, and he looked, too. But before he could do anything, there was a loud crack, and the doorknocker broke into pieces of dull bronze, which rolled and bounced and clattered down the stairs.

The pieces came to rest on the hall floor. The medicine man looked down at them with a sober face. "That's Coyote's idea of a warning. He's just reminding me that whatever I can do, he can undo and do again."

"We're not thinking of going upstairs after that performance, are we?" I said in a dry voice.

He sniffed. "I don't see what else we can do. Do you smell anything?"

I couldn't really, but I said, "Dogs?"

"I think so. It's faint at the moment, but it seems to be coming from upstairs."

The Indian set a foot on the first step, but I held his arm and looked him straight in the face. "George, I have to tell you this. I'm scared shitless."

He was silent for a moment, then he nodded. "So am I," he confessed.

Slowly, quietly, we climbed the first flight of stairs until we came to the landing. Just in front of us was the room where Bryan Corder had lost the flesh of his head. There was a window at the end of the landing, but it was so dirty and stained, and the sky was so cloudy outside, that only the weakest light could penetrate. Coyote, after all, was a lover of darkness.

We looked at each other. "Shall we check the rooms?" I asked.

"We'd better."

We went across to the first bedroom, hesitated, and then flung open the door. It was a silent, dreary room, with a dilapidated brass bed and one of those massive walnut wardrobes that looks as if it's veneered with strange feral faces. I could see myself in the dressing-table mirror, and I suddenly realized how rough and pale I looked. Two days of shock and tension don't do much for your outward glow.

"Nothing in there," he whispered. "Not unless there's somebody hiding under the bed."

"Are you going to look?"

He managed a lopsided grin. "Are you?"

"Forget it. We'll both look."

We got down on our hands and knees, lifted the bedspread, and peered into the shadowy darkness under the bed. There was nothing there except dust.

"Okay," he said. "Let's try the rest of the rooms."

One by one, we flung open doors and looked nervously inside. The bedrooms were silent, cold, unused. Depressing and run-down reminders of the people who had once lived in this house. They could never have been happy, not with the evil presence of Coyote built into their walls and their cornices and their chimneys, not with the demon's haunted breath whistling under every door with the midnight draft; and their unhappiness showed in the sparseness of their furnishings and the incongruous attempts at gaiety in their pictures. On one wall, there was a painting of mimosa. On another, a drawing of children dancing around a Maypole. Somehow, all these pictures did was emphasize the chilling sensation of dread that soaked through every wall, the dank terror that must have made every night under this roof a carnival of nightmares.

"I guess we'd better try further up," the Indian said. "There's one more floor, and then the attic."

I took a deep breath. "Okay, if you insist. But when we come to the attic, I think we'd better toss a coin for the privilege of going first."

We stepped out on to the landing again, ready to go up to the third floor, but all of a sudden we heard voices. They were coming from downstairs, in the hall. A man and a woman. I froze for a moment, but then I leaned over the banister, and saw Jim and Jane standing in the hallway. Jim was saying, "They must have been here already. The door's wide open."

"Maybe they were," Jane said. "But it doesn't matter. The main thing is that you're here."

I turned back to George Thousand Names. "It's *her,*" I hissed. "And she's brought Dr. Jarvis."

He tugged me gently back to one of the bedrooms. He closed the door, and gave me a long, intent look.

"This means one thing. Coyote must be here, in the house. She's probably brought Jim along as a sacrifice. A little wedding present from Bear Maiden to Coyote. Quite a succulent treat for a demon who's been dead for hundreds of years."

I pressed my ear to the door. I could hear Jane and Jim mounting the stairs, and talking in subdued voices. I whispered, "What can we do?"

George Thousand Names put his finger to his lips, and said, "Wait."

Jane and Jim reached the landing and walked along it toward the next flight of stairs. Jim said, "Are you sure John said he'd meet us up here? It seems kind of strange."

"Of course," asserted Jane. "Isn't the whole thing strange?"

As they passed our door, George Thousand Names opened it, and stepped on to the landing. I came out after him, my heart palpitating and my throat tight with fear.

"John! You're here!" said Jim, grinning. "What's going on here? Hide-and-seek?"

George Thousand Names snapped, *"Don't move!"*

"What?"

"Don't move! Stay right where you are! That woman you're with is dangerous!"

Jane looked at me and then at George Thousand Names as

if she really couldn't understand what we were talking about. I said, *"Jane?"* but I saw that her face was unusually white, and that her eyes were as blank as two clams on the halfshell. There was no trace of the cut that I'd inflicted on her forehead, but then after all I'd seen in the past two days, I believed Coyote capable of healing and mending anything that he felt like.

"John . . ." said Jane, in a slurry voice. "How nice to see you . . ."

George Thousand Names butted in, "Don't answer. Don't talk. She's not human right now, and anything you say can help her destroy you."

Jim frowned. "Not *human?* What the hell are you—"

"Shut up!" barked the medicine man. Then, quieter, "Shut up, please, I need to think."

Jane stood where she was in the dusk of the corridor, upright but very tense, and when I looked at her it seemed as if her face kept subtly altering and flowing, like a white drowned face seen through running water. I knew she wasn't Jane, not the Jane that I knew. But she looked so much like her that it was impossible for me to feel anything but affection. Almost involuntarily I stepped forward, but George Thousand Names was quick and he held my sleeve.

"I know what you feel," he said softly. "But have patience."

Jane suddenly laughed and snarled at the same time. It was such a horrifying sound that Jim, in spite of what George Thousand Names had told him, jumped away. In front of our eyes, Jane was melting and changing like one photograph overlaid on top of another, layer after layer, until I could see that dark hair was covering her hands, and her nails had become curved claws.

Jim said, "Oh, my God."

But George Thousand Names had this lesser demon under control. He lifted one of his amulets, and Bear Maiden shied back against the wall of the landing, snarling and growling, her eyes blank and red.

"I command you to obey me," he said. "Bear Maiden of the southwest, sister of those who loved you, constant until Coyote beguiled you. I command you to obey me."

Bear Maiden stood on her shaggy hind paws and roared, her eyes blazing like a devil. At her full height, she almost touched the ceiling, and I was far from sure that George Thousand Names could control her. The medicine man raised both of his hands and shouted, "Your mind and your will are mine. I command you to obey me!"

Jim was shaking his head in fear. "I don't *believe* it," he whispered. "That girl was at my apartment. I was *kissing* that girl. We had drinks."

For a moment, George Thousand Names faltered. I could sense his wavering control. I guess our combined nervousness and lack of faith wasn't doing much to help him, and the fierce strain of keeping a monster like Bear Maiden at bay must have been enormous.

"Don't speak," he hissed. "Don't speak, don't speak."

"But I can't believe it," said Jim, in a hollow, frightened voice.

The control snapped. I could feel it go like a dam bursting, like a tidal bore. With a shattering growl, Bear Maiden launched her massive bulk at Jim, and her jaws crunched into his neck with a noise that still makes me feel cold all over. He shrieked in an agonized falsetto, and then with one jerk of her massive head, she ripped the skin away from his neck and chest in one bloody rag. He collapsed to the floor, twitching, while she turned on George and me with her eyes blazing.

"Stop!" shouted George Thousand Names, lifting his arms once again. "By the powers of the Great Spirit, by the powers of the woods and forests, *stop!*"

Bear Maiden snarled and tossed her head. But then she gave another softer growl and turned away, dropping on to all fours. The medicine man stepped forward with his amulet held in front of him.

"I command you to obey me for one night and one day by the unbreakable spell of the greatest of those who lived at Sa-nos-tee. I command you to obey me until the sun's second sinking, and *you* will not defy me. This I command you in the name of the Navahos of old and the Hualapai of ancient times. Now, be silent and sleep."

Bear Maiden snarled once, and then sank down on her haunches. In a few moments, the red eyes closed, and she slept. I looked at George Thousand Names, impressed, but I saw what a toll that spell had taken. His face was glistening with sweat and he was shaking.

I knelt down beside Jim. His eyes were still open, and he was rigid with shock, but he was still alive.

"Jim," I said gently. "How do you feel?"

He whispered, "I think my neck's broken. Just get me to Elmwood and I guess I'll be okay."

The Indian said, "There's a phone in that bedroom. Be quick, because Coyote's upstairs, and he's going to be aware of all this."

While George Thousand Names waited impatiently and anxiously on the landing, I dialed Elmwood and spoke to Dr. Weston. I told her that Jim Jarvis had gotten involved in an accident, and asked her to send an ambulance across town straight away.

"It's nothing to do with what happened last night, is it?" she asked. I could see the medicine man beckoning me. "I'll explain later. I have to go. But, please, get that ambulance here fast."

"Come on!" urged George Thousand Names. "We don't have any time to lose!"

"I have to go. It's going crazy down here," and I slammed the receiver down. Then I followed George Thousand Names out on to the landing. "What do you want me to do?"

"Just keep close. And whatever you do, don't panic. If Coyote's still up there, you're going to get frightened out of your brain. But hold on. Provided you keep yourself together, you'll survive it."

I took a last worried look at Jim lying sprawled and bloody on the carpet, and the dark furry bulk of the slumbering Bear Maiden, and then I followed the Indian along to the second flight of stairs. It was even darker and more forbidding than the first. Its treads were threadbare and scuffed, and from somewhere upstairs a stifling draft was blowing, a draft that even I could smell. A draft that reeked of dog.

George Thousand Names went slowly up ahead of me, pausing every now and then to listen. It was so gloomy up there on the third floor that we could hardly see where we were going, and all I had to guide me was the rotting banister rail on one side and the damp wallpaper on the other. The smell of dog grew thicker as we climbed higher, and when we reached the second landing, it was almost nauseatingly strong.

"Oh, Coyote's here all right," he whispered. "He must have hidden up in the attic until nightfall. But he's here all right."

We paced along the landing, staring up at the ceiling to see where the attic door could be. George Thousand Names said softly, "He knows we're here. You hear how silent it is? He's waiting to see what we're going to do next."

I felt distinctly depressed and afraid. "If I had my way, I'd run like hell."

"Ssh! Listen."

I froze, and listened. At first, I couldn't hear anything, but then the sound of *scratching* reached my ears. It seemed to be all around, but George Thousand Names lifted a finger and pointed toward the ceiling.

"What do we do now?" I asked hoarsely.

George Thousand Names beckoned. We walked a few paces further along the dark landing until we were standing under the attic's oak-stained trapdoor. There was a frayed cord dangling down the wall, and I guessed this was one of those traps you pull down, and a built-in ladder slides out.

"Well," said the old Indian quietly, "we have the demon bearded in his den."

I coughed, and looked up at the trapdoor apprehensively. The scratching continued, soft and repetitive and creepy, like the fingernail of someone buried alive scratching hopelessly at the lid of their coffin. "George, I don't really think I want to go up there."

He frowned at me. "We have to. Don't you understand who this is? This is Coyote! This demon is like every medicine man's Moby Dick! I could have his scalp on my balcony rail, along with the pelts and the snowshoes! The scalp of Coyote, the First One to Use Words for Force!"

"George," I said anxiously, "I'm not in this for the scalphunting. I'm in this because innocent people are going to die if we don't do something about it."

"You're not a saint, and it's no good pretending you are," he said, and there was more than a dash of caustic in his voice.

"Maybe I'm not," I told him. "But I'm not a bounty hunter either."

"We knew this was happening at the last great council of the medicine men at Towaoc in the Ute Mountain Reservation; many of the wise men said they had seen and experienced warnings and omens. The gray birds were seen, and the old voices were heard on Superstition Mountain that haven't been heard since they laid Red Cloud to rest. And the coyotes and the dogs have been as restless as if a storm was brewing up."

"You *knew* Coyote was coming? Why didn't you say so before?"

"We didn't know. We guessed. But there will be much honor for me in defeating Coyote. I will be seen for the greatest wonder worker of any age, past or present; and I will then do something I have dearly wanted for years. I will unite the medicine men into a strong and powerful council, and bring back Indian magic to the glory it used to have, in the days long ago when the grasses were free and the tribes had dignity and strength. The signs said that Coyote would come in the Moon When the Geese Shed Their Feathers, and he has."

I stared at George Thousand Names's face in the dim light of the landing, and I could see what he meant. These days, there was no way for a medicine man to prove his powers, no test worthy of his magic. What good was an ancient skill for mesmerizing buffalo in a country where buffaloes only roamed in zoos? What use was the power to make a spear fly amazingly straight in a society of handguns and tear gas? That's why George Thousand Names relished this conflict with Coyote so much. No matter how hideous and terrifying Coyote was, he was a match for George's frustrated talents.

"All right," I said. "We'd better get to it."

He reached out and squeezed my shoulder with his old horny hand. "If the great spirit sees fit to take us, my friend, then let us remember the good words and not the sour."

"Okay, you're on."

I tugged the cord which hung down from the trapdoor. It seemed to be stuck, but then I pulled it harder, and, with a rusty groan, the door came shuddering open and the lower rungs of the ladder sank unwillingly toward us. From out of the dark space above us came a hot fetid breeze, and a restless scratching and rustling, as if something or someone was waiting for us impatiently.

"Let me go first," he said. "I have the power to hold the worst at bay."

"Don't get the idea I was volunteering," I told him.

The medicine man took hold of the ladder, which swayed and creaked and finally came to rest on the landing floor. Then, rung by rung, he climbed slowly upward, pausing now and again to listen and to look. His head and then his shoulders disappeared into the gloom. "For Christ's sake, don't do a Bryan Corder on me," I said.

"He's here. He's in this attic. Is there a light switch down there? I can sense him. I can smell him. Give me some light!"

I looked around, and there was an old bakelite switch on the opposite wall. I flicked it down and a weak dusty bulb suspended from the rafters inside the attic lit up.

George Thousand Names screamed. He dropped from the ladder, and his old body thumped awkwardly on to the floor. I thought he was dead for a second, but then he yelled, *"Shut the door! Shut the door! Shut the door before it's too late!"*

I seized the bottom of the ladder and tried to wrench it upward, but it was jammed on one side against the opening in the ceiling. I quickly clambered up four or five steps, and tugged at it as hard as I could to clear it.

It was then that I saw Coyote. I didn't see much. He was at

the far end of the attic, where the light scarcely penetrated, and the whole loft was alive with thousands and thousands of diseased gray birds, crawling and flapping and scratching their claws on the floor. It was almost impossible to see any kind of shape, any kind of form, but through the fluttering crowds of birds, the Gray Sorrow, I could make out something dark and enormous, with demonic eyes that glowed in a bristling face, and a terrible beastlike presence that was more evil and more vicious than any thing I could ever have imagined possible. On the floor of the attic, not far away from me, stood the statuette of the Bear Maiden, except that it wasn't a statuette anymore, but a tiny living replica of the gigantic Bear Maiden that slept downstairs. The statuette turned and grinned at me with bared teeth, and then she scuttled back toward the shadowy protection of her master, the demon Coyote, like a kind of rat.

I knew why George Thousand Names had screamed. Coyote, his slanting eyes fiery with hate, was unfolding his body from his gloomy corner of the attic, and in the half second I stayed at the trapdoor, I saw something unrolling from his sides, something greasy and pale and writhing like millions of maggots.

I came back down that ladder about fifty times faster than I went up it. My system was so pumped up with adrenalin that I seized the bottom rung and slammed the attic trapdoor upward with one hefty bang. Then I picked George Thousand Names up from the floor and half dragged him back along the landing.

At the head of the stairs, the medicine man gasped, "Wait, wait, he won't follow us yet."

"*Wait?* I'm getting out of this damned place as fast as I can! Did you see that thing! Did you see it?"

George Thousand Names resisted my tugging. "John," he

said. "John, you mustn't forget Big Monster's hair."

"So what?"

"John, it's the only way we can defeat him. If we find the hair first, we've at least got ourselves a chance!"

I let go of his jacket and rested my back against the wall. Upstairs in the attic, through the thin ceiling, I could hear noises that didn't bear thinking about. Slimy, soft, scratchy, shuffling noises.

"George, I'm asking. Let's get out. I can take bear-people but I can't take that thing."

"Wait. Remember what the symbol said. Look north from the lodgepole of the tepee of the beast. That's where Big Monster's hair is hidden."

I lifted my hands in temporary surrender. "Okay. So which way is north?"

He fumbled in his pocket and produced a small round box.

"What's this?" I asked him. "Another magic trick?"

He opened the lid. "Kind of. It's a compass."

It took us a few seconds to locate which way was north, because every time Coyote moved upstairs in the attic, the compass needle shivered and swung. But then we got our bearings, and George Thousand Names pointed along the landing to one of the dingy windows at the very far end. "That's it," he said. "That's the north window."

We hurried along to the end of the landing and looked out. There was a dull view of the backs of the houses on Mission Street, but beyond there was one obvious prominent landmark. It stood tall and stately and shrouded in low-lying fog, its piers and wires glistening in the gray morning light. The Golden Gate Bridge.

George Thousand Names breathed, "That's it. That's where the hair is hidden."

"The bridge? How can you hide hair on a bridge?"

He smiled at me triumphantly. "They said in the legends that Big Monster's hair was as gray as iron and as strong as a whip."

I listened uncomfortably to the noises of Coyote moving across the ceiling above us. "What does that prove? That doesn't mean anything to me."

He gripped my arm tight to keep my attention. He said fervently, "Where would you conceal anything that was as gray as iron and as strong as a whip?"

"Listen, George. I really don't know. I think we'd better—"

"John, *think!*"

I wrenched my arm away. "I can't damned well think! I just want to get the hell out of this house before that trapdoor comes bursting down and that demon comes down here and does whatever demons do. I'm not interested in scalps, George, and that's all. I want out!"

At that moment, a shower of plaster dust sifted down from the ceiling, and I heard rafters cracking beneath the weight of something unspeakable. The air was filled with the husky sound of fluttering wings as the Gray Sorrow clamored around their abominable master.

"Think!" he snapped. *"Think!"*

"Don't play games!" I screamed at him. "Just tell me!"

George Thousand Names pointed to the Golden Gate, and his eyes were cold and intense. "Wire!" he told me. "The Big Monster's hair must have looked like wire!"

"Wire? But the only wire on the bridge is the cables. You mean it's woven into the suspension cables? In the Golden Gate? George, you've got to be nuts!"

He tersely shook his head. "It's the kind of joke the ancient ones adored. Maybe they did it to humiliate Coyote and make it impossible for him to discover where the hair had gone to. They could make jokes in the future as well as the past, so my guess is that they intervened in the building of the bridge, and had Big Monster's hair wound into it. Maybe some Indian worked at the cable factory, and had the orders passed down from generation to generation to do what he did. Maybe it was done by potent magic. I don't know. But I know enough about the ancient gods and what they used to do, John. And, believe me, that's where Big Monster's hair is hidden."

"Oh, come on, George," I said nervously. "You're guessing."

"No guesses," he said. "Look."

What I hadn't seen before was a tiny symbol engraved on the glass of the window. It was the same symbol that I had drawn when I plotted out the views of Mount Taylor and Cabezon Peak. George said, "Put your eye to that mark and tell me what you see."

There was a rumble from the attic and a long strip of plaster molding, the kind of plaster molding that Seymour Wallis preferred to fiberglass, dropped to the landing floor with a heavy thud, filling the air with dust. I looked at him worriedly, but he said, "Go ahead, look."

I peered through the mark, and he was right. It lined up directly with one of the suspension cables on the seaward side of the Golden Gate Bridge. Maybe the Indian's guess was inspired, or maybe his magic told him more than he would ever admit, but right then I was willing to put money on what he'd said. That hair was right there, twisted and woven into the suspension cables of the West Coast's most celebrated landmark. From what George Thousand Names and Jane had said about Big Monster, he was one of the most evil demons of all southwest America. And the city authorities wondered why so many people chose to jump from that particular bridge?

"I know what you're thinking," he said. "And, yes, it's probably true."

"George," I told him, "you're a damned sight more psychic than you look."

But time was running out. Already the shufflings and the heavings from the attic were shaking the walls and sending cascades of dry plaster down on every side. I looked up and saw long cracks spreading at frightening speed across the ceiling and electric wires being tugged out of the walls like nerves being pulled out of flesh. Then, with a thunderous collapsing sound, the whole house began to fall down around us, and we were half buried in an avalanche of dust, plaster, splintered timber and shattered laths. The gray birds came flapping and fluttering around us, and for one moment, glowering triumphantly through the skeleton of the ceiling, I saw those demonic eyes and that body that writhed and twisted like some thing putrescent.

"Get out!" I yelled at George Thousand Names, and together we slithered over the dust and the wreckage toward the staircase. The head of the stairs was almost completely blocked with fallen rafters, but we managed to heave two or three of them aside and crawl through the small triangular space that was opened up. George went first, and I came after, with the gray birds already beating their wings around me and the hot dry blast of the demon Coyote scorching my back.

There was another fierce explosion of power, the same kind of explosion that had first concussed Dan Machin, only five times stronger. George Thousand Names and I were hurtled down the last few remaining stairs on to the landing, and I struck my shoulder painfully against the banister. We picked ourselves up and we both looked like bedraggled ghosts, white with fear and plaster.

"Next time you call me a paleface, just remember what you look like now," I told the old Indian, wiping grit and dust from my mouth with the back of my hand. George Thousand Names coughed and almost laughed.

Above us, the ceiling began to shake again, as Coyote ripped 1551 apart floor by floor to reach us. We ran along the landing, and Bear Maiden was still there, deep in her trancelike sleep, while Jim lay beside her with his eyes rolled up in shock and concussion.

"We have to get them out!" snapped the medicine man.

"For Christ's sake, we can get Jim out, but what about the bear?"

"Coyote wants her. He needs her. She's his love and his passion from ancient times. She's also his messenger, his closest helper. We have to get her away. Without her, he's much weaker."

The walls of the landing began to creak and shake, and one of the bedroom doors was twisted off its hinges and banged flat on the floor with a sound that made me jump with fright.

"Come on," he insisted. "Let's take the doctor down first."

Awkwardly, keeping our shoulders bent to protect ourselves from falling plaster, we picked up Jim and carried him to the top of the stairs. George Thousand Names was panting now, and his eyes were red-rimmed in his dusty white face. I didn't know how old he was, but he had to be the wrong side of sixty, and running away from destructive demons wasn't particularly good for the heart. As the house rumbled and shook, we staggered down the last few stairs into the hallway, and out of the front door.

In the street, the ambulance was just arriving, its siren whooping and its red lights flashing. I could see police cars turning up Pilarcitos, too, and there was already a jostling crowd of staring faces on the sidewalk.

Two medics came hurrying across, and took Jim out of our hands. Two more brought a wheeled stretcher, and they lifted him carefully on to it.

"What happened here?" asked one of the medics, a small Italian with thick eyeglasses. "Are you guys demolishing this place, or what?"

"This guy's been bitten," remarked the other medic, in a puzzled voice. "Something's bitten his neck."

There were more rumblings behind us, and we looked around to see part of the roof collapse inward. The brick chimney stack slowly toppled after it, and there was a crash of glass and timber. Through the murky windows on the second floor, we could see the dull and evil glow of the demon, flickering with malice and hatred.

George Thousand Names held my arm. "We have to go back, John. The Bear Maiden."

"The what?" said the Italian medic. "The *bare* maiden?"

We were just about to go through the front door again, when a hard, familiar voice said, "Hold it! Mr. Hyatt, Mr. Thousand Names! Just hold it there!"

Through the gathering crowd came Lieutenant Stroud, followed by two patrolmen. He came up the steps with a face as grave as an undertaker. "What goes on here? I picked up the call from downtown."

George Thousand Names brushed dust from the sleeve of his jacket. "We've found your demon for you, Lieutenant. He's upstairs, and he's fighting mad, and the sooner we get in there and rescue the Bear Maiden, the better. It's almost too late."

"Bear Maiden? What the hell are you talking about? You guys are staying right here. We have a SWAT squad on the way."

"Lieutenant," I told him, "we have to go. The Bear Maiden is Coyote's helper. She's vicious and savage, and she acts like his eyes and his ears during the day. Most of the time she's a woman, but she can become a kind of werewolf whenever she wants."

Lieutenant Stroud stared at me as if he had a mouthful of lime and salt and no tequila to go with it.

"A werewolf?" he asked flatly.

Another siren howled in the street. It was the gray SWAT truck, swaying and bouncing into the curbside. Three SWAT officers in combat uniforms clambered out of the cab and came trotting athletically up the steps. Their senior officer was a short, fit man with cropped silver hair and hazel eyes like the rivets on a pair of Levi's. He saluted and said, "You located your fugitive, Lieutenant? What's he doing up there?"

Lieutenant Stroud continued to stare at me, but said out of the side of his mouth. "It seems like he's tearing the place apart. These gentlemen say he has a woman accomplice."

George Thousand Names said, in a trembling voice, "Are you going to let us go in there or not? I warn you, Lieutenant. I am the only one who can subdue the Bear Maiden."

"The what maiden?" queried the SWAT officer.

Behind us, there was a hideous groaning and tearing sound as Coyote brought down the ceiling of the second floor. Dust rolled in clouds down the stairs into the hallway, and broken windows shattered and tinkled through the plaster. The whole house seemed to pulse and throb as if it was a tortured beast, and through the gloom and wreckage we could see the malevolent light of the demon's eyes. Even the sky above the house seemed to thicken and grow darker, and the gray birds were fluttering and circling around overhead, silent and ominous as ever.

The SWAT officer didn't wait to hear what kind of maiden

it was. He turned around to his team, who were busy assembling teargas launchers on the sidewalk, and rapped, "Three and five, around the back, move! Jackson, you come with me!"

George Thousand Names said, "Lieutenant, please, don't let them. I must go in there alone. It's our only hope."

The SWAT officer took out his automatic. "Will you just stand aside, please, sir? We have to get in there and deal with this maniac fast."

George Thousand Names raised his arms, blocking the front door. "You don't understand, *you'll die!* Please let me get in there! I beg you!"

"Will you move!" ordered the SWAT officer.

But as he came forward to push George Thousand Names out of the way, the old Indian reached into his open-necked shirt and produced his golden amulet. I saw it flash momentarily, and then I didn't seem to see anything at all. The next thing I knew, we were still standing on the porch but George Thousand Names had gone. The SWAT officer turned to Lieutenant Stroud and blinked, and they both turned and looked at me.

"Where'd he go? He just vanished!"

A frowning SWAT officer called from the sidewalk, "He just walked in there, sir. You let him."

"I let him?"

"Yes, sir. You lowered your gun and let him go."

The SWAT leader frowned at Lieutenant Stroud suspiciously, but then there was another rumbling crash from inside the house, and a sudden hot wind sprang up, howling and shrieking, and sending grit and dust spraying out of the door. All of us dived back from the doorway, and the SWAT officer took cover down behind the porch steps.

"Right!" he yelled. "We're going in!"

There was another explosion, another burst of power, and I was sure that George Thousand Names must have been hurt. But there was nothing I could do except crouch down by the front gate and pray. Jane was up there, too, and Bear Maiden or not, she was the girl I used to love. I glanced up at the house, and the gray birds were turning and swooping excitedly, as if they expected a feast of death.

The SWAT team scrambled through the moaning wind into the hallway, and hit the floor with their guns held up toward the stairs. More splintered glass flew around them, and one of them cried out as his hand was cut open.

The leader raised his arm, ready to signal an assault on the stairs, but at that moment George Thousand Names appeared through the blizzarding debris, and he was carrying something on his back.

"Hold your fire!" bellowed the SWAT leader, although none of his officers looked as if they had any inclination to shoot.

I couldn't see what was happening very well from my position by the gate. Maybe the SWAT men saw better than I did, although they never admitted it. But I was sure that George Thousand Names wasn't *walking* down those stairs at all. There seemed to be a curious radiance around him, and he was *floating.* He was carrying Jane on his back, not as a bear, but as a girl, slumped and naked over his shoulders.

"What did I tell you," muttered the Italian medic. "A bare maiden."

George came across the hall and I swear that I saw an inch of daylight under his feet. His head was raised serene and proud, the head of an Indian who had known magical days when the grasses spoke and the tribes were closest of all to the great spirit. He was sixty years old and more, and there was no way that he could have carried Jane like that, no way at all, down the stairs and across the hall, with his back so straight and his face so calm. At that moment, he was the holy vessel of the powers of Gitche Manitou, who looks after his servants, even those who are deaf to his whispers in the prairie winds.

As George Thousand Names floated out of the front door, all hell broke out behind him. The house seemed to shriek in anger, and I saw the floorboards literally boiling upward and the walls rush together in one hideous spray of plaster and wood. The SWAT men were caught right in the middle of it, and I saw one of them smashed through a solid oak door. The crowds in the street shouted and shrieked, and ran back in terror.

George Thousand Names knelt down beside me, letting Jane slide off his back. She was bruised badly, and there was a red weal across her stomach, but she was still in her deep trance, and still unhurt.

It was George who worried me right then. I looked up at him and he was shivering and sweating, and his face was blue.

"George, we'll get you a doctor," I insisted.

He shook his head. "There's nothing you can do now. I'm too old for that kind of trick. Too much out of practice. You need strength, you see, mental strength, and I suddenly realized how little I had. We've grown soft, you know, John. Even the best of us. There was a time when men could fly like eagles. But not now. I'm done for, John. I'm truly done for."

"George, listen, you're going to be fine. Just rest right now and tell me what I have to do."

He was breathing in husky, painful gasps. "Take Bear Maiden with you. Until I die, she'll stay in that trance. Take her down to the Golden Gate. See if you—see if you can bargain with Coyote—but don't let him get the hair—don't let him—"

He collapsed and fell to the side of the porch steps in a heavy coma. An ambulance team was already running across the road toward us, and I said, "Quick, please, he's had a heart attack."

I pulled one of the blankets off their stretcher and wrapped it clumsily around Jane's naked body. Then I dragged her out of the front gate past the milling crowds of police and SWAT officers and bystanders, and over to a yellow Pinto that was parked across the street. The keys were still in the ignition, so I wrestled Jane's limp arms and legs and blanket-wrapped body into the passenger seat, climbed in myself, and started the motor.

I took a last look at 1551. It seemed to be quiet now, a collapsed shell of a house. But the gray birds were still circling around it, and as I signaled to pull away from the curb I saw a dim reddish light penetrating through the dark clouds of dust that still rose upward from its sagging roof.

Then, hanging in the grimy air itself, enormous and terrifying, I saw the evil wolfish form of the demon Coyote, his face drawn back in a savage grin, the same face that I had seen on the doorknocker but magnified beyond the realms of nightmares. He was cloaked in birds and darkness, and the ground shook and cracked under his malevolent power.

The street was suddenly clattering with the sound of running feet. The crowds were rushing down toward Mission Street, away from the sinister apparition that hung over the house on Pilarcitos, and they were screaming and shrieking and dragging their children with them. Even police and the SWAT officers were running. I pulled the Pinto away from the curb, and sped down to the corner as fast as I safely could.

I turned north on Mission, toward Van Ness and the bridge. I didn't have any idea what I could possibly do to prevent Coyote from stealing back Big Monster's hair, or how I could bargain with him, but that's what George Thousand Names had told me to do, and at least I was going to have a try. My heart was racing, and I was breathing like an Olympic runner, and all the time I was willing myself not to look back.

Mission Street seemed so completely normal that day that I couldn't believe that a thing worse than the devil himself was behind me. People were shopping, walking, eating, laughing, and I was driving desperately northwards toward the Golden Gate, not even sure if I was going to come out of the next few minutes alive.

The Golden Gate was even foggier now, and the outline of the bridge's stately structure was limned in spidery shadows. Cars were moving across it with their headlights on, and when I rolled down the Pinto's window I could smell the chilly flat smell of fog, and hear the ships mournfully calling as they steamed slowly out of the bay toward the ocean. As I came down Lombard Street to the bridge approaches, the fog grew denser still, and despite my panic I had to slow down and crawl along behind a line of other cars.

I glanced at Jane. She was still slumped in her seat, her head back, and for all I knew she could have been dead. I said another prayer for George Thousand Names right then, partly because I didn't want him to die, and partly because the Bear Maiden would wake up if he did. The last thing I wanted to do was fight a supernatural grizzly in the confines of a Ford Pinto.

The car ahead of me suddenly stopped. I blew my horn a couple of times, but he stayed put. I opened my door and climbed anxiously out, and then I saw what the trouble was. Two policemen had halted the traffic, and they were standing around in the road, pointing upward. I ran toward them, leaving Jane in the car.

"What's the hold-up?" I asked, trying to sound normal.

All the same, I guess my voice came out pretty high-pitched.

"Some kind of disturbance up there. Some kind of structural disturbance. You see that?"

I peered up into the fog. The policemen were right. The suspension cables of the bridge were swaying alarmingly from side to side, and there was some kind of strange encrustation on them. When I peered harder, I saw what the encrustation was. The birds. The Gray Sorrow. Coyote had gotten here before me and was extracting the hair of Big Monster from the cables.

"That's real strange," said one of the cops. "You see that? Up there? Now, does that look like a kind of a darkness or doesn't it?"

He was more observant than he realized. The darkness, which clung around the bridge's uprights like a stain in the sky, was the substance of the demon Coyote. He was in his shadowy, amorphous form, the form that he took when he traveled with the sandstorms of the desert and the hot winds from the south. Now, up there, he was taking the prize which he had won for himself centuries and centuries ago, when Mount Taylor was the home of a giant and Cabezon Peak hadn't even been created. *The demonic scalp of Big Monster, the trophy that guaranteed him invulnerability and immortality.*

One of the suspension cables sagged and then swung downward, frayed and broken. It must have weighed tons, but it fell over the side of the bridge and did nothing but lash backward and forward in the air, a frustrated steel snake.

Right then, I didn't care about the police or anyone. I knew that Coyote had the hair, and there was no way that I could explain that to anyone. I cupped my hands around my mouth and shouted out, *"Coyote! Coyote! Coyote!"*

The policemen looked at me pop-eyed.

"Coyote!" I bellowed. *"Come out and face me, Coyote!"*

One of the cops stepped forward and took my arm. "Hey, mister, just keep it down a little, will you."

"Coyote!" I screamed. *"I challenge you! Coward! Lecher! Treacherous murderer!"*

The cop said, "What the hell—"

But then the sky darkened even more, and the bridge shook with a rumbling vibration, and when the policemen looked up they saw what I was doing. There was a sigh of surprise and fear from all the people around who'd gotten out of their cars, a moaning sigh that could have been the sound of mourners at a foggy funeral.

Around the upper reaches of the bridge's spires hovered Coyote's ugliest and most feral form. It squirmed and changed with every dull breath of wind, but the malicious eyes burned down at us, and the racks of demonic teeth glistened through the fog.

Motorists and policemen scattered. One of the cops tried to pull me away with him, but I shook him off. Behind me, I heard feet running down the roadway, and the sound of more car doors opening and more people dragging their wives and their children away.

"Coyote!" I shouted. I was bathed in sweat, and trembling. *"I have your Bear Maiden, Coyote!"*

The gruesome demon's form rolled and twisted, and grew clearer in the fog. Now I could see that around its horned head, the iron-gray hair of Big Monster was wound, a ghastly garland of primitive magic. The bridge vibrated under me, and there was a deep, shuddering sound like thunder over nearby hills.

"Coyote! Give me the hair and you can have Bear Maiden back! Can you hear me, Coyote? Can you hear me?"

There was another rumble. Fragments of steel and concrete dropped from the top of the bridge on to the roadway, bouncing off abandoned cars.

I turned and started to hurry back to the Pinto, glancing over my shoulder at the hovering demon as I did so. I kept imagining its devilish claws sinking into my back, or its teeth ripping my flesh off, and my body was so hyped up that I walked like a tennis player on the crucial edge of a major tournament. I had to wipe the sweat from my face with my shirtsleeve.

I reached the car. The demon's wind was beginning to blow, a scorching hurricane that blasted my ears and made my face feel as if it was raw. I wrenched open the Pinto's passenger door, and tried to lift Jane out of her seat and onto the road. I was sweating and cursing, and all the time the bridge was heaving under my feet so that I could hardly stay upright.

At that moment, three uniformed SWAT squad men came running past me with carbines. One of them slapped me on the shoulder and shouted, "Okay, feller, just get out of here as fast as you can!"

"I can't! I have to destroy it!" I shouted back, but the man didn't understand, and went running off along the bridge toward the horrendous dark form of Coyote.

It was only when the three SWAT officers ran into Coyote that I really understood what I was up against. One moment they were pelting along the roadway with their guns raised, and the next second the wolfish shape of the demon descended on them with a crackling of electrified air, and a thundering sound that made the Golden Gate Bridge tremble.

The man in front was spun around; and as he spun round I saw that his front was cleaved open like meat in a supermarket freezer. Then all three of them were hacked to pieces in front of my eyes by some fearful invisible force that chopped away their hands and their heads and their legs and their arms, and knocked the pieces in all directions. I think I probably screamed.

Now the demon was rippling toward me, only a few yards off, and the full power of his hatred and malevolence was directed my way. I desperately dragged Jane toward the rail of the bridge, then turned to face Coyote with as much defiance as I could manage, which wasn't very much.

"Keep away!" I yelled. *"Keep away or I push her over!"*

The demon kept coming, and now the terrible hot wind was searing my face and drying my eyeballs so that I couldn't even blink. Everything around me was darkness and fear, and those evil red eyes were fixed on me with cruel intensity.

I heaved Jane up on to the rail. Below us, through the fog, the gray waters of the bay heaved and foamed.

"I mean it, damn you! I mean it!" I shouted. And in that moment of total panic, I *did* mean it. I willed myself to mean it. If Coyote moved any nearer, his beloved Bear Maiden, his passionate werewolf mistress, was going to go over the rail and die.

I saw a disembodied snarl in the turbulent darkness in front of me, a snarl of terrible phantom teeth. I saw, too, Coyote's head, with its crown of magical hair. But he paused for one second. He paused. And it was then that I gambled everything, and let Jane fall to the sidewalk.

It happened in strange slow motion, like a nightmare of running in which you can never escape. As Jane slid down to the road, I dodged sideways and made a run for Coyote himself. With one hand, I reached out for Big Monster's hair, and I forced as much strength and energy through my body as I possibly could, and more. All the same, it seemed to take forever, and I could actually see Coyote beginning to turn toward me, and his teeth baring in animal hatred.

It was like throwing yourself into boiling water. The heat

and the turmoil of Coyote's presence was unbearable. I snatched, missed, and snatched again, and suddenly I was tumbling and roiling back across the road with a handful of long gray hair that fizzed and buzzed like live electric wires. I was thrown right back against the wheel of an abandoned Plymouth, and I grazed my face and my arm, but I knew that I'd done it. I'd actually stolen the Big Monster's scalp away from the demon Coyote.

There was a shattering roar of supernatural fury. I thought the bridge was cracking, the sound was so loud. I pushed myself sideways between two cars, and then I had to jump even farther back as those cars were lifted and smashed against each other in an ear-splitting collision. I dragged the hair around behind a Cadillac, and raised it above my head.

In that moment, I remembered what George Thousand Names had told me. *If a mortal man attempts to wear the scalp of a giant or a demon, he will be destroyed by what he sees. In other words, for as long as he could survive it, which wouldn't be long, he would become a demon himself, and his mind just couldn't take it.*

I said only one thing. It was a whisper against the scorching wind, but it was all I could think of. "George, help me. Wherever you are, help me."

Then, closing my eyes in dreadful anticipation, I wound the strange slippery hair of Big Monster around my head.

I didn't think anything was going to happen at first. I raised my head, terrified and disappointed. But then a feeling like a dark depth charge went through my whole body, and I was suddenly aware of a strength both physical and mental that I had never imagined possible. It was a frightening, evil strength. It was the strength of all my most violent and carnal desires amplified a hundred times. But it gave me such a wild jolt of exhilaration that I shrieked out loud, not a shriek of fear, but a shriek of sheer joyous overwhelming malevolence. I felt lustful, and vengeful, and I felt swamped with urges to rape and wreck and destroy everything and anyone I came across. I stood up from behind the cars, and I seemed to rise to amazing heights, taller and stronger than any human being could ever be.

I saw Coyote then clearly. Not a murky shadow, or a turmoil of cloud, but the demonic beast himself, crouching over Jane's body with his robe of worms and coyote skins on his back. I knew, too, what he was going to do. He had a gray bird perched on one of his bristly shoulders, and an armful of guts and blood from the dead SWAT men. He was preparing to reward Jane for her failure with his most loathsome specialty; sewing a bird into her stomach and then forcing her into the dead intestines of the SWAT men. The Ordeal of Three.

I felt anger so far beyond human anger that I roared out loud. I saw Coyote for what he was; and I also saw that the air was curdled with other demons and spirits, the ghosts of the wind and the fog, the manitous of earth and fire.

"Coyote!" I bellowed. *"Coyote!"*

The demon turned, his jaws dripping with blood. I raged across the roadway toward him, and all the time I felt with black delight that I was fearless, that I was not afraid of him any longer. I seized him, and felt the coarse and revolting bristles of his body, the maggoty softness of his insides. He struggled and screamed, but it was Big Monster's hair that was giving me strength, strength far greater than Coyote could cope with.

I tore him open like a sack, and out of his insides came living things that crawled and twitched, smothered in blowflies. I seized his jaws and stretched them so far apart that they snapped, and then I put out those blazing eyes. There was no blood. But there was a stench of evil that was centuries old, the sour and sickening smell of the dog-beast, Coyote, the First One to Use Words for Force.

I stood away from his ruined body, and his breath fled with the wind. His heartbeat palpitated for a few moments, and then went still. His eyes dulled over. The breeze of San Francisco Bay tossed away the bristles, the crumbling bones, the leathery skin. Soon there was nothing but a fragment of hairy scalp and a scorch on the sidewalk. A scorch that, if you walk across the Golden Gate today, you can still see.

Right then, with Coyote dead, I felt as if something as black and as vast as a locomotive was rushing into my brain. I knew that I wasn't going to survive these minutes in my demonic form, but I didn't care. I was almost elated, as if the ultimate high was rushing my way to hit me.

In the back of my mind, though, I still heard the voice of George Thousand Names. Maybe he knew what my plight was, and he was making one last supreme psychic effort. Maybe the strength was my own. But I heard him say, *If a mortal man attempts to wear the scalp of a giant or a demon, he will be destroyed by what he sees. For as long as he could survive it, which wouldn't be long, he would become a demon himself, and his mind just couldn't take it.*

With an agonized cry, I pulled Big Monster's hair from my head and hurled it as far as I could into the dull waters of San Francisco Bay. It curled and unwound with the wind, and blew away. I felt a desperate sensation of loss and exhaustion go through me, and I sank on to my knees on the roadway.

It was then, through clouding vision, that I saw Jane. She was lying on the sidewalk, and for one fleeting moment, I saw claws and teeth and black hair down her spine. But as the last of Coyote's dust was whipped away, she opened her eyes and she was Jane Torresino again, my once and perhaps even my future love.

She reached out her hand to me, and said softly, "John . . . oh, John. I need you. . . ."

And then the sirens were warbling in the distance, and we heard the welcoming sound of running feet.

It was September before I could make it up to Round Valley Reservation again. I borrowed a slightly clapped-out Pacer, and Jane and I traveled up over the weekend, stopping the night at Willits, in Mendocino County. It was afternoon by the time we reached George Thousand Names's house, overlooking the valley, and we parked the car. We climbed the stairs to the balcony, and a stern, quiet, middle-aged Indian was there, Walter Running Cow, and he shook our hands ceremoniously.

We had some tea, and in gentle voices we told Walter Running Cow about everything that had happened at Pilarcitos Street, and the emergence of Coyote, and what George Thousand Names had done to help us destroy him. We told him, too, how George had succumbed to a massive coronary at the moment of Coyote's death. Walter Running Cow listened in silence, and nodded now and again, while the sunlight crossed the room and the birds called long and plaintive from the distant woods.

Finally, the Indian said, "It was a brave passing for George Thousand Names. By modern standards, you know, he was one of our greatest magicians. Maybe he could never have flown like an eagle, as the wonder workers did in days gone by, but he used his powers to their utmost, and I believe we can all be grateful for that."

"I needed to tell someone who believed," I said softly. "In San Francisco, it was treated as a straightforward homicide.

The official explanation is that it was all the work of a maniac, and in the end he leaped off the bridge."

"Well," said Walter Running Cow, "I suppose that all cultures need their rationale. Even Indian magic has its blind spots."

"Will Coyote ever return?"

He looked at me, and his face was quite serious. "Not in our lifetime, maybe. But sometime. I am not deprecating what you did, but one such as you could never dismiss a demon like Coyote forever. And Big Monster's hair still floats in the tides of the ocean."

"Talking of hair," I said, "there's one thing I want to do."

I opened up the plastic shopping bag I'd brought with me and took out the dried bristly scalp of the demon Coyote. Walter Running Cow looked at it for a long time with a mixture of apprehension and respect, then said, "It is good that you have brought it here. George Thousand Names will thank you for this, in the skies."

We went out on to the balcony in the last light of the day, and I tied Coyote's scalp to the rail, along with the pelts and the snowshoes. Then I stood in the vastness of the Indian evening, while the breeze ruffled the long grass and set the trophy that belonged to George Thousand Names spinning in the faded warmth of the year, in the Drying Grass Moon, the month after the Moon of the Demon.

The employees of Five Star hope you have enjoyed this book. All our books are made to last. Other Five Star books are available at your library, through selected bookstores, or directly from us.

For information about titles, please call:

(800) 223-1244

or visit our Web site at:

www.gale.com/fivestar

To share your comments, please write:

Publisher
Five Star
295 Kennedy Memorial Drive
Waterville, ME 04901